Addicted to You

Addicted to You

PORSCHA STERLING

KENSINGTON PUBLISHING CORP.

www.kensingtonbooks.com

DAFINA BOOKS are published by

Kensington Publishing Corp.
119 West 40th Street
New York, NY 10018

Copyright © 2019 by Porscha Sterling
Originally published by ROYALTY PUBLISHING HOUSE © 2019

To the extent that the image or images on the cover of this book depict a person or persons, such person or persons are merely models, and are not intended to portray any character or characters featured in the book.

This book is a work of fiction. Names, characters, places, and incidents either are products of the author's imagination or are used fictitiously. Any resemblance to actual events or locales or persons living or dead is entirely coincidental.

All rights reserved. No part of this book may be reproduced in any form or by any means without the prior written consent of the Publisher, excepting brief quotes used in reviews.

All Kensington titles, imprints, and distributed lines are available at special quantity discounts for bulk purchases for sales promotion, premiums, fund-raising, and educational or institutional use.

Special book excerpts or customized printings can also be created to fit specific needs. For details, write or phone the office of the Kensington Sales Manager: Kensington Publishing Corp., 119 West 40th Street, New York, NY 10018. Attn. Sales Department. Phone: 1-800-221-2647.

Dafina and the Dafina logo Reg. U.S. Pat. & TM Off.

ISBN-13: 978-1-4967-2609-4
ISBN-10: 1-4967-2609-X

First Trade Paperback Edition: July 2020

10 9 8 7 6 5 4 3 2 1

Printed in the United States of America

Table of Contents

~

Addicted to You

Chapter One

~

Sage

"We should get tattoos."

Frowning, I glanced in the passenger seat at my best and only friend, Lola, knowing for sure I hadn't heard her right. I loved her to death but, right then, I wasn't so sure that she hadn't lost her mind.

Every girl needed the type of friend who was loyal to the end, the kind of friend who would fight first and ask questions later for you if it came down to it. For me, that was Lola. We had become close on my first day of boarding school. I was the awkward Black girl, pushed into a world that I'd never experienced before after my father had sent me away. I didn't want to leave; I didn't understand why I couldn't go to a school in the city so I could stay home with him. Unfortunately, that wasn't an option. He'd told me that Calvin's Preparatory School for Girls was the best and he'd only have the best for his little girl. Turned out, he was right, as usual.

When people saw me, the words 'entitled,' 'spoiled,' and

'brat' were probably what first came to mind but, if they had known my story, they would've known that I was anything but that. It was true, I had everything that money could buy, never spent a single day of my life being denied the things that I wanted, and it could've been argued that I was entitled because I only felt that I deserved the best. But the difference between the average rich kid and me was that I had worked hard for every single thing that I had and if I wanted something, I didn't mind putting in the effort to get it.

I was like my father in that way. He was the hardest working man I'd ever known.

My daddy came from nothing and made something, and not in the way that people say when they finally get a job making enough to cover the rent. He'd built an empire that provided enough wealth to take care of his great-great-grandkids. He was a hard worker in the greatest sense of the word. Because of that, he had a legacy that would live forever and he'd started it by carrying it on his back. He never met a challenge that he couldn't conquer; never saw a deal that he couldn't close on. He was relentless, powerful, strong-willed and, when he died, all of those traits continued to live through me. His only child.

After graduating with honors from Calvin Prep, I had my pick of Yale, Harvard, and Princeton. I wanted to go to Spelman so I could be home with my daddy but he wouldn't have it, so I chose Princeton since that was Lola's pick as well. Spending those four years with her, getting our Bachelors, were the best of my life. But the worst day ever came about a week before graduation when I was told that my father had died. Two years had passed since then, but I didn't think I'd ever fully get over living my life without my daddy in it.

"Tattoos?" I replied, shaking my head. "No, I don't think so."

Lola sucked her teeth, crossing her arms in front of her chest. I sighed and looked out the front windshield at the packed interstate in front of me. There was an accident that slowed traffic down to the point that it was stop-and-go...more 'stops' than 'gos,' that is. As it was, we'd been in the same exact spot for over five minutes.

I broke my stare away from the thick Atlanta traffic to glance once more at my sulking best friend and sighed again at her stubborn expression. She had a trump card that she could use in order to get her way and, even though I was praying to God that she wouldn't, I knew she would use it.

"Sage, this is my birthday and I flew all the way down here so that I could spend it with you before I go to medical school and you become an..." She curled up her nose at me. "...official adult."

My lips broke into a smile at the way she said the words like they stunk. If Lola could have, she would've been a child forever. The only reason she was even going to medical school was because it delayed the time until she would be responsible for her own bills.

"With my schedule in medical school and with you being officially placed on the board of your father's company, there's no telling when we will see each other again. I've wanted a tattoo forever, but I haven't gotten one yet. So your birthday gift to me can be you getting one with me. Please?" She clasped her hands together as if in prayer and gave me a sweet smile that was the tool she used to always get her way.

I pursed my lips for a few seconds to think but there was no point because I already knew what I was going to do. Lola was my best friend and that wouldn't be the first time she'd pressured me into doing things that I didn't want to. She would call it 'making memories' and I had to admit that those times when I gave in did lead to some of the funniest or most adventurous moments in my life.

"Fine," I said, rolling my eyes. "Let's make a memory."

"YES!" Lola shouted and then squealed with her hands in the air. She pressed a button in between us and the roof of my Mercedes convertible lowered right in the middle of traffic. Rays of sunlight burned into my eyes and I grabbed my shades to place them on my face.

"Girl, what are you doing?"

"I'm living!" Lola said, standing up with her face and arms pointed up at the sky. "You have a few more days before you'll be on the board, Sage. You're not an adult yet. You should live, too."

With that said, she reached down and turned on my radio, cutting the volume up high before dancing to some new jam by the City Girls. Mortified, I looked around at the cars around us and noticed that all eyes were on Lola, who was dancing like she was in the middle of the dancefloor at the club. She worked her hips like she was earning bill money to do it, laughing and singing to the top of her lungs without a care in the world.

"Work them hips, ma! You sexy!" I heard some man yell, followed by several hoots. That only encouraged Lola all the more.

"Oh God!" I said, laughing with my hand over my mouth.

I couldn't believe what she was doing but I also couldn't say that part of me wasn't a bit jealous. Lola was the carefree, adventurous one who lived her life without regret. Everyone loved her because she was that way. She was so fun to be around because she knew and loved herself. I wasn't that way at all. I was much too concerned with what others thought of me. The only time I was able to break free of that was when Lola was with me.

"C'mon, Sage! Traffic won't be moving for a while. Let's dance!"

Reaching down, Lola grabbed me by my arm and pulled me up with her as a new song started. This one was a hot new song that I couldn't resist. A week from now, I would be an official board member of my father's company, under heavy scrutiny and pressured to ensure the success of the empire he'd built. But, in that moment, I was simply me.

Here's to making memories, I thought.

With my eyes closed and my arms lifted in the air, I started to dance.

"Do you think it will hurt?" I asked, suddenly feeling uneasy.

The time of dancing was over, the woes of disaster traffic was a thing of the past, and now I was being forced to make good on my promise to Lola, who was still adamant about getting tattoos. After thinking for a short while about what I wanted permanently drawn on my body, the idea came to me. It felt right but the thought of needles made my stomach queasy.

Lola laughed and rolled her eyes. "Even if it does, that lil' thing you picked out won't have you hurting for long."

Chapter Two

Sage

I wasn't persuaded and she could see it in my eyes.

She came over and peered down at the picture on my phone. "Why'd you pick that anyway? I would've thought you would get a rose or something."

I shrugged my response and then lifted my eyes to the glowing sign in front of me that read *Official Ink*. Catching my lower lip between my teeth, I shifted my feet nervously. According to Lola, the owner of the shop, a guy who called himself Ink, was somewhat of a celebrity in the city and was the best at doing tattoos. He'd received several offers to film a reality show in his shop, something more like Miami Ink than Black Ink with more tattoos and less drama, but he'd turned each offer down. Lola said he was the type of celebrity who seemed to hate the spotlight, which only added to his allure.

"Let's go," Lola said, grabbing me by the wrist. "I made our appointment back when I booked my flight and we can't be late."

My jaw dropped. "So you *plotted* on me!"

She laughed and then rolled her eyes. "Don't call it plotting. Call it advance planning. Besides, I scheduled your appointment with Ink so you should thank me. You're welcome!"

Without another word said, she walked ahead, pulled open the front door, and disappeared into the shop, leaving me staring in shock on the sidewalk outside.

"This is the *last* time I'm letting her trick me into shit," I mumbled to myself.

***

My stiletto nails drummed along the arm of my leather chair as I bounced my leg nervously, waiting for whatever was coming next. I was all checked in, and had been taken to a station towards the back of the shop to wait. The inside of *Official Ink* appealed to the senses. Not only was it beautifully designed and decorated, but there were essential oil lamps around, blowing a scented vapor throughout that was somewhat calming.

The walls were covered with artwork that almost seemed too good to be true. Tattooed portraits of people that looked so real, you could see the reflections in their eyes. I scanned the pictures of their past clients and recognized many celebrities and political figures in the city. I swallowed hard and tried to calm my nerves, telling myself that I was in good company.

"Ink will be with you in a few minutes," the receptionist, who had introduced herself as Indie, told me with a smile. She was pretty with a gentle face and soft eyes that provided me some comfort. But not much.

"He's the best at this. You'll be fine."

I could tell that she knew I was nervous and was trying to put me at ease.

A guy named MiKale was doing Lola's tattoo in a closed room behind where I sat. She was getting a thorny rose bush on the left cheek of her ass. Though she let it be known that she didn't mind having it done out front in the open, she was escorted to the back.

"Alright. Let's get this shit started," a deep voice spoke from behind.

I closed my eyes. I didn't have to recognize his voice to know that it was Ink. Chill bumps rose up across the skin of my arms, though it wasn't cold. For some reason, I was terrified, and I wasn't completely sure why. I wasn't a punk; being brave was in my pedigree. But there was something about that moment that made me feel like what I was doing would completely change the course of my entire life.

"That's all you want? The lil' bird on your phone?"

I opened my eyes, feeling a presence hovering above me.

"Yes, I—"

I lifted my eyes to his face and my words instantly caught in my throat. He was a beautiful man, taller than average height, thick with muscles that put the perfect finishing touches on his athletic physique. Tattooed art nearly covered his body; he even had a few markings on his face. Dead center on his neck was a tattoo of a red lipstick kiss. My eyes lingered there for a moment as I stared at it.

This man is fuckin' fine!

I couldn't remember a single time in my life when I'd been so immediately attracted to a man. Not ever. I wasn't the type to lose my words in front of anyone. Though I was a controlled person and modest, in comparison to Lola, confidence was something I didn't lack. I wasn't afraid to speak to anyone but… damn. Ink had me speechless.

With brooding eyes, he stared down at me under hooded lids, waiting for me to answer. There was such intensity in his expression that it was hard for me to even recall the words that I was searching for.

"Um…"

"The bird. That's what you want? You know my minimum is a grand, right?"

My brows pinched.

No, I didn't know that. Lola must've forgotten to mention it.

"It's okay. And yes, this is all I want."

I saw judgement in his eyes. He probably thought I was crazy or maybe even one of the many fans I saw sitting around the front of the shop—girls who were there to get a tattoo but with the real motive of getting closer to him in the process.

"Where do you want it?"

My cheeks warmed.

Anywhere you wanna put it, was my first thought.

"Right here… on my wrist," is what I said instead.

He lifted one brow to catch my eyes.

"That's a sensitive spot. Might hurt more than other areas, like your shoulder, back, or upper thigh."

The image of him running his hands across my upper thigh, holding the skin in place as he first sketched out the design before making it permanent, made my stomach flutter.

"Um..." I swallowed hard, cutting my eyes away from him. "It's okay. I'll do my wrist."

He shrugged and a slight frown knotted his brows.

"Your choice."

Chapter Three

Ink

"Yo, Ink, you left your phone in the back. The shit been ringing back to back. I could hear it from my station and it's messing up the vibe I'm trying to set up with ole' girl."

Lifting my head, I gave Kale a pointed look as he walked up from the back holding my phone in his hands. His ass was always trying to fuck the clients, no matter how much it was bad for business. I'd only messed with a client once and I was still dealing with the blowback from that shit.

"Man, I heard it, but I ain't trying to answer it. I already know who it is."

"Nah, don't tell me," Kale said, smirking so hard that his already slanted eyes were nearly closed. "It can't be that Brisha chick."

I snorted air out through my nose and nodded. "I hung up on her crazy ass before I came out here. I should've known she would've started blowing up my phone. I should've turned it off."

Kale laughed as I pulled out everything I needed for my next tattoo. I didn't crack a smile because I didn't find anything funny. Brisha was a reminder of why I had to stick to certain rules. Once broken, there was always a consequence and dealing with the drama that came from a crazy, clingy chick was too high a price to pay.

"I saw her last night. I had an appearance at that new club in Midtown. She was standing in line to get in and I guess she thought I was gon' let her ride my clout to score a seat in V.I.P. I curbed her ass and now she's threatening to come down to my spot and put on a show that would have me on *TMZ*, *The Shade Room*, and *Baller Alert*."

Kale erupted into laughter at that and I shook my head. The girl in my seat shifted, looking in the opposite direction from us. I could tell she was trying to act like she wasn't listening but she was definitely all ears. Who wouldn't be? If it wasn't happening to me, maybe I would've found the situation entertaining, too.

"It ain't funny, man. The shit is pissing me off." Lifting my tool in my hand, I let it run for a few seconds to warm it up. "That's why I'm solo from here on out. The next one that I get with will have to be the one. Until then, it's just my daughter and me."

Kale's brows jumped. "Solo? I'll believe it when I see it."

"Better believe it, nigga." I looked at him with all seriousness. "I'm sick of this shit."

Shaking his head, he left to tend to the client that he was neglecting so that he could poke fun at my misery, and I began to get to work. He didn't believe me but what I'd said was true.

I was definitely done with the 'fly-by-night' chicks. From then on, I was going to be on my grown-man shit, find a good girl, marry her, and have a family. The American Dream, I guess was what they called it. I wanted that life. The celebrity life was whack.

Outside of being able to effortlessly get my dick wet, being considered a so-called celebrity was bullshit and, during times like that, I felt more disgusted with it than others. I'd never meant to be famous. Doing tattoos was a skill that I had learned during the two years of my life that I spent locked up after a chick lied on me about something stupid. Now that it was over, I didn't feel any kind of way about having to do the time because I'd learned a lot while I was away. To be honest, I'd expected to get locked up at some point in my life. I was guilty of doing a lot of things in my past except the one thing I got locked up for.

Focusing on my business kept me out of the streets, which kept me out of trouble. But what I hadn't expected was for the success of my business to lead to me getting what Kale liked to call 'fans' and that's where all the drama in my life began.

In the beginning, I figured if I could stay out the club unless for paid appearances, I wouldn't get caught up in no bullshit, but those hoes were smart. When thirsty chicks couldn't get at me in the club, they would make appointments to take up space in my shop, praying that a nigga would pay them some attention. I could always tell which ones were around for tattoos and which were coming in to fuck with me based off what they chose to get. My work started at $1,000 and went up from there. If a girl was willing to drop that much on a small ass butterfly tatt, I knew right then what she was really there for.

The entire time I had done the tattoo on Brisha's thigh, she sat there with her legs open, dick-teasing the hell out of me in a short-ass dress with no panties on. To be honest, she wasn't even my type and, outside of her doing that, I wouldn't have given her the time of day. Plus, I had a rule about not messing with clients.

When I was finished, she followed me in the back and grabbed my dick through my pants. Another reason why she wasn't my type; she was too bold. After she dropped to her knees, I let her know that I wasn't trying to be nobody's man and when she replied with 'and I'm not tryin' to be nobody's bitch,' I thought we had an understanding. Obviously, I did but she didn't. My head was so messed up from dealing with that broad, I didn't want to put up with another woman for the rest of my life.

"Hold still," I said to the chick in my chair.

Though she hadn't tried me yet, I suspected that she was one of the thirsty chicks that came in to swing pussy. She hid it well, though. She wasn't half-naked, was avoiding looking in my direction, and her body language said she wanted to be anywhere but sitting in my chair. However, the fact that she was about to drop a grand on a tattoo that was smaller than the palm of her hand gave her away.

Sighing heavily, I grabbed my marker to begin the sketch. As soon as the tip hit her skin, she flinched like I'd pricked her for blood.

"Oh!"

Pulling back, I then waved the marker in front of her face.

"It's just a sketch. I haven't even started yet."

I leaned over to start and then stopped to address her again.

"Sorry, this is my first tattoo."

"Obviously." I snorted.

She snapped her neck in my direction and narrowed her eyes.

"The only reason I'm even getting this tattoo is because it's my best friend's birthday, she made me promise so cut me some slack."

For a few seconds, I froze. No lie, I wasn't expecting that one. Shorty had attitude.

"Chill, ma. It'll be quick. And it ain't that bad, I promise."

She didn't seem convinced but didn't bother to respond either way. With her jaw tight, she focused her eyes away from me, her lips forming a slight pout. Part of me found the shit funny. It was definitely attractive. Physically, she was bad to death and the fact that she didn't come off like other chicks that came in there piqued my curiosity.

"I'm about to start again, a'ight?"

A slight nod was the only indication that she'd even heard me speak.

"I'm armed with a marker. Brace yourself," I said.

She sucked her teeth. From her peripheral, I saw her roll her eyes and couldn't help but chuckle at that. The more I pissed her off, the funnier it was to me.

Leaning in, I made my first mark on her wrist and the more time that passed, the more her staggered breaths became normal. The rise and fall of her chest called out to me and, after fighting my curiosity for what I figured was a respectable amount of time, I glanced at her chest. The smooth, ebony cleavage of her perfectly round breasts greeted me. Her nipples pebbled out the front of her shirt, a telling sign that she wasn't wearing a bra. I fought the urge to lick my lips.

Finish this tatt and get her ass out of here. Brisha ain't taught you shit?

Apparently not.

Chapter Four

Ink

Inhaling, I continued to work, forcing my eyes away from her chest. Her skin had a scent to it, something fresh and fruity. Women didn't understand how much perfume, lotion, and that body spray shit intoxicated men. There was nothing better than a woman who smelled good. It let me know that she took care of other things when it came to hygiene.

"That kinda tickles…"

She squirmed and her thighs parted slightly with the movement, drawing my attention.

And that's the same shit that got you caught up with Brisha.

The voice of reason was echoing in my mind, but it was my dick that needed the reminder. She had me on brick.

Refocusing, I quickly finished up my sketch, working with quality but also speed. Obviously, my body wasn't cooperating with my mind. The sooner I got her ass out of my chair, the sooner I would be able to lay to rest the battle between the head on my shoulder and the one in my jeans.

"Check out the sketch and tell me what you think."

She first looked at me and then bent her head to look at her wrist. Her brows furrowed, then softened, and her tense lips slowly curved into a smile.

"I love it." She raised her arm and gave it a closer look. "It's perfect."

Tears shined in her eyes when she turned to me. "I wasn't expecting to like it." She paused and then added, "I mean, no offense."

"I'm not easily offended."

She nodded and then dropped her head, staring into her lap. I could tell her thoughts had gone to something else. Most likely whatever had tears come to her eyes.

"This design mean something to you?" I couldn't help but ask, wondering if I'd misjudged her. I was so used to women coming in for silly shit to be able to sit in my seat that I'd assumed she was the same.

"Yes," she replied quietly and dropped her head. "I wanted it in honor of my father. He died two years ago. This is…was his favorite bird. I wanted it green because that's his favorite color. Sage… like my name."

She brushed away a tear with her free hand and then went silent. I grabbed my machine in hand, dipped it in ink, and prepared to make her dedication to her father into my latest masterpiece.

"You need tissue?" I asked.

She shook her head.

"No, I'm fine. But thanks."

I couldn't resist looking at her again.

She was beautiful by anyone's standards; kinda reminded me of a young Gabrielle Union but was lighter on the eyes. They were hazel, the most vivid of colors being the green. Her eyes were a perfect match for her name.

"He died about a week before I was about to graduate. He was so proud about it. I wanted to surprise him with the news that I was the Valedictorian. My plan was for him to find out on graduation day when I stood to make my speech. But..."

She didn't finish her sentence and I knew it was because she was trying to hold back her emotions. I wanted her to keep talking but not about anything that would make her cry. She didn't seem to even know it yet, but I had already started on her tattoo. Talking provided the perfect distraction.

"Valedictorian, huh? Where did you go to school?"

"Princeton."

I stopped and looked at her with wide eyes. "Real shit?"

When she glanced at me, there was a smile on her lips.

She nodded and said, "Yeah..." Then she shrugged. "But I went to a prep school that is known for getting students into Ivy League colleges so I kinda had a leg up."

"Nah, don't do that," I said, starting back on her tattoo. "Don't discount your achievements. Not only did you get in, but you rocked that shit and came out as the Valedictorian. Motherfuckers out here didn't even want our Black asses in that school unless we were mopping the floors and you gave them your ass to kiss. Shine, shorty. You deserve it."

She paused and, though my head was down, it was like I could feel her smile.

"Yeah, I guess you're right."

"Hell yeah, I'm right. I might put your pic on my wall. Right next to Michelle Obama."

She gasped. "Oh my God! You did a tattoo on her?"

When I looked up, she was squinting at the wall display with my previous clients, searching for the one of the First Lady. I laughed so hard that I had to cut my machine off for a second.

"Nah, I wish! She ain't on that wall, ma. If Mrs. Obama got some ink, best believe it wasn't in here. You would know if I did it because I'd clear that whole damn wall off to get a poster board made to commemorate that shit. She's right there." I pointed behind me to the photo I'd printed, framed, and hung on the wall.

"Outside of my daughter and my moms, she's the only other woman that I love."

Sage smirked and then rolled her eyes. "Mr. Obama might have something to say about that."

"He can say what he wants. She still gon' be bae," I joked with a smile.

"Ink, you over here disrespecting that man's wife again? Didn't I tell you 'bout that?"

The voice was none other than Indie who, as usual, was acting like she ran things.

"Sage, have you met Indie, the mama of the shop?"

She laughed and nodded as Indie rolled her eyes. "Yes, I have. She tried to keep me calm while I waited for you."

"Shit didn't work," I teased, cutting my eyes at Indie. "I don't know what I pay her for."

With one hand on her hip, Indie narrowed her eyes at me, playing like she was mad while trying to hold back the smile on her lips.

"You pay me to keep this shop in order. Which I do very well." I lifted my head and gave her a doubtful look, then she continued. "Anyway, is it okay if I leave now? You don't have any more clients and neither does Kale. I have to pick up Davin from the sitter."

"Yeah, that's cool. Everything alright with lil' man? You need to bring him 'round here to see me. It's been a minute."

She released a long and heavy sigh. "Yeah… I do. He's been asking a lot of questions lately that I can't answer. I think it may be good to have him come around and chill with you and Kale for a little."

I glanced up, trying to read her facial expression. She was guarded, didn't talk much about her personal life, but all of Indie's emotions could be seen in her eyes. Even now, I could tell that there was something she was holding inside and trying to deal with on her own. She was the strongest and most stubborn woman that I knew.

Her son, Davin, was born as a result of a rape. Now he was older and asking about his father and the other side of his family. She was a great mother and Kale and I were the father figures that he needed, but nothing could take the place of a dad. If anyone knew that, I did.

"When I leave, I'm going to give you a call so answer your phone. If you ignore my call, just know I'ma pull up."

She sucked her teeth. "Whatever!" she said over her shoulder as she walked away. Indie stayed acting like she didn't want Kale and me to look after her but I knew the truth. She appreciated it.

"I'm done," I said to Sage, releasing her wrist. "Check it out."

Lifting her arm in front of her face, she looked at the artwork, observing the details. When she turned to me, her smile was bright enough to light up a whole neighborhood.

"It's perfect!"

I checked it out again myself. I had to admit that it was dope.

When I looked up, I caught her staring right at me. For a moment, we said nothing as our gazes locked. Her eyes were alluring; so packed full of emotions that they pulled you in. I wasn't sure if that was the effect that they had on me or if the shit worked on all the men that she met. I would gamble on the fact that she had them white boys tripping over their feet to get with her when she was at Princeton.

And now she was in the ATL where men more of her caliber where everywhere. Brothas out there were stockbrokers, bankers, doctors, and lawyers. I'm sure her daddy wouldn't have been proud to see her bringing a nigga from the streets like me home. I wanted to shoot my shot with her, but I wasn't even about to put myself out there to get dissed. So, I decided to stick to business.

"Let me show you how you need to take care of it for the next few days," I told her, holding a tube of ointment and spray. "Pay attention. You don't want it to get infected. That'll fuck it up and I'm not in the business of fixing shit."

Chapter Five

~
Sage

You deserve love, Sage. You're looking for it everywhere and you're willing to accept it from everyone but the person who should be giving it to you. You need to learn how to love yourself and how to accept the love that comes from you. You can't expect someone to make you happy and fulfilled when you can't even do it for yourself.

But I do love myself.

No... you don't love yourself. You hate being alone. You take medication because of how sad you are when you're forced to deal with yourself. You have to find happiness in yourself. You have to learn how to not need anyone else.

When I opened my eyes the next day, my head and my heart both ached with the same pulse. I groaned and hugged my pillow, stretching my curvy frame out across my queen-sized bed, and then ran my hand through my hair. It had been such a task to even get myself in the bed the night before that I hadn't tied it up and, thanks to the tossing and turning I'd done through the night, my thick coif was strung out all over my head.

I rolled onto my back and looked at the ceiling.

You deserve love. You deserve love.

I had money, beauty, and freedom. I was a young woman in my mid-twenties with no children so I wasn't tied down and, according to what the world told me, I should've been happy. But I wasn't. I wanted a husband. I wanted kids. I wanted to not be alone.

I had no siblings, no mother, and my father was dead. I couldn't even spend the holidays with my dad's side of the family because my stepmother wouldn't let me. I was the love child born to him and his side chick. His only child because she hadn't been able to conceive. She wanted nothing to do with me.

Though my daddy said the decisions to always send me away had been made for my own benefit, I didn't believe it. *She* was the one who wanted it that way. *She* hated having me around. My stepmother had stolen my father from me. Had it not been for her, I would have spent his last days and all the time before by his side. I would have lived in his home, under his roof, instead of spending most of the year away at boarding school. *She* couldn't stand to look at me and, to keep her comfortable and happy, he had distanced himself from me.

Lola had become my family but now we were on two different paths, leading two separate lives. I missed her and she had only been gone a week.

You deserve love, Sage. You're a beautiful girl. You'll be a beautiful woman. You'll make a wonderful mother.

Another thing I craved… the endless love of a child.

As a little girl, I had always fantasized about the day when I would have children of my own to take care of. I had cradled my baby dolls in my arms and pretended that I had daughters. After braiding their hair, I would tie ribbons on the end and whisper my love for them in their ears, hugging them tight in my arms while promising to give them what I never had. I didn't have a mother; I had a host. She had given birth to me in order to gain possession of a man. When she failed at that, she no longer wanted me. I was left in front of the gate of my daddy's mansion for the help to find.

You're not a victim. Your past doesn't control you. You control your own destiny.

My head throbbed and the more sunlight that hit my eyes, the worse the pain became. Reaching on my nightstand, I grabbed two pills from the bottle there and swallowed them dry. With my eyes closed, I repeated the phrase in my mind, hoping that it would work its normal magic and help me pull myself from the bed. The opposite happened. Time crept on and drowsiness settled in.

You deserve someone who loves you. All of you.

Chapter Six

Sage

"Your boy is going to be out and about in the city tonight. I saw the promotion on his Instagram page."

"Stalker much?"

The sound of Lola loudly sucking her teeth in my ear made me flinch. I pressed my thumb to the side of the phone to reduce the volume.

"I wasn't stalking *him*. I was trying to find out if the other one, Kale, had an Instagram page. It was only supposed to be a one-time thing, but I've been thinking about him ever since. I may have to fly down during a break to find his ass again."

I rolled both my eyes and my body, turning over in the bed so that I was staring at the ceiling. After sitting alone in the waiting room of *Official Ink* for Lola to get her tattoo done, I learned once she appeared that Kale had spent about thirty minutes doing her ass tattoo and spent the rest of the time doing *her*. I wouldn't have been as pissed about having to wait during her 'THOTivities' if I hadn't been made to do it alone. Once he was finished with my tattoo, Ink ran out of the building before my signature had a chance to dry on the receipt. I'd thought we had a connection but obviously I'd misread something. It was weird.

"As hard as he was grinning when he walked you out of that room, he might end up flying to you. I don't know what you did in there, but he didn't want to let you go. He asked for your number like five times. If you hadn't turned him down, you wouldn't have to snoop around for his page."

"Whatever!" she snapped. "And anyway, I found his page already, not too long after I saw the promotion that I was telling you about. We've been texting back and forth for about an hour. Girl, it's going down in the D.M.!"

At least she was getting some action. But what else was new? Lola had had plenty of boyfriends during the time I'd known her. I'd only had one. And, to be honest, I wasn't sure if he really counted. Do you count a man that you were sleeping with and thought you were in a relationship with if you found out that he had a wife?

"Anyway, I didn't call you to talk about me. I called you to talk about Ink. You should go see him. Kale said that he thinks he was feeling you."

I scoffed and grabbed a pillow, hugging it to my chest. "He had a funny way of showing it. After he finished with me, he was on to the next. Before he even got out the door, he was already on the phone with the girl who was sitting up front. Indie."

Something about thinking on that moment made a sour

taste form in the back of my throat. There was nothing worse than rejection, especially when it came when you least expected it. Mentally, I had already been asking myself if I would give Ink my number when he asked while I was sitting in his chair. Turned out, there was no point in wondering because that moment never came. I guess that's why they say don't count your chickens before they hatch.

"That Indie chick is a charity case. Kale told me all about her. She's like the little sister of the shop. Single mother, no father, blah-blah-blah. Don't worry about her. Just go see him tonight."

"Lola, I—"

"What else do you have to do? Nothing! You're probably laying in the bed right now, hugging your *pillow companion* when it should be a man. A man like Ink. We shared an apartment for four years. You know I know you!"

I couldn't even respond as I dropped my head to look at the pillow that I was squeezing between my arms. She'd called it. She was absolutely right. Literally hit the nail right on the head. Was I that pitiful or that predictable?

"If you don't promise me right now that you'll go, I'm going to call you back to back and fill you in on every little detail that's been happening in my life. I'm not going to let you sleep your life away on my watch. And classes haven't started yet so I have nothing but time. You know I'll do it."

Her defiance was all in her tone.

"Fine, I'll go." I lifted my hands as I gave in, though she couldn't see me. "I'll get the info from his page."

"No need. I already texted it to your phone," she informed

me. "And I already called the club and reserved you a table in V.I.P. right near the front. You're welcome!"

Covering my head with my *pillow companion,* I let out a long groan. Lola had played me once again.

Chapter Seven

~ Sage

"My name is Sage McMillian. There should be a booth reserved in my name. In V.I.P."

The bouncer was looking so hard at my body that I wasn't positive he'd even heard the words that had come from my mouth. Licking his lips, he rubbed his hands together before finally meeting my eyes. He was a bear of man, large and built like a linebacker with a grizzly beard and dirt caked up under his fingernails.

Yuck!

My lips curled with disgust. How could he expect any woman to want him touching her with nails as dirty as his?

Just before walking to the front, I'd seen him ogling another group of women while rubbing his hands together like one of them was going to give him a chance. They hadn't, and I wouldn't either.

"I would pat you down, baby girl. But from how that dress

is huggin' them hips, I think you're good." He dropped his gaze, dipping his eyes into the crevice of every one of my curves. I sucked my teeth when he fixated his eyes on my breasts.

"I mean, unless you want me to," he added, lifting his brows.

Nigga, please!

No matter how desperate I was for a man, I wasn't interested. I was way out of his league. Did he really think he had a chance with me? Then again, men in Atlanta thought that the only thing it took to get a woman was a big bank account and an even bigger dick. Actually, in some cases, the bank account was optional. Straight, available Black men were an endangered species there, steadily decreasing in size on the daily. Some poor woman with too much to offer would someday give him a chance but it wouldn't be me.

"Actually, my boyfriend should already be here. Thanks, but no thanks."

Before he could fix his mouth to respond, I'd already slipped by and was walking in the door.

The club was packed nearly to max capacity. I made my way through the crowd, bopping my head slightly to the rap song blasting through the speakers. Instantly, I loved the vibe. Expertly dressed young professionals, entrepreneurs, and hipsters were all around, networking, drinking, eating, and having an overall good time.

My eyes trailed over to the bar and a man caught my eye. Attractive, white, blond hair, nicely dressed in a shirt, tie, and slacks that I suspected were custom-made. A slow, boyish smile rose up on his lips. He lifted the glass in his hand and nodded his head to me in greeting. Bashful, I did the same and then moved on. If I hadn't been there to see Ink, I would have loved to give him some of my time.

A cheering roar coming from a crowd near the back grabbed my attention. Once the noise died down and the crowd began to settle, I was able to see why.

Sitting dead center, right across from the V.I.P. lounge, was Ink. The second my eyes fell on him, my breathing hitched. A week had passed since the last time I'd seen him but the effect that he had on me hadn't lessened one bit.

He was *gorgeous*. Dressed in a pair of intentionally worn designer jeans and a black tee, his muscles bulged from his sleeves as he worked on a tattoo. His customer was a sexy woman who probably had a million followers on Instagram, double-clicking all of her seductive poses. My suspicion was that the crowd of mostly men hovering around was more interested in the show that she was putting on than anything. While Ink tattooed her thigh, she was biting her bottom lip seductively, moaning, and writhing like a sex kitten against the chair.

"You've *got* to be kidding me."

I had half a mind to leave but my feet had a mind of their own. With my head down, I began moving towards the booth with my name scribbled on a tent card placed above. I'd picked a short, form-fitting, canary-yellow maxi dress for attention, specifically Ink's attention, and I was counting on it to work in my favor.

Sliding into my private booth, right in view of where he was stationed, I watched him hard, mentally beckoning him with my mind. My stomach filled with nervous energy as I looked him over, feeling the same chemistry and connection to him that I'd felt that day as soon as I'd seen him in *Official Ink*. It was too strong to ignore, and there had to be something to it. Like in another life, he was mine. It may sound desperate, even crazy, but something in my soul told me the man was for me. Like we were meant to be.

My cell phone vibrated against the tabletop. I snatched it up, knowing exactly who it was.

Lola: *Are you there?! What's happening?*

Instead of answering with a text reply, I lifted my phone and took a quick video. Lola's reply came back almost seconds after the video finished uploading.

Lola: *WTF!!!*

I was about to reply when another text came in from her before I could.

Lola: *Give me two seconds. Bitch, I got you!*

There was no telling what the hell Lola was planning and, to be honest, I was a little afraid. But not enough to wipe the smile off my face. Lola was insane but always effective.

I placed the phone back down on the table and refocused my attention on Ink. The woman leaned in to him and whispered something in his ear that made him smile. It made me frown. How the hell long did it take to finish the tattoo? It couldn't have been that hard!

Almost as soon as I had that thought, Ink paused and pulled back in his chair. Lying his machine down on the table in front of him, he reached in his pocket and pulled out his cell.

I watched him as he spoke to whoever was on the other line, loving the way he moved his lips.

His brows bent as he focused on whatever was being said on the other end. I admired his chiseled jawline and perfectly trimmed goatee. It was cut lower than the last time I had seen him, like he'd just left the barbershop. I lifted my eyes to check out his hairline and then froze.

He was looking right at me.

"Can I get you a drink?"

I jumped in my seat until I realized the question had come from a waitress right next to me. There was no telling how long she'd been standing there. There was a small smile on her lips and a knowing look in her eyes.

"Yeah… he's pretty damn sexy."

My cheeks flamed.

"Um, I'll take a lemon-drop, please. Make it a double."

She nodded, gave me a polite smile, and then left to fulfill my order. My phone vibrated once again.

Lola: I told Kale to let Ink know that you were there to see him and you didn't have panties on. If you don't get none tonight, it's your OWN fault!

I gawked at the words on the screen, reading them over and over as if they would somehow disappear or morph into something else. Unfortunately, they didn't.

I glanced over the top of my phone at Ink, just in time to see a smile curl his lips. Even in the midst of my misery, the grin still ignited a burning sensation straight to my center, between my thighs. Absentmindedly, I squeezed them together, and Ink's eyes trailed down to them and then back up to me. I could see the hunger there from a mile away.

Chapter Eight

~ Sage

Lola: I told Kale that you would die if you knew Ink knew you didn't have panties on. So just act normal. He doesn't know you know that HE knows!

Me: But I DO have panties on!

Lola: So then it shouldn't be a big deal for you to act normal!

I couldn't even begin to describe how embarrassed I was but it was done. There was nothing left for me to do but roll with it. So when Ink stood up and began to walk my way, leaving the Instagram model looking lovesick in his chair, I looked up and gave him a smile.

"What are you doing here?"

He slid into the booth beside me, coming in so close that I could smell his cologne. It had a smoke cedar scent, strong and robust, like the essence of what made a man a man.

"This place is new. Thought I'd check it out."

His smirk only reached one half of his lips. "Oh? And it had nothing to do with the fact that yo' boy was here?"

I looked at him under bent brows. "*My* boy? You mean… you?" I scrolled my eyes to the ceiling, pretending to think for a minute and then said, "Nah."

He laughed at that. "A man can wish."

Eyeroll. "Yes. On a star."

"Well…" He shrugged. "You're a star."

More dramatic eyeroll. "And you're corny."

"If you tell me you don't like it, I'll stop." He licked his lips.

My hands flew up in the air. "Okay, okay, *okay!* I can't take this anymore. Lola lied! What Kale told you about my panties— or lack thereof—isn't true. She made it up. So you don't have to do this."

I couldn't continue with the con. I liked the flirting, but somehow I felt like it wasn't genuine. I didn't want Ink to show interest in me because he wanted to have sex with me. I wanted him to sincerely be interested in me for *me.*

"Wait… what?" Ink frowned and backed a little away from me. "Panties? What the hell are you talkin' about? Kale didn't tell me anything about panties."

My jaw dropped and I searched his eyes, trying to figure out whether or not he was serious. From the looks of it, he was. Everything about his expression said that he was genuinely confused.

"So…. You didn't get a call from Kale telling you that I was here with no panties on to see you?"

His eyes widened in shock right before he broke into a fit

of laughter, like what I'd said was the funniest thing on Earth.

"Hell nah, you serious?" he asked and I nodded. "Kale did call me about you. But all he said was that your friend told him that you were here. He said I choked up before but it was my lucky night because now I had another chance. Then I told him that I didn't think I was your type and he said that he had a feeling that I was wrong."

My jaw dropped again for the second time in two minutes. "I am going to *kill* Lola."

Ink laughed again and placed his hand on my knee. "Don't do that. Yo' girl got a crazy way of doing things but, you gotta hand it to her; she gets it done."

I couldn't argue with that. Her methods were insane, but she wasn't able to maintain a 4.0 average while partying every weekend and all through the week because she was an idiot. Part of the reason why Lola and I had bonded was because we were both smart.

"For some reason, she has it in her mind that I should give you a chance." When he pulled his hand away, the longing I felt made me realize how much I'd enjoyed his touch.

"And what do you think?" he asked, shifting.

I took a moment to look at him. His elbows were sitting on top of the table and his hands were clasped as if in prayer. I sucked in a breath and tried to keep my composure.

With a shrug, I decided to play it coy. "I think you a'ight."

Shock registered on his face and it was so funny to me. He wasn't accustomed to women turning him down. For someone as sexy and accomplished as he was, I could see why. Then, suddenly, he began to laugh. It was infectious. Not too long after, I found myself laughing, too.

"Damn, that's all I get? Yo, you're a trip."

He ran his thumb across the bridge of his nose and then turned his body even more towards me, closing in on the space between us.

I sucked in a breath and tried to play it cool. Bringing my hand up, I toyed with the length of my ponytail nervously, hoping that I didn't look anything like I felt. I glanced down at his feet. They were big. I couldn't push away the instant question swirling in my head as to whether that was proof that he had a big dick.

"I'm just being honest."

"Honest, huh?" He ran his tongue over his lips and then used his teeth to pull in his bottom lip. His eyes dipped low as he admired my style, taking all of me in. My breathing came to a halt.

"I got another tatt to do and then it's a wrap. You think you can stay until I'm done?"

His focus was on me and although the room was packed, in that moment, it felt like it was only us. I pretended to give it some thought and then checked the time on my phone, as if I had a busy schedule full of something other than returning back home, crawling in my bed, and going back to sleep.

"I can do that."

"Cool."

Ink brought his hand up and ran it over the top of his head as he looked around the crowd uneasily. More than a few women were stealing glances at us, cutting their eyes. They were jealous. They'd come there to catch the attention of a man who had all of it focused in on me. Ignoring them, I watched Ink closely, observing the expression on his face. His jaw was tight for a moment and then he let out a heavy breath.

"You look nervous," I said.

I placed my hand on his thigh. Not in a seductive way, although a volt of electricity seemed to pulse through me as soon as my hand made contact with him, but in a way to draw his attention back to me. He shifted some, turning his body towards me.

"Nah, I ain't nervous. I'm not a fan of this shit." He lifted his hand and pointed with his thumb over his shoulder. "The appearances... the thirsty chicks. I do it because I have to. It's good for business and I make money off of it but I ain't a fan of the extra attention and all this celebrity shit."

I raised both brows. "So you're telling me that you don't like being a man sought after by so many women?"

He smiled a little, blowing air through his nostrils. "I love women but, after a while, the shit gets old. Fuckin' random chicks that you don't really connect with on any level leads to drama. I'm done with it."

I couldn't tell if he was saying all the things I wanted to hear or if he was telling me his truth. Either way, I felt like I could swoon.

Clearing my throat, I said, "Well, why don't you find someone you can connect with and be with her?"

He paused and looked away from me. Suddenly, I felt him closing off and I knew my question had put something in his mind that he didn't want to think of in that moment.

"It's complicated. I wish shit was that simple for me."

I let his words hang in the air and simply watched him, thinking about how much alike we were. Like me, Ink was someone who seemed to have everything but was missing one thing that would make his puzzle complete: someone to share it all with.

"On second thought," he began, pausing long enough for me to guess about what would follow next. "Maybe it's not a good thing for you to wait up for me. I got a lot of shit going on."

"I can tell," I responded. "It sounds like you need a friend. Someone you can be real with."

"A friend?" He looked shocked, almost humored by what I'd said. "At my age, I've made all the friends I plan to make. I don't trust easily. But why? You want to be my friend?"

I raised my hand to stop him. "I don't do friends."

"Why not?"

"Because I'm not friendly."

At that moment, the waitress returned with my drink. I took a sip as Ink ordered something for himself.

"I thought you had another tattoo to do."

He nodded. "I do."

Clutching my hand, he stood, pulling me up. I nearly lost my balance and fell into him.

"What are you *doing?*"

I dug my heels into the floor when he began pulling me to his station. He tugged harder and I gave in to avoid falling on my face.

"I told you. I'm about to do my last tattoo," he replied, over his shoulder.

"But not on *me,* crazy. I've already gotten one and I'm done!"

Once he had me in front of the chair, he stood in front of me, still holding my arm as I glared stubbornly back up at him. There was no way I was about to sit down in the middle of a packed club and do that with him. Not that day and not ever.

"Sit down."

"No."

"So, you don't trust me? I thought we were friends." He smirked and then licked his lips. I almost lost strength in my legs. The man was so fuckin' sexy, it was ridiculous.

"*We* aren't friends. I said *you* needed a friend, but I never said the friend was me."

"Well, I choose you and this is your initiation. Sit down and relax."

I felt my defenses crumble under the intensity of his stare. My skin prickled from the feel of his thumb running over the top of my hand. It was calming but turned me on at the same time.

"Trust me," he said.

Those two words sealed my fate.

"Okaaaayyy." I dragged the word out as I reluctantly gave in. "How should I sit?"

His stare was still intense as he observed me under hooded brows. "Face me. Put your back to the crowd."

"But they won't be able to see anything." I frowned,

wondering what he was up to.

He winked. "That's the point."

With my lips firmly pressed into a straight line, I did as he asked.

"Alright, everybody, Ink is about to begin his last tattoo of the night. If you didn't get a chance to get inked by the god of ink himself, you'll have to visit him at his shop, Official Ink, *to get it done at another time. Now I'm about to drop the beat to something sexy for the sexy lady he got in his chair. If you think you sexy, too, wind your muthafuckin' hips to this muthafuckin' beat. Let's go!"*

The beat came in and I watched Ink carefully as he lifted a tool in his hands. It looked different from the one that he had used the other day in his shop, but I didn't ask any questions. Without looking at me, he dipped the tip into a small container of black ink.

"Spread your legs."

Knotting my brows, I hesitated, wondering if I'd heard him right.

"Not happening."

"Not wide," he clarified. "Just enough so I can slide my hand inside."

I sucked in a breath and separated my knees a bit, feeling like I could hear my heart beating in my ears. Strobe lights danced through the room around us, enveloping us in a kaleidoscope of colors.

"Can you see?" I asked, suddenly feeling nervous about the dim lighting in the club.

"Not everything. But I can see enough."

I wasn't sure exactly what he was referring to, but I left it at that.

He slid his left hand between my legs, gripping my thigh, and the other he used to hold firmly onto the tool in his hands. Flickering his eyes up to mine, he widened them a bit.

"Ready?"

"Yes," I replied almost breathlessly.

His head dropped and my sex throbbed as he went to work. He pressed the machine on my thigh, and I groaned in pure ecstasy, closing my eyes. The vibration went right to my clit, quaking it just right. I bit down on my bottom lip, trying to keep myself from crying out.

My legs parted further, and my body jerked when I felt Ink's hand creep even higher up my thigh. I tensed and opened my eyes, searching his face, nearly on the brink of panic. I wanted that feeling so bad, but we were in public, sitting dead center in the club.

"Relax," he said.

With a slight frown bending my brows, I looked around us, thankful for the dark and the fact that Ink had me positioned so that my back was to everyone sitting in the club. Suddenly, he pushed a button, speeding up the vibration on his machine and my eyes nearly rolled back when the sensation hit my clit. My lips parted slightly, and I closed my eyes once more.

"Oh god…"

I nearly came.

Ink's hand moved again, and that time I didn't try to stop

him. I welcomed his touch. Using his middle finger, he nudged my panties to the side and parted my southern lips. My passion flowed like a river and I gushed honey all over him. He sent the tool into another setting and the vibration increased as he continued to probe me, no longer even trying to pretend that he was holding my thigh. With all fingers forming a fist, except for the one that was deep inside of me, he pumped into my moistness, curling his finger towards him as if beckoning my body to release. His knuckles rubbed against my clit as he sunk his forefinger as deeply as he could into my pussy.

"You're sexy, right? Then wind your hips," he commanded, repeating the words of the DJ.

"You have to stop. Ink…" I gasped out my words, feeling short of breath.

"You're so fuckin' wet, baby. Cum for me."

I opened my eyes and saw his attention zero in on my chest, where my rock-hard nipples had pebbled up through the thin material of my dress. He licked his lips with longing and dove his finger in deeper inside of me. I was so turned on that I began to do as he'd asked, winding my sex against him. I drenched him in my sweet love potion.

I felt my legs begin to shake. My cheeks flustered. I couldn't believe what I was allowing him to do to me in a public place, but it felt so good, there was no way I could make him stop.

"You need this." He beckoned my mind with his words while doing the same to my body with his fingers. "Release it for me."

"Not here…"

"It's only you and me here," I heard him say. "There is no

one around but you and me. Let go of it for me, baby."

Still kneading my center, he used his thumb to press down hard on the most sensitive part of my clit and I had to gnash my teeth together to keep from crying out. My body jerked and my toes curled. With my mouth open, forming a perfect 'O', I released onto his fingers, bathing them in my sweet and sticky juices. He removed himself from inside of me and I couldn't help the twinge of disappointment that I'd felt once he was gone.

"Mmmm."

I opened my eyes to the sight of him dipping his finger into his mouth. He ran his thumb across the top of his lip, spreading my scent right under his nose.

"You fuckin' taste and smell as good as you look. You're perfect."

Unable to respond to that, I dropped my head to look at the tattoo on my thigh. There were two words that read "Infamous Ink."

"I branded you so you're mine," he said before laughing at the horrified look in my eyes. "I'm kidding. It's a different kind of ink. Like henna. Just give it a minute and it'll wash off."

"It better."

Huffing out a breath, I tried to fix my clothes, suddenly feeling self-conscious and stupid about what I'd allowed him to do. That wasn't like me. I was controlled, thoughtful, careful. I wasn't spontaneous and I never did things without thinking through the consequences or making sure I had myself covered. Getting fingered in the middle of the club was the opposite of me. It was something Lola would do.

But, crazy enough, I loved it.

"I've got to get out of here." I was speaking more to myself than to him.

Running my hand over my head, I wiped the beads of sweat from my forehead and smoothed them on top of my hair.

"Don't be in a rush to wash me off," he joked with a smile.

Lifting one brow, I glanced at his fingers and then remarked, "I could say the same to you."

"But you don't have to." He lifted his hand to his nose and inhaled my scent. "Real shit, I ain't never washing this hand again."

My cheeks were blazing hot.

"Have a good night."

With weak legs, I struggled to my feet and stretched the hem of my dress over the fresh ink on my thigh before stalking away. Leaning over the V.I.P. booth, I snatched up my clutch and then made a beeline for the exit.

Ink didn't even try to stop me from leaving. I wasn't sure if I wanted him to.

Chapter Nine

Ink

I've had enough of this ratchet shit.

With my jaw tight, I stared out of the third-story window of my building and took in the scene of the city. Atlanta was a beautiful place but so much had happened since the day I made it my home that it was hard for me to still see the beauty in it.

"What do you mean, you won't be home?"

I could hear Tami's annoyed sigh come through on the other line. Before she even opened her mouth, I knew that whatever she was about to say, I wouldn't like it.

"That's *exactly* what I meant, Ink. I won't be home. I'm going out and then I'm meetin' up later with Tracyi."

My brows pinched. "Tracyi? Who the hell is that?"

Another sigh. This one much heavier.

"I already told you 'bout her before. See? This is what I'm talkin' about. You never listen to me, barely act like you know that I'm here. You don't give a damn about me, Ink, but you always have shit to say when I want to go out and hang with people who do!"

"Because you have our daughter. Mothers don't do this shit, Tami. You're not some lil' young chick who ain't got shit to do but party hop. What's so hard about stayin' home and takin' care of your kid? That's the only damn thing I ask you to do!"

My temples throbbed. I ran a hand over my face, trying to suppress my rage but it was getting harder and harder to control myself.

"I deserve to have a life, Ink," Tami replied with a flat tone. "I'm more than a mother so if you got a problem with me goin' out and bein' with my friends, that's on you."

With that said, she ended the call.

I shoved the phone in my pocket and held my arms behind my back. As a man, I had no problems assuming responsibility for the decisions I made, whether good or bad. But marrying Tami was the one thing I'd always regret.

"Yo, Ink, I hate to bother you but that chick from the other night is back."

I turned around to Kale and my mind instantly fell on Sage. I hadn't seen her since she'd stormed out of the club about a week before. All the fuckin' talking we had done, and I still didn't get her number. I could easily pull it from our system but that felt too much like some stalker-shit. I would rather she gave it to me when I saw her again. My assumption was that she would have surfaced by then, but I was learning that Sage wasn't as predictable as the other women that I'd met.

"Is it Sage? The one with the hummingbird tattoo?"

The smirk on Kale's face said that he knew I was hoping it

was, but the slight shake of his head told me that it wasn't.

"Nah, not her. The one with the red hair."

I frowned. "Brisha."

Shit.

With a slight chuckle, Kale nodded. "Yeah, that's the one."

"Why you ain't tell her I left for the day?"

He threw his hands up in the air. "I did! So did Indie. She told us we were lying. Said she saw your car out front. I told you a while ago to start using your parking space 'round back so these crazy ass broads won't know when you here."

He was right so I couldn't say shit, but I made a mental note not to make the same mistake again. In fact, there were a lot of mistakes I wouldn't be making again. Including fuckin' around with crazy chicks like Brisha.

"I'll be down in a minute. She on some bullshit, I already know." I sighed and ran my hand over the top of my head. "I should've never fucked with her. I knew something wasn't right 'bout her when I first saw her."

Kale shrugged. "Don't blame yourself. Shawty fine as fuck. Who would've known she was the clingy type? She looks like she could have any nigga out here so I don't know why she actin' all thirsty for your ugly ass."

That got a laugh out of me. "Shut yo' dumb ass up, nigga. Don't you got clients to tend to?"

With a salute, he turned on his heels and began to walk away. "I got the hint, boss."

"Fuck outta here with that *boss* shit," I said to his back right before he slipped out the door.

With another deep sigh, I ran my hand over my face and tried to get my mind right to deal with Brisha. I wasn't a heartless man and I hated to hurt a woman's feelings, even if she deserved it. Even when it came to Tami, I had enough respect for her to not have her out there looking stupid. I had done my dirt with other women, but I was choosy with who I decided to share my dick with, making sure that I never dealt with messy broads or women who could step to her about me. I only messed around with women who had pride and something to lose.

Brisha had seemed like that type at first. She was sexy as hell and was working towards a law degree… or so she said. Thinking back on it, it was more likely that she was the type of girl who only went to college to find a husband to take care of her ass. After she had given me head at the shop, I had met up with her in the club. It was on a rare night when Kale was able to convince me to go out: his birthday.

I was sitting in V.I.P., minding my own business, when I decided to take a trip to the bathroom and Brisha ran dead into me. The glass of Hennessey that I was finishing up flew out and spilled straight down the front of her all-white dress. It was Versace, something I only knew because she screamed the shit at me once she saw it was ruined.

I apologized and shot her some cash for a new dress and then one thing led to another and then another, which led to me fucking her inside of the V.I.P. bathroom. That wasn't my style, but I was backed up *as fuck*. Tami had started wilding out and how she was acting when it came to our daughter disgusted me so much that I couldn't even get my shit hard enough to do anything with her. Plus, Brisha was gorgeous. The problem was, I didn't know the chick was crazy, too.

"Ink, I was about to come up and get you," Indie said, nearly running into me the second I stepped off the elevator. "That girl is here and she's getting loud."

The judgment in her eyes was clear and obvious. Indie was always getting on my case about the women that I chose to deal with, telling me that I didn't know my worth. What kind of shit was that to say to a nigga? To me, that seemed like stuff chicks would only say to other chicks. And even if it wasn't, I knew what my worth was. That's why I wasn't dealing with those basic broads on no real level. For me, it was simply sex. It wasn't my fault that they couldn't understand that.

"I'll take care of her."

"Ink…" She paused, and then looked down as she sighed.

"What?" I asked, slightly annoyed because I knew she was about to get started. I didn't need that right then. I'd just been pissed off by one woman and was about to walk right into a situation with another.

She opened her mouth to say something and then stopped and shook her head.

"Nothing. Just… just handle your business."

That said, she walked away swiftly, as if I was a bomb about to explode and she was trying to get away as quickly as possible.

Women, I thought, cutting my eyes at Indie before following her towards the front of the shop.

"What the fuck you doin' here?" I said as soon as I saw Brisha, speaking low enough to not be overheard but stern enough for her to know that shit wasn't going to go the way she planned it.

Pouting, she poked her lips out and ducked her eyes. It didn't move me at all because I'd seen the act a million times before. She would go from sad to a fuckin' crazy bitch in less than five seconds and I wasn't in the mood for her theatrics after arguing with Tami.

"Why are you so mean to me, Ink? I only came to say that I'm moving soon."

My eyes widened with relief. That was the best news I'd heard all day.

"I finally got in law school," she continued, running a hand through her long braids. "I have to do some prep program during the summer before the fall semester starts so I'll be gone in a week or so. I thought you should know."

With hopeful eyes, she looked up at me, expecting for me to say something that meant I gave a damn. I didn't even have the heart to lie to her. What was the point in giving her false hope? Hearing that she was leaving for good made me a happy man.

"Congratulations. I wish you the best."

My tone was flat, my face had no expression. Behind me, I heard Indie make a sound—a grunt of some sort, which let me, as well as Brisha, know that she was all ears. With narrowed eyes, Brisha cut her eyes behind me to where I assumed Indie was sitting before flashing her pretty browns back to my face. I had to admit, she had such soft, attractive features for a bat-shit crazy lunatic.

"That's *all* you have to say?"

I couldn't help but frown. What was it with that chick? I didn't want to be rude but shit like that was why people took me for an asshole. I didn't want to be all that but when it came to women like Brisha, it's what I had to be. They couldn't take a hint, so I had to dish it to them raw.

"What else you expect me to say?" I shot back through gritted teeth. "We ain't friends. You ain't my chick. You ain't even a client anymore. If you came all the way over here expectin' a nigga to give a damn that you ain't gon' be around here no more, you wasted ya time."

Movement behind her caught my attention and when the door to the shop opened, my expression softened when I saw who was strolling in. My shoulders relaxed as the tension left me. I felt my dick began to swell in my jeans. Never in life had any woman ever had that kind of effect on me.

It's her.

She walked inside with her eyes low and then looked up, searching the back before her eyes landed on me. A smile began to creep up on her face once she saw me standing up front and, for a moment, I forgot Brisha was even there. When she cleared her throat, I was quickly reminded.

"Oh, I get it," I heard her say.

I watched as her pupils trailed from me to the woman standing behind her, near the door. A harsh chuckle escaped her lips.

"Yeah, I *definitely* get it now, Ink. I guess it's *on to the next bitch...* that's how you move."

Brisha's nostrils flared and her eyes filled with rage. My chest tightened as I glanced around my shop at the potential customers looking at the artwork on the walls showcasing my past work. The bitch was about to cause a fuckin' scene and it was my fault for even walking down there to talk to her in the first place.

"You need to get the hell out of here. I got work to do." I kept my tone low and tried not to look at Sage standing behind her.

"So you fuck me and then treat me like this?" she said, speaking through her teeth. "This must be about your *wife*, huh? You didn't think I knew 'bout her? Well, I do. Is she the bitch that got you treatin' me like this? Everybody knows you only with her because of your daughter. From what I heard, y'all don't even sleep in the same room together."

I clenched my jaw. God knew I didn't have time for that shit.

"Ink?" Indie piped up from behind me. "Should I call—"

I waved a hand to stop her from speaking. "Nah, I got this."

With cold eyes on Brisha's face and my jaw tight, I kept my tone low as I spoke to her—not like Ink the tattoo artist of the A, but Infamous Ink, the nigga who had earned his name by running the Chicago streets. I wasn't that man anymore but, every now and then, I had to bring a piece of him out.

"Yo, listen to this. I been trying to be nice to yo' dumb ass but you don't know how to respect that shit. I'mma tell you this once and after it's said, I ain't gon' repeat myself again. Don't bring yo' ass down here no more with this shit. Trust me when I say, I don't give a damn 'bout you and if you want to know you how much I mean that, I ain't got no problem with showing you."

By that time, Brisha's eyes were so wide, they could've doubled as dinner plates and her skin was as pale as a sheet.

"As for my daughter," I continued, "Mention her one mo'

fuckin' time and it's a wrap for you. They'll be zippin' you up in a body bag and takin' ya ass to the morgue so ya moms and pops can identify you. Now, play with it."

As if frozen by fear, she stood completely still; frozen into place as I glared down at her. I didn't need her to say a thing; one look told me that I wouldn't have to deal with her coming around anymore.

"This is the last time I'mma let you play me, nigga. I'm done with you," she spat. She was trying to save face, but I let her have that. The fact that I didn't respond only pissed her off even more.

With her hand lifted, she pointed her finger close to my face and said, "You'll miss me when I'm gone. Have a nice life."

I couldn't even respond to that. The bitch was delirious. After giving me head and one fuck in the bathroom of a club, she had the nerve to have an attitude about the life of a nigga who wasn't even hers. She wouldn't have even been tripping so hard if I was any other random man in the city. Like I said, that celebrity shit wasn't for me.

After Brisha made her exit, Sage stepped forward cautiously with her brows raised as she looked at me. From the look on her face, I knew she'd heard everything.

"Let's walk outside," I said before giving her a chance to say a word.

Taking the lead, I walked to the door and held it open as she stepped outside. Once there, we stood in front of each other and I waited in silence for her to speak. The crazy part about it was that I was nervous like my girl had caught me creepin' or some shit. She wasn't my girl, I barely knew her, but there I was, ready to explain something that wasn't actually her business anyway.

"Your *wife*?"

Her tone was low. With her arms folded in front of her body, she cut her eyes around us, glancing over the busy streets. When they came back to me, there was so much emotion in them that I couldn't help but feel guilty.

"She's lying, right?"

With my head lifted, I ran my hand over my mouth before lowering my eyes.

Damn, I thought, looking at her. She was beautiful as fuck and it was making the conversation that much harder.

"Lyin' about what?"

"Your wife," she fired back, her eyes seeming more green than brown in her anger. It fascinated me. I swallowed hard, taking a moment to weigh my words before I spoke again.

Normally, I didn't go for chicks like her. She wasn't my normal type. I grew up in the hood and I had a thing for hood-ass chicks that could be the Bonnie to my Clyde. True shit. My type was the kind of woman who knew how to roll a blunt, help me smoke that shit, and then fuck until we fell asleep. That's the kind of girl Tami was; in fact, she was rolling a blunt when I met her.

We both grew up in the same hood, were birthed by the same streets. When I came up in the dope game, she was right along with me. I cooked my first pie in her crib and, being that her pops was a low-level hustler back in the day, she told me a lot about the game. We had puppy love. When it was time for work, we worked hard but when it was time to play, we fucked even harder.

Growing up, I always knew that Tami would be my wife because I'd never loved any woman like I loved her. I figured there was no point in wasting time, and I bought her a ring with all that money I'd hustled up. We got married in the courthouse when we were fifteen years old. Our parents happily gave us consent because they didn't give a damn about what we chose to do with our lives as long as they didn't have to pay for any of it. I didn't have a dollar in my pocket and no home to put her in but neither one of us cared. We came from nothing and had nothing but each other. In our young minds, that was enough.

But all that changed when she changed.

The more I made a name in the streets, the more I had to be in them, which left her home alone more than she wanted to be. She started to become suspicious and paranoid, complaining that I was running up in random hoes when I was actually putting in work to build a life for the two of us. Eventually, I got enough of her shit and told her that I needed a break.

During that break, she ended up fuckin' around with my enemy, a slimy nigga by the name of Dolla. When I heard she got pregnant by him, that shit almost killed me. I would've gotten over it but my stash spots started getting robbed and Kale found out that Dolla was behind it. He suggested that Tami was the one giving him all the information he needed about how I ran things in order to come at me, but I couldn't believe that she would betray me like that.

I put word out that I wanted Dolla dead. My lil' homies ran up on him while he was in his car one night and lit that shit up with bullets. With the windows tinted, they had no idea that Tami, who was eight months pregnant at the time, was in the car with him.

Something about seeing a baby fighting for her life because of some shit that I'd put into play crushed me. With Tami in a coma, her baby's father dead, and her baby girl fighting to survive after I called the hit that almost ended her life, there was no one to be there for the baby but me.

Tamiyah was six months old when I was told that Tami would probably never recover from her coma. Since we were still legally married, by law, I was Tamiyah's father and I happily took on the responsibility. By then, I couldn't see living my life without my daughter. She wasn't biologically mine, but I was the only father that she knew.

Once Tami recovered unexpectedly, she tried to take Tamiyah away from me, said she wanted a new start in a new place, but I wasn't having that. I moved to Atlanta and bought a house so we could stay under one roof but there was nothing going on between the two of us; we didn't even share a room.

I was single in my mind, so I acted like a single man. I never brought up getting a divorce to make it legal because no relationship ever became serious enough for me to want to deal with the drama that would follow. Now, with Sage standing in front of me staring with unspoken accusations of my doggish ways in her eyes, I wished I'd gotten all that over with.

"It's not a lie. I do have a wife but it's not what you think."

"Oh my god... not again. Why does this always happen to me?"

She placed her hands over her eyes and blew out a breath.

"I'm not with my wife like that," I continued on, hoping it would make a difference. "She does her thing and I do mine. The only thing we have between us is a daughter. We got married young on some stupid shit. That's all."

My words were met with skeptical eyes, judging and mocking me at the same time.

"Am I supposed to believe that? If you don't want to be with her, why don't you get a divorce?"

I raised my arms and laced my fingers together as my palms rested above my head. That was the question everyone asked me.

"I've tried to cut ties with her more than a few times. And the next thing that comes out her mouth is how she will move across the country and I'll never see my daughter again. I've never met a woman who I wanted something real with, so that legal shit never mattered."

"She threatened to move your daughter away from you? Who would do that to her kid? What a miserable bitch!"

I wanted to agree but I knew better than that. Tami and I had our issues but she was my daughter's mother and, personal shit aside, she was one of my closest friends. I wouldn't disrespect her.

"She doesn't have anyone else and she's scared. I've been in her life since before she could walk. We fell in love when we were young and then, when she thought she was losing me, she made a mistake that she could never bounce back from. The threats are her way of trying to make me stay. She thinks that one day, I'll love her again."

"Well, will you?"

I leveled with her hazel eyes and spoke with all sincerity.

"Nah." I shook my head. "Loyalty means everything to me.

The second that she proved she wasn't loyal, everything that I could have felt died. I will always respect her because of our history but I could never go back to someone who would betray me. Ever."

I watched the beautiful woman in front of me, wondering what was on her mind as she looked down at her feet, thinking to herself. I waited because I knew that once she collected her words, she would share them. She was a woman who didn't hold much in. She led with her feelings and I picked up on that, even though she tried to play it hard.

"I'm not anybody's side chick," she said finally. "I deserve more than that."

I frowned. "I'm not tryin' to make you no side chick."

She gave me a pointed look and I could almost read what was on her mind. How could I say that when only a week ago, I had my finger in her pussy while inking my name on her thigh? As soon as I went there in my head, I felt my manhood swell in my pants. When she dipped her eyes to my bulge, I was caught.

"Make no mistake about it," I began, speaking honestly. "I want to fuck you. Anybody who says they don't is a gay ass nigga."

Somehow, my words were able to soften her up. She bashfully dropped her head and tried to hide the smile curving her lips, but I saw it anyways.

"But I won't go there with you until I have my shit together. That's why I told you not to wait for me the other night at the club. I got a lot going on in my life and I don't want to bring you into that until I get all that together. Until then, I don't mind bein' your friend." I took a step closer to get her attention and then smiled. "I mean, if the offer still stands."

She rolled her pretty eyes to the sky and then laughed.

"There was never an offer. I told you that I'm not friendly."

"I can't tell..." I licked my lips, thinking about the scent of her womanhood on my upper lip after that night at the club. "You may not have asked me to be a friend, but you've definitely been acting friendly."

Another laugh escaped her lips and I smiled at her. I couldn't ignore the chemistry between us. For a nigga who didn't like talking, she had me doing a lot of it. It came easy, too, like holding a conversation with her was a natural thing. Right then, I knew she wouldn't be just any other female to me, and I made up my mind to treat her different than the ones before. Maybe it was a good thing that she had standards and that I wanted to respect them. It would give me the chance to get to know her without sex coming into play.

"What brought you out here? I know you ain't stop by because you wanted to pull up on a nigga." I shrugged. "Although I wouldn't complain. I expected to see you sooner."

Her eyes widened. "Oh? How did you know you would see me at all after I left the club?"

"God's been answering my prayers so far when it comes to you," I replied with a shrug. "I guess I figured He would keep it going."

The smile that followed could've brought a grown-ass man to his knees.

"I was wondering if I could get a consultation with you... on another tattoo," she said in a quiet voice. She spoke like she was unsure of the words that were escaping from her lips.

My brows shot to the sky. "Word?"

She nodded and gave me a long look before pulling out a folded piece of paper and then unfolded it slowly. Once opened, she held it up to reveal a photo of a phoenix flying out of the flames. I got excited looking at it. The colors, the depth of talent that was needed to create such a work of art… it was a challenge that I was more than ready to accept. I was fully engaged.

"That's gonna be a long session," I told her, speaking simply, not allowing my voice to show how amped I was at being able to get the job done. "Where you want it?"

"On my back," she replied with certainty and a steady tone, like a woman who knew exactly what she wanted. I could respect that.

"When you want to get it done?"

"As soon as you have an opening."

I looked at my watch. I'd finished my last client for the day and was supposed to be on my way home. Being that Tamiyah was with the sitter because her mama was out hitting the club, I was more than ready to leave, but by the time I got there, she would already be in bed.

"It's your lucky day," I told her. "If you don't mind staying after hours, I got some time to start it tonight. I'll do the outline and get you on the schedule next week to color it in. Cool?"

She smiled her response and then nodded her head.

"Cool."

Chapter Ten

Sage

Ink said that the outline for my tattoo could take a couple of hours.

Was two hours too soon to fall in love with someone? How about one? I couldn't say whether there was an answer to that but, the facts were, he was only about halfway through outlining it and I felt a way that I had never experienced before. I didn't want to say it was the 'L' word… or maybe it *was* the 'L' word. You know, the other one.

Lust?

I couldn't be sure but all I knew was I didn't want the night to end.

"How did you start doing tattoos?"

Hugging the back of the chair with my arms, I looked at the images of his work on the walls while listening to the buzzing sound behind me as Ink outlined the tattoo on my lower back. We had been talking nonstop since he started. About random things, mostly, but I'd enjoyed it. So far, I knew how old he was, where he was from, and how much he loved Atlanta but hated being in the spotlight. He knew about my family's business and how nervous I was to be running it now that I'd completed my degree. He even knew my favorite things to do and favorite foods to eat. It was small talk, but it felt like it was the beginning of something real.

"I always liked to draw. As a child, my moms would beat my ass for scribbling shit on the walls at the crib." He chuckled and I joined in, trying to suppress my laughter as much as I could so that I didn't mess him up. "When I got older, drawing on the walls turned into me spray-painting shit on buildings, signs and streets… I almost got picked up the cops one time after getting caught spraying graffiti. I stopped all that once I started hustling but, when I got locked up, I did tattoos in the pen to pass the time. I was good at the shit and went back to it when I decided to go legit."

I frowned. "Hustling? You sold drugs?"

Although Ink looked like he knew his way around the streets, I was shocked to hear someone admit something like that in casual conversation.

"Yeah… *hell* yeah. Growin' up the way I did, seein' the things I've seen, it's almost an expectation that you have for your life. I didn't see any other way. It wasn't until I had my daughter that I put that shit to rest and started *Official Ink*."

That was admirable. My heart swelled and I felt my body respond to his words. A man who loved his daughter enough to sacrifice his normal way of life to take a different and better path? I was impressed. If he could love his child like that, imagine how he could love a woman.

"Why did you go to prison?"

The buzzing behind me stopped for a few seconds before starting up again. I felt like it was a fair question; plus, he was the one who had opened the door for me to ask once he mentioned it. I wanted to know and I didn't want to assume that his history of selling drugs was the reason for it. However, the longer he delayed in answering me, the more unnerved I felt.

"I mean… you don't have to tell me. It's your personal business but I—"

"Nah, it's cool," he said, no sign of anger or irritation in his tone. "I mentioned it so I can't blame you for asking. To answer your question, I messed with the wrong chick and she got me caught up. She was a good girl who wanted a taste of a thug. When shit went south, she told her pops that I drugged and raped her. I didn't but, when it comes to a man with a background like mine, it doesn't matter either way. She was pregnant and had to explain to her family why she was about to have a Black baby. She didn't have money for an abortion and I wouldn't pay for no shit like that. So she went to her dad with that lie."

"That's crazy."

He nodded. "Yeah… but I was young and dumb. While I was in, Tami held me down, even though I never would've gotten caught up if I hadn't cheated. I guess that's why I don't do her dirty, though she's been a headache to deal with most times. She fucked up eventually. After I got out of prison and hit the streets hard, she thought I was cheating again, but I never did no matter what she believed. Getting locked up gave me a reality check about life that I needed."

"We've all had our young and dumb moments."

My mind immediately went to my ex, Grey, and I felt sadness take over me. I was over him, but the time wasted and the hopes and dreams that I had about what was supposed to be our future together still affected me.

"You sound like you're speaking from experience. What somebody like you know about being young and dumb?" He laughed a little and I felt nervous energy course through my stomach. "It seems like you've always had your shit together."

I paused and twisted my lips to the side before speaking. Through my hesitation, I wondered if I should tell him my story and how much of it I should share. I felt pressed to say something since he'd been so open and honest with me.

"My ex was my first love and he took me through hell," I suddenly heard myself saying. "So, believe me when I say that I know how it is to be dumb when it comes to love *and* life." I stopped speaking but when he didn't say anything, I felt like I should continue on. Crazy enough, Ink made me feel comfortable enough to speak my truth.

"He made me fall in love with him and then, after I was too attached, I found out that he had a wife. Not like in the way you say—he had a *real* wife who he had no intentions of leaving. He said he loved her and would never leave her for me."

"Damn, that's fucked up," Ink said and blew out a breath. "What crazy ass chick did he think would go for that?"

I hung my head in shame. "Well, I did."

His eyes widened and I continued.

"I went along with it for some time after because I was in love and I didn't know how to live without him. But I got tired of being his secret… my feelings were involved. I was stupid— I believed what he said about being a prisoner in his marriage because he was trying to look out for his kids. But then I thought about it one day. There was no way he could love me but put me in that situation. He wanted me but didn't want to give me the love I deserved. When I told him that I was leaving, he turned into someone else. He said I was ruining him. He even hit me."

Tears came to my eyes as I thought back to my ex, Grey. I was thankful that my back was to Ink so that he couldn't see.

"That's one thing I don't do—put my hands on a woman. Ever. Which is why it's so fucked up that I got locked up for the shit. Everybody that knows me can tell you that shit ain't in me but, to them white boys in the courtroom… I guess it didn't matter."

We continued talking as he worked on my back, I didn't share much because there wasn't all that much to my life beyond private schools and college life. I'd always lived the model life, never stepped out of line, and always did the things I was expected to do. My only issues came from out of my experiences with love.

Listening to Ink speak about his past was interesting. His upbringing was so different from mine that it was fascinating. I was born into a world of wealth; never had a day passed by where I knew how it felt to not be catered to or live the privileged life. To hear about how it is for someone living on the other end of the spectrum was like reading a book that I couldn't put down.

"You're finished. For tonight anyway," he added with a sigh.

My brows jumped. I hadn't realized that time had passed by so quickly.

"I wanna see it!"

Before he could say anything, I leaped up from the chair with only my arms covering my double D-sized titties. When Ink had started the tattoo, he offered me a blanket to wrap up in after taking my shirt off, but I hadn't really used it. I was playing with fire, especially after I was the one who placed him into the 'friend zone,' but I wanted him to see my body. I thought about the look in his eyes at the club when he was staring at my perky breasts. It was shameful but I would've given anything to see that lustful stare again.

"It's so pretty," I said, staring at my fresh new tattoo through a mirror on the wall. It sat high, and I had long ago slipped out of my heels, so I had to get on my tiptoes and toot my booty up on a small shelf in order to be tall enough to see into it.

Through the reflection, I saw Ink purposely not looking directly at me, respectful of the fact that I was half-clothed. I liked that about him—he was a gentleman now that I'd laid out the rules. But I wanted him to be a little more of the thug that I'd met the other day.

"Same day and time next week work for you?" I asked him.

He nodded. "Yeah…"

He kept his head down and ran one hand over the top of his head. When he shifted his feet, somewhat spreading his legs, I couldn't help but shift my gaze down.

"Ahh!"

As I tried to get off the shelf, it tipped forward and, though I reached out for something to break my fall, there was nothing there and I busted my ass, falling right onto the floor.

"Oww!" I whined, bringing my hand to my head. I

scrunched up my face and started to laugh at myself as Ink ran over to help me up.

"You good?"

I laughed through my embarrassment, steadying myself before reaching out to grab his outstretched hand.

"Yes, thanks."

My perky tits bounced when he hoisted me to my feet and, though I was dead wrong, I didn't move to cover them. Being that the shop was closed for the night, the blinds on the front windows were closed as well, preventing me from giving the entire street a show. The only person able to get a good look at me was Ink.

"Sage… you gotta put your clothes on, ma."

The way he said the word 'ma' only made me want him that much more. He placed more distance between us and sat down on a stool a short distance away. His body was doing one thing, his mouth was saying another, but his eyes were still on me.

"Ink." I licked my lips. "I—I think I changed my mind." Walking in closer to him, I positioned my body between his thighs and grabbed his hands in mine. "I know what I said but… I know what I feel, and I want what I want. We're connected. Can't you feel it? We are meant for this."

With that said, I placed both of his hands on my breasts and groaned when he gave my nipples a squeeze. Pushing both of my large melons together, he positioned my nipples between his thumbs, forcing them together and then leaned over, sucking them both into the warmth of his mouth.

"Oh god…" I moaned, letting my head fall back.

His tongue danced around my nipples and my pussy puckered, gushing honey. Ink released my breasts from his grasp and ran a hand to my backside as he sucked hard, nearly swallowing one half of my chest in his mouth. He kneaded my ass through my jeans, and I allowed him to pull me forward, pushing my center right into his. I felt his hardness through his sweats, and I began to wind my hips against it, wanting nothing more than to rub it against my clit before allowing him to force his girth inside.

"You want that?" he whispered against my neck.

With one hand on my ass and the other under my chin, he jerked my head upwards and then sunk his teeth into my neck. At the same time, he nudged my thighs apart and jerked his manhood forward, rubbing against my center. I sucked in a breath, loving the way he was balancing me in between pleasure and pain.

"Yes, I want it… so bad."

I was in heaven. The man was creating in me a feeling that I'd never felt before. I wanted to say that I was in love, but that couldn't be love. Or could it? It seemed like it was too soon to tell but it felt so right.

"Once we go there… you know that means you're mine, right?" His words made me shutter as he spoke them against my neck. "The way you got me feelin', I'mma be territorial about this pussy. I don't share. Won't nobody be able to even sniff her but me."

And with that said, he released my chin and the next thing I felt was him slipping his fingers into the waist of my pants. The material stretched to give him room. He dipped his finger into my center, hard, pressing on my clit with his thumb, working it with expert precision.

"Fuck…oh god," I cried out. We were alone so I didn't even try to stay quiet.

I leaned into him, feeling my body go limp as he held me in his arms. Whispering in my ear, he said everything that I needed to hear to bring me to a gushing climax. I let go while screaming his name, clutching on to him for dear life.

"Damn," he said, suckling my juices from his fingers. "I can't wait to taste the real thing. But I'll wait." He added the last part and I shot my eyes open.

"Wait? After all of this?" I questioned, pointing eyes to my exposed chest. "After what we just did, you want to wait?"

He nodded. "There's no turning back once we cross that line. I know the kinda man I am and I don't like to share when I feel like something is mine. But I can't claim somebody who can't claim me. Once I can find a way to get my issues in order, we can go from there."

Longingness settled over me but I tried to ignore it as much as I could in order to collect my things. I'd waited a long time for love and, once again, it was so close but other things were in the way. I wasn't sure how long it would be until Ink got his situation together but the way he had me feeling, I couldn't wait much longer. From the look in his eyes as I pulled on my clothes, neither could he.

Chapter Eleven

Ink

Laughing to myself, I turned onto the ramp for I-285 and began the long ride home. Although it had been almost a half-hour since she'd left, Sage was still on my mind. I guess she'd made sure of that with the 'oops, my titties are out' trick.

The chick was slick as fuck.

That stunt shouldn't have worked on someone like me; I was a professional at curving beautiful chicks. But she got me on some sucker shit, and I couldn't resist touching her again. She was right; something about our interactions felt supernatural, like we were meant to be. It was beyond the sexual, even though my shit was rock hard after being around her for hours. I couldn't stop staring at the soft skin on her back, the curve of the top of her ass poking out of her low-rise jeans and the pretty, caramel sides of her breasts as I outlined her tattoo.

When she'd shown her bare chest, I'd bricked up like never before, but I couldn't let myself slip. I'd dodged a bullet once I got rid of Brisha but I didn't want to fall back in my old ways. I didn't have the patience for that shit. I wanted something real. My daughter was getting older and the last thing I wanted was for her to read one day in the blogs about how her daddy was fuckin' around on her mother because he didn't love her. Tami and I kept no secrets; she knew we were only playing house, but I didn't want news of that getting to Tamiyah.

It was almost five in the morning by the time Tami strolled her drunk ass into the house, talking loudly on the phone with one of her bird-ass friends. I was in her room when she arrived. I wasn't asleep because I'd been waiting for her to get home. Although there was no love between us, Tami and I had a history that made it so that I would always care about her and would always look out for her no matter what. She did some stupid shit when we were younger—we both did—but though that made it so that I could never look at her the way I once did, I still made sure she was safe. The truth was, if it hadn't been for her, I wouldn't be me.

"Why the fuck are you still up?" she asked as she entered the room, like that was a new routine for me. "And why are you in my room?"

"I'm always up waiting for whenever you decide to bring yo' ass home. And lower yo' voice. Your *daughter* is sleeping," I purposely put emphasis on 'daughter' which, from the sound of her sucking her teeth, must have pissed her off.

She rolled her eyes. "Right… she's *sleeping*. The same way she would be if I were here. So you can drop the attitude, Ink. You got so much to say but you're just gettin' home, too."

I watched her from the chair I was sitting in near the closet as she pulled off her stiletto heels, stumbling to keep her balance since she was clearly intoxicated. Once they were off, she stomped by me into the closet, making sure to cut her eyes sharply in my direction as she passed by. I caught a whiff of something and, before I knew it, I'd jumped up from my seat.

"Yo, what nigga you was all up on to the point that you wearin' his cologne? I can smell the shit on you so don't lie."

Tami sucked her teeth as she headed into the closet, stripping along the way, not at all bothered about the fact that I was right behind her, damn near standing on the back of her heels.

"I wasn't on no nigga and what if I was? You don't care. *Clearly.*" She snatched the zipper down on the dress and then began to step out of it. "You know we ain't like that so why the attitude?"

She had a point. The same way she didn't trip about what I did, I never said a word about what she did. My only stipulation was that she told me before she did it. But according to her, she wasn't interested in anyone else because she wanted things to work out between her and me. No matter how much I told her that I couldn't see that happening, she refused to move on.

"Are you done with the twenty-one questions?" she asked, stepping out of her panties. "I had a long night of dancing with my *friends* and I need to get in the shower."

She didn't wait for me to answer and, instead, stomped by me butt-ass naked to walk to the adjoining bathroom. I wasn't able to stop myself from turning around to get a glance at her fat ass. Tami had a ghetto booty and she was thick as hell. No matter how determined I was to not want to be with her on a real level, we still messed around every now and then. Her body always caught my attention and she knew it, often using that knowledge to her advantage.

When I heard the shower start, I left the closet, walking back into the room only to see that Tami had left the bathroom door wide open, giving me a clear view of her in the shower. The glass was slightly fogged, but I could still make out the sight of her rubbing her body down, covering it with soap.

My dick sprung to life when she caught me looking, wiped away some of the fog, and began to cup her fat pussy in her hands. She lifted her head to look at me before dipping a finger inside, jerking it in and out slowly as I watched.

Captivated, I stood in silence and enjoyed the show. The whole thing was a set up but, unlike what Sage had pulled earlier, I didn't have to use restraint. Technically, Tami was still my wife. Meaning, I had a license to fuck with zero consequences.

I watched her intently as she put on a show, rubbing her breasts, pinching her nipples, and stroking her clit. When she turned around and spread her ass cheeks apart, bending down low so that I could get a clear image of both of her holes, my dick was hard as a baseball bat. Holding the muscle in my hand, I stroked it as I watched Tami continue with her visual seduction, rubbing her hands in her wetness before sucking it off her fingers as she poked each one in her mouth.

"Want a taste?" she asked, and her words were like a remote that controlled my feet.

With a mission in mind, I strode over to her and opened the door to the shower, stepping right inside after removing my clothes. As soon as I closed the glass door behind me, I twisted her body around and pressed her back down so I could enter her from behind. With her hand on the tile wall, she braced herself as I deep-stroked her from the back, squeezing my eyes as I imagined that I was splitting Sage's pussy in two instead.

"Mmm, I love that juicy dick!"

Tami's pussy hugged me like it was a custom-fit. No matter how many women I'd been with, I had to admit that her sex was one of the best. She was always soaking wet and when I fucked her, she fucked me back. When giving me head, she could swallow me whole like she was born without a gag reflex. If only I could've trusted her, we could've been the perfect couple. But I couldn't and the saying was true: there was no love without trust.

Finishing fast, I unloaded into her without thinking twice. Tami didn't want to get pregnant as much as I didn't want another child from her. She took her birth control religiously. The shower rained down on my body as I breathed heavily, hanging on to the memory of Sage's body in my mind's eye. I lifted my hand to my nose and sucked in the sweet remains of her fleeting scent. Though I'd showered as soon as I got home, I avoided removing her natural aroma from my fingertips. I pulled back and leaned against the back of the shower, massaging my manhood in my hands. Thinking about Sage made me rock up again, and the moment Tami saw it, she dropped down to her knees.

"Nah, you good, T. Listen, I don't need—"

Before I could protest further, she opened her mouth and nearly covered my entire twelve-inch dick with her mouth. Hers weren't the lips that I wanted wrapped around me, but it was too late for me to object.

Smacking loudly, Tami gobbled me between her jaws like I was a full-course meal. She was relentless when it came to that. All her life, she'd been competitive. She kept her body tight because she wanted to look her best. When it came to men, she wanted to be with the best. And when her bedroom skills came into play, she was like a porn star with it; no lie. That time, however, her masterful skills weren't having the same effect because the erection she was trying to satisfy was one she hadn't caused.

"Aye, you good," I told her, tapping on the top of her head. "I'm tired so I'm about to get in the bed."

Jerking away, I pulled out of her mouth while softly nudging her back. I could feel myself going limp. It wasn't her fault, but she was going to take it personally regardless of what I said.

"Some other bitch must got your attention... again," she said.

She already knew I wasn't about to respond so I didn't feel any type of way about ignoring her as I grabbed my clothes and started to walk away. Behind me, I sensed that she was staring, heating my back with her rage. The things that she wanted from me, the emotions she wanted me to feel for her, she would never again experience. Dick was all I could give her but with Sage fuckin' up my head, pretty soon, I wouldn't even be able to give her that either.

"I hope you enjoyed that because I'll never let you fuck me again!" Tami shouted as I walked out of her bedroom door.

Her ego was bruised, and I was used to her talking shit when she was trying to work through her pain. She would get over it. She always did.

Chapter Twelve

~ Sage

"Bitch, you lyin'!"

With her mouth wide, Lola ogled me incredulously like I'd told her that I'd seen a three-legged man walking down the road. She was sitting Indian-style, listening intently, as I filled her in on everything that had happened the night before at Ink's shop. We were video-chatting because I needed her to see every bit of my expressions so she knew I was real.

"I'm *definitely* not lying," I replied, smiling wide. My phone chirped and I jumped to check it, hoping it was Ink texting me. When I saw it was spam mail, I tossed it back on my nightstand, somewhat disappointed. Though I was still swooning over the night at the shop, I couldn't help but wonder why he hadn't contacted me.

"So, he got an eyeful of your boobs and then what?"

I shrugged a little before answering and then fell back on the stack of pillows behind me.

"I could tell he wanted to do something, but he tried to play it cool. His dick gave him away. That thing was hard as hell and I could see it through his pants. It's long, too… and thick with a curve."

Flicking my tongue over my lips, I squeezed my pussy lips at the thought of Ink's dick, imagining I was gripping it between my walls. I gushed, wishing that he was lying beside me on the bed.

"Let me get this straight," Lola spoke, interrupting my thoughts. "You and Ink were alone, your shirt was off, titties on display, and he was standing there with a hard dick but y'all ain't fuck? What the hell is wrong with you?"

"I don't know." I sighed and then rolled my eyes as I continued. "He said that what messed him and Tami up was that they argued all the time. She went in on him about everything and he wanted her to trust him. So I'm trying not to rock the boat. We are just getting started and I like him a lot."

"Kale told me a lot about her, too. She's a bitch!"

I snorted out a laugh. "Lola, that's rude."

She rolled her eyes and cocked her head to the side. "Well, it's true! And the craziest part of it all is that he talks about her as if she is a victim. Like it's Ink's fault that she is the way she is. I really feel like he blames Ink for her being a miserable bitch."

"Hmm… that's crazy," I said, thinking about what Lola was saying. "I actually got that feeling from Ink, too, though. He won't say anything against her. Makes it feel like she acts how she does because she's miserable in love."

"Nah, that bitch is just miserable."

I laughed so hard at that, by the time I was done, I was

wiping tears from my eyes.

"I can't mess with you anymore. I have to get ready for work."

"Work? Ew." She wrinkled her nose.

"I'm supposed to be in by now but I'm not since…" I raised my hands in the air like I was putting a crown on my head. "…I'm the boss."

"Yeah, yeah, yeah… you're still wasting time in an office when there is a whole world out here that you could be helping me explore, but I'll let you go. Call me when you're done. I need to hear about you about your new man that *I* hooked you with. When y'all get married, I want your firstborn named after me."

I rolled my eyes at that, but I couldn't deny that I loved thinking about Ink as my new man and me being the mother of his future kids.

Chapter Thirteen

~ Sage

"Welcome to McMillian Enterprises. We are excited to have you on the board."

I looked back and forth at all of the smiling faces in front of me, sporting a smile of my own, although I didn't trust any of the people around me.

"I'm delighted to be here," I said with honesty because I was.

Although everyone around me probably believed that I was there solely based off my last name, I knew the truth. Not only was I smart enough to be on the board and to take on the leadership role of running my father's business, I was more than capable of doing so. I'd trained for this moment my entire life. The art of getting what I wanted was a lesson that my stepmother had taught me very early on.

"I never let anyone tell me what I can or can't do or what I can or can't own," she said one day. *"A McMillian is a boss in every sense of the word. As a boss, we don't ask permission. If we*

want something, we create a plan and we take what should be ours."

After shaking hands and saying the necessary pleasantries, I left the boardroom and took the elevator up to my office on the top level of McMillian Tower, one of the tallest buildings in the city. The entire top floor belonged to me; my office took up half, with my receptionist sitting outside. On the other end, I had a private kitchen, a boardroom of my own for when I brought in clients and even a small exercise room, shower and bedroom for any late nights spent at the office. It was built and designed with a queen in mind; perfect for me.

"Good to see you again, Ms. McMillian," Sherelle, my assistant and receptionist, greeted me as soon as I stepped off the elevator. She raised a coffee cup to me and smiled. She seemed genuine. I wasn't pleased about not being involved in the process of selecting my assistant, but I had to admit that there was something about her that I liked immediately.

"Based on the questionnaire of your personal preferences that I emailed you, I saw that you enjoyed Caramel Lattes, so I grabbed one for you." She handed the cup over and I thanked her with a gracious smile before taking a sip.

"It's perfect. Thank you so much. You didn't have to do that," I told her.

"Of course, I did. That's what I'm here for... to make your days easy, pleasant and ensure that you stay on point. I typed up your schedule as well as a brief of everything that is happening this week that you'll need to be aware of. Let me know if you have any questions or need anything further. I'll be right outside."

With that said, Sherelle gave me a polite nod before leaving to take her place at her desk. I took a deep breath and then turned to walk towards my office, already loving the start of the day. Just as she'd said, there was a small stack of papers on my desk and as soon as I made myself comfortable in my large, leather office chair, I grabbed them in my hands to look them over. There wasn't anything there that I hadn't already seen and prepared for. Turns out... I was still rich.

My father started the McMillian empire from a cleaning company and then branched out into other areas of business, including real estate, interior decorating, furniture and other household products from there. He made something of a 'one-stop shop' for his clients and was able to continue doing business with them for years after the purchase of their home was final. Once he placed them in the home of their dreams, he would also fully furnish it with premium décor and then contract them through his cleaning service during the time they lived in it. When and if they decided to sell, he handled that as well, which led to him gaining new clients as well as keeping the old ones when he found them a new home through services that his other businesses provided. It was a business that continued to grow.

After a few minutes of going through my business emails, my mind went back to Ink and I found myself looking at the hummingbird tattoo on my wrist. It was peeling, as he said it would, so I grabbed the ointment that he'd given me and was applying it when my phone started to ring. My heart almost stopped when I saw the name that flashed across the screen.

"Hello?"

"Congratulations are in order, right? Tell me, how does it feel to be running your own shit, Ms. Business Lady?"

A smile curved my lips.

"Actually, it feels damn good. Better than I expected. But you should know that. Plus, you built your business from the ground up. I was handed mine, so I have a lot to prove." I rolled my eyes, thinking about all the fake smiles and kind words that flowed through them during the board meeting earlier. They could pretend but I wasn't dumb.

"What do you mean? Prove to who?"

I sighed and began clicking my pen against the top of my desk. "The other board members. They don't truly want me here. They don't think I've earned the right to be in charge of them. They've had decades in the business and I just happened to be the child of the founder."

"Fuck 'em," Ink said so casually that I snorted a suppressed giggle through my nose. "They old asses are just jealous. You're young, sexy, smart and now you're running shit and telling them what to do. It's human nature to be salty about it but you've worked hard to get where you are and, in time, they will see that you aren't some dumb chick who was given a company to run. You deserve to be there."

Sticking the tip of the pen between my teeth, I smiled, feeling my body go warm. He spoke to me in a way that I wasn't accustomed to but it was so real. So authentic. Maybe that's why it made me feel like he was right and I could trust him.

"Aye, listen... your building isn't too far from mine. Can I take you to lunch? Just to celebrate your first day."

"How do you know I don't already have plans?" I asked, though it didn't matter if I did. My schedule was clear but, even if it wasn't, I would've cancelled everything to meet up with Ink.

"You're a busy woman and you have a lot to do but you gotta eat… and I'm hoping you could do that with me. I'm easy. Even if we gotta grab something off a hotdog stand, it's cool. I wanna see you."

I couldn't play it tough any longer. He had said all the right things to make me feel the right ways.

"I'll be ready by noon if that works for you."

"Bet."

***

I was taught to always make a man wait. It was another of the few lessons given to me by my stepmother. She didn't teach me much because she didn't like to have me around that long. But one thing I do remember from when I had just turned ten years old was sitting in her room watching in awe as she got dressed to go out with my father.

It was my birthday but instead of spending it with me, he was taking her to a charity dinner for some women's club that she worked with. My daddy promised me that he would give me the best birthday party ever over the weekend if I forgave him for skipping out on me that night and I agreed with tears in my eyes.

Truthfully, I didn't want a party. I didn't have any friends to invite so what was the use? But when it came to my daddy, my stepmother always won out over me. Choosing her seemed to be his way of earning her infinite forgiveness for my existence.

"Even if you're on time, always be late," she had said that night. *"You must always make sure a man is reminded that you are the prize. Make him anticipate your presence. The more anxious he is for you to arrive, the more pleased he will be to see*

you. A gracious man is a man who won't forget what he has. He won't take you for granted."

With those words in mind, I glanced out of the tenth-story window of my office down to the front of the building, watching Ink who was sitting on a concrete ledge down below. It was twelve-fifteen and he'd glanced at his watch a few times already in between watching the double doors at the entrance, anxiously anticipating the moment when I would walk through them.

"I'm heading to lunch. I'll be back soon."

Sherelle looked up from her computer and nodded her head.

"I'll be here. Have a good lunch." She smiled and then went back to what she'd been doing.

Stepping onto the elevator, I frowned slightly when I felt something vibrating against my side. It only took a second to realize it was my phone.

"Hey," I said, answering as soon as I saw who was calling. "I'm heading down now. Sorry, I was caught up on something and fell behind."

"You're good. Just wanted to make sure I wasn't being stood up," he replied. I could almost hear his smile through the phone.

"Never that," I said, stepping off the elevator. "I would never stand you up."

"I like the sound of that."

My eyes focused on him through the glass double doors and I was able to see the smile in person. It was much sexier in reality than in my mind's eye. Hanging up the line, I slid the phone into my purse and stepped out the building, straight to Ink who greeted me with a hug and kiss on the cheek.

"You ready?" he asked with one brow lifted.

Was he serious? I was more than ready... and for more than what he was offering. Holding my words back for a beat, I checked him out as he stood before me in rugged designer jeans, a soft black tee that hugged his muscles just right and designer shoes. He was casual but dressy in his own way.

"Of course," I answered him.

He held his hand out to me and I hesitated briefly before giving in. He wasted no time lacing his fingers through mine and I relaxed into him, feeling like that moment was the most natural thing on Earth.

It felt so good. So right. I didn't want the moment to end.

Chapter Fourteen

Ink

Sage was growing on me like no other woman had before. It wasn't merely that I was finally in a place where I was ready for a grown-up relationship, but she was a different type of woman than what I was used to in every way.

Most women didn't demand me to level up when it came to how I treated them, but she expected it and wouldn't go for less. She made me behave like a man and I did it because I wanted her. When I took her out to eat, she wouldn't step foot in anything that wasn't five stars. I mean that *literally*. She checked the ratings on her phone before even walking inside. She waited for me to open doors, pull out her chairs and when the bills came, she acted like they weren't even there. She was a pampered princess in every way but that was cool with me. I considered myself a king so what else would I go for but a woman I could make my queen? I was convinced that Sage was it.

Every day for weeks, I showed up like clockwork to take her

out to lunch until it became our thing. Even if I didn't tell her I was coming, she would walk out her building, late as usual, expecting to see me.

What we had going was cool, but I wanted to take our relationship deeper than the lunchtime dates, texts and calls that we had going on. It was my idea to take things slow, but I was ready to go all in. My only problem was Tami. I had to find a way to get rid of her ass that didn't compromise me being around my daughter. Once I figured that out, then I could really make things official with Sage.

As if summoned, as soon as my mind was on Sage, she hit my phone. It was crazy how things seemed to always happen that way when it came to us.

Sage: What you doin'?

I didn't even notice the smirk on my face as I read the text until I heard Kale's nosey ass all in my business.

"Yo, Ink, what fine-ass shorty got you smiling like that? Bet not be Brisha!"

I waved him off. "Hell nah. I ain't fucking with that girl ever again."

Ignoring him, I went back to my phone and quickly responded.

Me: Working. The club I was at before asked me to swing through, pretend like I'm having a good time so they could take pics and shit.

Sage: Pretend? Lol. Why you gotta pretend?

Me: Because you ain't here this time so shit ain't sweet.

Anyways, what were you up to?

　　Sage: Definitely not thinking about you.

　　Me: Yeah? So you hit me up because you weren't thinking about me?

　　Sage: Yeah, that sounds about right.

　　Me: Why don't you swing through?

　　Sage: I'll think about it.

"Yo, tell me again why you ain't fucked hummingbird chick yet?"

Glancing up, I cut my eyes at Kale who was sitting across from me, his arms spread out across the booth. From the smirk on his face and the question he'd asked, he must've made an assumption about who I'd been texting.

"I told you already. She ain't the type of chick that you put on the side. When I take it there with her, I want to have all my shit in order so we can build something real. I can't have Tami fuckin' up what we got going before it even gets started."

"Am I talking to Infamous Ink right now or somebody else?" Kale laughed, rubbing his eyes for added affect. "Because you ain't sounded like the nigga I've known for damn near all his life." He turned to Indie who was sitting next to him, looking down at her phone. "Indie… do you believe this?"

With her lips pressed together, she slowly brought her eyes up, giving me a hard look before replying.

"Ink has the ability to do anything he decides to," she said before rolling her eyes and adding, "I simply want him to make better decisions about the women he chooses to deal with."

I chuckled at her attitude. Indie was always trying to sound like somebody's mama.

"Why it gotta be like that? I fucked up in the past but I'm with Sage now. Can't get no better than her. What you think?"

She scoffed. "You really don't want me to answer that."

"Damn!" Kale cut in, laughing at her. "Indie, if I ain't know better I'd think you were jealous. Why Ink can't get him some cutty from Sage?"

With her hand in the air, Indie held it in front of Kale's face and sucked her teeth.

"MiKale, don't go there with me. You know I don't give a damn 'bout y'all getting—" She curled her nose in disgust. "*Cutty*, if that's what you wanna call it. But if Ink is trying to settle down with somebody, especially someone who will need to be a role model to his daughter, I don't think Sage is it."

Amused, I watched them in action. They always went at it like brother and sister. It was funny as hell to watch. Some chick behind Kale shot me googly eyes before blowing a kiss. I ignored her and leaned forward to grab the glass of brown liquid in front of me, preparing to take it straight to the head.

"Why not?" I asked out of pure curiosity. Indie had never before been this determined to prove to me that some girl wasn't right for me. She usually said little stuff to let me know where she stood but the more we discussed Sage, the more upset she seemed to become.

"Because she has no idea about anything real. She's been rich her entire life. Everything has been handed to her. What do someone like that and you have in common?"

"That's not true," I replied back. "She didn't have it as good as you may think. Her mother was her father's side-chick and Sage was never accepted by her stepmom. Boarding schools raised her. In a lot of ways, our paths are the same. We never had nobody around who really had our backs like a parent should. We raised ourselves."

"Yeah, whatever." Indie rolled her eyes. "It's easy to raise yourself when you have an unlimited budget at your disposal."

"So what you're saying is, she's not good enough for him because she's rich? Hell, he's rich, too."

"That's *not* what I'm saying." Indie rolled her eyes again. "Ink needs someone who knows his struggle and can identify with it. Someone compassionate, not trying to use him for his money or to be in the limelight. Kind, honest, hardworking…"

"Well, tell me this, Indie. Who *is* good enough for Ink?" Kale asked with a smug smile that said he was up to some bullshit. "Because I'm feeling like the woman you're describing is you."

My eyes widened slightly as I looked from him to Indie, watching the expression on her face. For some reason, I was curious about what she would say.

"What?" She almost gasped. "No!"

The color seemed to drain from her face and then suddenly return. If I didn't know better, I would say she was blushing under her ebony brown cheeks.

"All I'm saying is that…" She shook her head, growing increasingly agitated. "You know what? This ain't my conversation so keep me out of it!"

That said, she snatched up her phone and placed it back in front of her face. Her pinched expression reminded me of the one someone made when they had bit into something sour. It was cute and, though I was tempted to fuck with her for a little longer, I let it go and tried to bite back my smile. Turning away from her, I focused back in on Kale who had a satisfied smirk on his lips, knowing he'd succeeded in stirring up some shit.

"Listen, we all gotta grow up some time, bruh. I'm tired of playing the same ole game I've been playing. How much longer you think I can put up with chicks like Brisha showing up, actin' crazy and shit before Tamiyah ends up reading 'bout it in some blog?"

He ran a finger over his top lip and nodded slowly. "Yeah, you got a point. Don't need my goddaughter finding out her daddy out here being a whole hoe in these Atlanta streets."

"Fuck you, man."

I snorted out a soft laugh and then glanced down at my phone. Sage hadn't hit me back since the last message. I wasn't sure if she was coming, but I definitely hoped that she was. I could never predict things like that with her because it could go either way. She wasn't the clingy type, but we did talk often. We usually talked or texted through the night until she fell asleep. Obviously, she enjoyed my company, no matter how much she tried to pretend that I was just something to fill up the void spaces of time in her day.

"Did you tell Tami that you were coming here?" Kale asked all of a sudden.

I frowned. "Nah, why?"

He nudged his head at something behind me and I felt my chest tighten. I didn't even want to look because I already had a feeling that I knew who would be there once I did.

"This is some bullshit."

Once again, Tami was partying it up in the club like she didn't have a child to watch over at home. Since I had to be out for work, I took off the entire day and spent it with Tamiyah because I wanted to be with her but also because I wanted to give Tami a break to do whatever she wanted before I had to leave out that night. Even after doing that, she still couldn't stay her ass at home.

"She looks drunk as hell," Indie said, shaking her head.

I was pissed off.

Tami was twerking up on one of her homegirls like she was the one getting paid for a show instead of the bottle girls standing around. A nigga came up behind her the second she turned around and started grinding up on her ass. Looking back at him, she smiled like she had sex for sale and began working up against him like he had flashed her his black card.

"Ink... hey."

My brows shot to the sky at the sound of her voice. Pulling away from the sight of Tami shaking her ass like it was a pair of dice, I turned to the voice and my temper cooled somewhat the second I saw Sage's beautiful face.

"Damn, you made it."

She bent her brows low. "You aren't happy to see me?"

"Of course, I am." I ran my hand over my mouth and then cut a quick glance to Tami before bringing my focus back. "Just didn't know for sure if you were coming or not."

"It was a surprise." She smiled wide. "After you said that you were pretending to have a good time, I'd already made up my mind. I was already close by and didn't have anything else to do."

She shrugged and I allowed my eyes to drop, taking in her swag. She had on a tight-fitting tee with a pair of little ass shorts that had me thinking all kind of nasty things. Her high heels matched her top as well as the bag she held at her side and, for a change, she had her long hair curled in ringlets, hanging down her back.

"Damn, you look... right," I said, not wanting to come on too strong. Honestly, I wanted to say that she looked sexy as fuck.

She giggled. "I look *right*?" she repeated. "That's new." Turning towards Kale, she waved. He nodded and then leaned over to shake her hand.

"How's that crazy ass friend of yours doing?"

Sage laughed and shook her head. "Lola is the same as always. You already know."

From there, her eyes scrolled over to Indie who had her head bent and her eyes glued to her phone as if she were in her own world.

"Hi, Indie. It's nice to see you again."

She took her sweet time lifting her head. "Oh, hi... It's Sage, right?"

I narrowed my eyes at her, wondering why she was acting like she didn't know Sage's name although we had just been talking about her.

"Yes, that's right," Sage said slowly, like she didn't quite believe that Indie's question was innocent.

"Why don't you come up here and sit next to me." I patted the space I was referring to.

As soon as I said it, I could feel Kale looking at me and I could've sworn I heard Indie suck her teeth. She was still focused on her phone, but her body language was saying it all.

"Nigga, is you *crazy*?" Kale mouthed but I waved him away. Tami couldn't say shit to me when she was on the other side of the club shaking everything her mama didn't give her, but my bank account paid for her to get.

Sage slid into the booth right next to me, in a way that told all the chicks around staring that she was my woman. She even cut her eyes at Indie who, thankfully, didn't catch it. I couldn't blame her. She was probably reading her body language, which clearly said she wanted Sage anywhere but there.

The more I watched, I laughed a little to myself. In our conversations, Sage was always trying to play it like she wasn't feeling a nigga as deeply as she was but every now and then, she couldn't help but let it show. Especially now. She was posted up next to me with an expression on her face that said she was staking claim.

Her possessive ass.

It was funny to me, but if Tami caught her sitting there, she would start some trouble.

"Aye," I said, leaning over to speak to Kale as Sage bobbed her head to the beat of the new jam the DJ was spinning. "I need you to do me a favor."

"Yeah, I got you," he replied. "What's up?"

"Go over there and tell ole girl that you gon' take her home. She's drunk as hell and I don't want her starting drama."

Kale nodded and then looked over to Tami who was letting some nigga pour a shot in her mouth while others stood around watching. Cameras were flashing all around her. She was putting on a hell of a show.

Narrowing his eyes, Kale stood. The look on his face showed that he was as irritated as I was. We'd all grown up together and he had known her as long as I had. He thought of Tami as his little sister so I could see why he was feeling some kind of way about how she was acting. It didn't look good and Tami had to be doing it on purpose. It was no coincidence that she was showing her ass in the same damn club where I was doing a paid appearance.

"Yeah it's time for her to go," he said. "She's officially doing too damn much."

Kale pushed by me like a damn linebacker, bolting past like he was ready to shake some shit up. Initially, I thought it would be better to send him because he would've been calmer than me, but now I wasn't so sure. From where I stood, it looked like he wanted to choke the life out of Tami's ass about as much as I wanted to.

"It's time for me to go, too," Indie announced, grabbing her bag.

She cut her eyes at Sage who was looking the opposite way, still dancing as she mouthed the words to the song. I felt like she was catching Indie's negative vibe but was choosing to ignore it. Indie, on the other hand, was on some other shit.

"Wait... what?" I frowned. "Indie, it's like that?"

Ignoring me, she snatched her sweater from behind her and pulled it on. This wasn't the same Indie I knew. What was her problem? I slid over to her so I could speak without yelling over the music.

"Yo, I hope you don't think I feel any kind of way 'bout what Kale was sayin' earlier. I know it's family between you and me. He was playing and it was a bad joke. We good, fam." I held out my fist for dap and she frowned, glaring down at it. After a few quick seconds passed, her expression relaxed and she began to nod slowly.

"You know what? You're right," she said, returning my dap. "That's exactly what we are... family. That's what we will *always* be."

Before I could respond, she stood up and darted away, leaving me wondering what the hell I'd said wrong. I rose to my feet, about to go after her, but stopped when Sage grabbed my hand.

"Do you know this song?" she asked, moving her body to the beat. "It's really good! Reminds me of the one the D.J. was playing that night at the other club."

"Yeah..." I replied and then turned back around. But that quickly, Indie was gone.

"It's nice here. I've never been to this club before." Sage snapped her fingers to the music and then signaled for the waitress. I took a seat and put all of my attention on her so that she could give me hers. She didn't seem to be at all aware of the fact that my wife was in the same building and I wanted to keep it that way.

"You're looking good as hell tonight," I told her, licking my lips as I looked her up and down. "Good enough to eat."

She rolled her eyes and smiled. "Don't play me when you

know you're not ready."

I frowned. "I never said I wasn't ready. I only said that I wanted to take it slow. Do things right."

"Exactly," she replied, giving me a pointed look. "So in other words, you ain't ready for me."

"But I'm making moves to be."

"Oh yeah? What moves have you been making to settle the issue of your *wife*?"

She put emphasis on the last word and cut her eyes behind me in the direction of where Tami was.

Ah shit. I didn't have time for any more drama.

"Why would you have me come out here if she was here?"

"Listen, I can handle my—"

I stopped when I saw Sage's facial expression change. She was still looking behind me but her eyes had widened and her lips parted, forming a circle of surprise.

"Oh my God... something is happening over there."

I stood to get a better look, my ears picking up on raised voices. I heard Tami's clear as day. It wasn't like her to go off on Kale, but she was drunk so I couldn't put it past her. But when I focused in on the source of the yelling, it wasn't him that she was shouting at. He was there, standing not too far from her as she held an envelope in her hand and snaked her neck, jerking it back and forward while spouting a slew of four-letter words at a man standing in front of her who I hadn't seen around her before. Once she was done giving him a piece of her mind, she pivoted around, and her blazing eyes met mine.

"How *dare* you!" she said. I couldn't hear her, but I could read her lips clearly.

Before I knew what the hell was going on, she took off in a mad strut across the room, heading directly towards me. The crowd around her parted to allow her room and I stood to my feet, my composure calm and my expression blank, even though some ratchet shit was fast approaching.

"So, this is how you do me?" she yelled and tossed the envelope at me like a frisbee. It hit me square in the chest and the papers inside flew out, spraying all around the V.I.P. booth.

"The fuck?" I growled back, looking from the papers up to her. "Listen, you need to take yo' drunk ass home."

"You obviously don't want me home because then you couldn't publicly embarrass me!" She spat. "You planned this whole thing, huh? Had them send me the message on Instagram telling me to show up here for a paid appearance only so you could have me served with divorce papers?"

I narrowed my eyes at her, confused as hell. "What the hell are you talking 'bout, Tami? I ain't have nobody ask you to be here or serve you with no papers. Are you crazy?"

Folding her arms across her chest, she cocked her head to the side.

"You really want to tell that lie when the papers from some lawyer are right there in your face?"

Still not completely grasping what she was talking about, I leaned over to grab the paper closest to me and my frown deepened when I read what was there.

"I don't know who the hell sent this but…"

Brisha.

Only a fake ass wannabe attorney would send some fake-ass shit like this. Brisha was feeling some kind of way about me not wanting her but, being that she had been gone for a while now, I thought she was over that. Apparently, she wasn't.

"Tami, I didn't send you this shit so—"

"And who is this new bitch? Oh, this some real bullshit!" she said, leaning over to the side so that she could get a good look at Sage who was still sitting behind where I stood. "Don't try to hide now! I see you, hoe! I guess this *bitch* is the reason you're talking about divorcing me now? You're trying to get legit to be with this green-eyed hoe? Well, guess what? Not happening! I'm not going nowhere! And even if I were, you already know who would be coming with me."

I began to get heated and my hands clenched into fists at my side. I hated when she brought my daughter into shit.

"Um… I'm not tryin' to get in the middle of no drama," I heard Sage saying, followed by some shuffling as she began to move. "So I'll be on my way."

"No, bitch! How 'bout you stay? Don't act shy now. You obviously don't have no problem fuckin' a married man!"

The alcohol had her mad as hell. She was going in so hard on Sage that she wasn't even focused on me anymore. Her drunk ass wanted to start a fight and Sage seemed like an easy and obvious target.

"And *you* don't have any problem being a married woman in here shaking your ass for the next nigga, so what's your point?"

Well, damn!

Sage was in rare form. I cut my eyes in her direction and I immediately saw the fire in her eyes. She wasn't no chump and that was for sure. It was a nice surprise for me but I knew that Tami hadn't expected it. Even so, it wasn't a good look having my possible girlfriend fighting with my current wife so I had to step in.

"Tami, don't start throwing around this *wife* shit. You know we ain't like that. And you also know I wouldn't serve you no divorce papers in public."

She continued to glare at me but didn't respond. Even drunk, she knew me well enough to know, for a fact, that what I was saying was true. That wasn't like me but it was also dumb. Why the hell would I send somebody after her ass while she's in the same damn club I was in?

"Aye, Kale, do me a favor and take her ass home, man."

Tami cocked her head back and scowled at me. "I don't need anybody to take me home!"

"You may not but I got you," Kale said before walking up to Tami's side. He whispered something in her ear and slid his arm around her waist in a way that showed how comfortable he was touching her. They looked more like a couple than she and I did.

"Let's go," he then said in an authoritative way that she didn't argue with. He grabbed her by the arm to lead her away and she allowed him, although she made sure to keep her eyes lasered in on me.

"I'm not going anywhere and not signing shit. So have fun with your side bitch and then bring your ass home!" she yelled out before Kale drug her the rest of the way out of the club.

The moment she disappeared, I ran my hand over my face and exhaled heavily. The shit was stressful, and I hadn't even done a thing to earn it. I halfway wished that I had actually served Tami the divorce papers so at least I could be one step closer to being done with her ass.

"You didn't send her these?"

Turning around, I watched as Sage collected all of the papers from around us, staring hard at them.

"They look legit… like they came from a real law firm."

"Hell nah, I didn't do no shit like that and I didn't send her no message to show up here either." She handed me the papers and I grabbed them, balling them up without even looking. "That dumb chick that I was messing with—Brisha. She's the one behind it. Fake-ass attorney."

Sage's entire face went blank and I began to wonder what she was thinking. More than likely, she was second-guessing if she really wanted to be involved with someone like me. I had a whole lot of drama coming with me that I was sure she didn't have room in her life for. I wanted her but if she didn't feel the same, I couldn't make her stay.

Then, as I was about to cut my losses and tell Sage that we needed to put some distance between us for a while, she began to laugh. I watched her, in awe and confusion, wondering what was so funny to her all of a sudden. She was nearly roaring with laughter, like what had happened—whatever it was that I obviously missed—was the funniest thing in the world.

"I'm sorry, I just—"

Before she could even complete her sentence, she began laughing again. This time, even harder than before. It was infectious. Before I knew it, I was letting out a few chuckles myself.

"Yo… what happened just now?"

Placing her hand on her stomach, Sage inhaled sharply and then exhaled slowly to calm down her laughter.

"It occurred to me that you have *terrible* taste in women! Like…" She threw up her hands as she scanned the area around us incredulously. "This right here is only something you hear about in movies. The jump-off is a wannabe lawyer who writes up fake divorce papers and serves them to your wife after tricking her into being at an event that you'll also be at so that she can start drama and embarrass you. It's crazy but you have to admit, it would be good for T.V."

Running my hand over my mouth, I laughed a little. She had a point there.

"What can I say? I mind my business and the drama follows me."

She snorted. "That's for sure."

"Is all this too much for you?" I asked, feeling crazy about how much I really cared about her answer.

Looking up, her eyes softened when they met mine. "No, it's not. I'm not fragile and I'm not easily intimidated. Though I like to avoid drama, if and when it comes, I'm able to deal with it. Especially when it concerns the ones I care for."

Damn.

This chick was absolutely perfect in all ways. She was the complete package and I needed her to be mine. But I didn't want to be like other niggas I'd seen good girls get wrapped up with. The ones who pulled a good woman into his situation and ended up fucking up her life because she gave so much when he could only offer her so little. I wanted us to be together on equal grounds. I didn't need to be her burden. That said, I *definitely* didn't want her to leave and become another man's blessing.

Stepping forward, I closed the space between us, very much aware of all the eyes that were on us. People were no longer staring like we were the main event as they had been when Tami was raising hell, but Sage and I were still very much the focus. I lifted my hands to touch her but stopped, knowing that any wrong moves on my part could make her the subject of some gossipy article written by a blogger with no life. I'd already given them enough to go on already; no need to make Sage the confirmed 'homewrecker' in the story.

"You should leave and let me finish up here," I said as I took a few paces back. "Too many eyes on us right now and I can't control myself."

"I didn't ask you to control yourself." She was baiting me. "You can do what you want."

My eyes narrowed in on her. The effect that she had on me was strong. With words and looks alone, she was making my nature rise.

"And I will," I vowed. "Call me when you get in."

Smirking, she pulled a spiral of hair behind her ear. "I might."

As soon as those words left her lips, she slid by me, so close that her hair rubbed against my nose as she walked by. I inhaled the sweet scent and kept my eyes glued on her as she strolled out of the club, grabbing the attention of nearly every man around her as she passed by. All of them wished for a chance with her but I wasn't about to give any of them the opportunity. The time for waiting around and worrying about Tami's feelings was over. I had to make Sage mine.

Chapter Fifteen
Ink

The humming of my machine was the soundtrack to my thoughts as Sage sat in front of me in my chair. We were alone once again in the shop. Kale had no clients the entire day and Indie left as soon as she saw Sage walk in. I still couldn't understand what her issue was those days. It was almost like she wanted nothing to do with me. I wasn't one to force people to do anything, so I gave her some space. Maybe it was some hormonal female shit.

"Oh!" She squeezed her eyes closed. "That spot is tender."

"Don't worry, I'm almost done," I told her. "The chick who normally watches Tamiyah for me when I work late went to Boston to visit her folks. I gotta be back in time to grab my daughter so her mother can go to the club and shake her ass."

My disgust was palpable but as soon as the words were out of my mouth, I regretted them. I wasn't the type of man to talk about my child's mother in front of the next chick. No matter how much I couldn't stand her in that moment.

"I shouldn't have said that. Tami is Tamiyah's mother and she deserves my respect because of that. I'm mad as hell because she's been hitting up my phone back to back for the last hour and I already know why. She's only had Tamiyah for two hours since she picked her up from school and she's already trying to get rid of her so she can go out."

"You have a reason to be upset," Sage replied, speaking softly. "I think you and Tami misunderstand each other and that's why you're always at odds. You both need to learn how to communicate. You used to love her at one time so she can't be all bad."

Her response gave me pause. Whereas most chicks would jump at the opportunity to talk shit about a man's ex, especially one like Tami, Sage wasn't.

"Didn't you call her a 'miserable bitch' a while back when I told you about her trying to keep my daughter away from me?" I teased with a sly smile. Though her back was to me, I could tell by the way her cheeks moved that she was grinning.

"I did but I may have been dishing out judgment too soon. Now that I know more about you, I can see why she acts the way she does sometimes. She wants your attention… it's like how a spoiled child does a parent."

"The difference is I'm not Tami's parent, I'm not her man and I'm only her husband by circumstance."

Sage giggled. "That kinda rhymed."

"I'm multi-talented," I replied with a shrug.

The only sound around us became the sporadic buzzing of my tool as I colored in her tattoo, dipping the tip in the various colors of ink on my desk as I finished up what was becoming a masterpiece. We settled into a comfortable silence that I wasn't in any hurry to break.

"Ink, tell me something."

Cupping the top corner of her ass in my hand as I colored in the lower half of her phoenix tattoo, I was more than a little distracted. When I heard myself say, "Go ahead," I almost confused my damn self. I'd been so focused on the softness of her skin and her sweet butterscotch scent that I was barely paying attention to what she'd said. However, what came next snapped me right out of that shit.

"Tell me more about when you got locked up. You said the girl accused you of rape when she got pregnant. What really happened?"

My brows bent so far down on my forehead, they probably connected at the center.

"I don't really talk about shit like that."

"I know. I want to know everything about you. Your past, your present." She shrugged. "I mean, people say you shouldn't ask questions about a person's exes but I think it gives you a lot of insight on what kind of partner they will be."

"Really?" I chuckled a little. "You don't think people change? That was a long time ago. What does it have to do with me now?"

She paused for a few seconds, working either my question or her answer around in her mind.

"People change but, in many ways, they stay the same. Past trauma, hurt or experiences shape the way we view the world and the people in it. It shapes our interactions and how we view and solve problems. It's important to know."

She had a point there. I didn't want to say I was a man who was emotionally affected by previous relationships but I knew, for a fact, that my dealings with Tami did shape my outlook on many women who followed after her.

"The first girl, the one who accused me of rape, I didn't have a relationship with her. We knew of each other. She used to flirt and shit but I didn't really take it further with her. She got drunk one night, came on to me at a club and it wasn't the smartest thing to do but I had sex with her anyway. She was in that rebel stage that rich white girls go through. Partying every night, fucking around with whoever. She got pregnant and told me the baby was mine. I wasn't trying to hear that shit because I knew what was up. Out of all the men she had dealt with, I was the one moving weight, riding in an expensive whip, dressing nice, and she saw dollar signs. She asked me to pay for an abortion and I wasn't with that shit. I don't kill babies, period. Mine or anyone else's. Her pops ended up finding out she was pregnant after she used her parents' insurance for her doctor's appointment. They saw the bill and when he asked her about it, she lied. Said she was raped and that I was the one who did it."

The days that followed after that had been some of the worst in my life and I could remember them vividly. It felt like my whole city had turned its back on me. I was a nigga from the hood, but I was well-liked by everyone; it didn't matter their race or financial status. That was how I was able to make moves with my money that others couldn't do. You couldn't tell by talking to me that I wasn't college-educated so I'd been welcomed into arenas that were closed for many niggas that I grew up with. But when I caught that charge, everything changed.

Sighing, I dropped my tool, thinking back to that moment

when I found out what I was being accused of. Tami had been there. When I'd first told her about how I'd cheated on her after the chick tried to pin her baby on me, she was devastated but, on the day I was arrested, she stayed by my side from then on out.

"The chick's father was a known businessman so he had clout. They found the videos from the club, saw she was drunk. They made it seem like I drugged her. They said I gave her a roofie and that's why she couldn't remember everything."

"The date rape drug?" Sage shook her head. "That's crazy."

"Nah, what's crazy is that a lot of other dudes were trying to speak up for me, to talk about how wild she was and how she was fucking everything moving. Even Kale tried to be a witness for me because he was there that night, but her father was able to get all their testimonies thrown out. The jury never heard them."

"But didn't you have an attorney? Why wasn't he able to help you?"

It was a question I'd had all along the way but didn't find out the answer to until after I was locked up.

"I made the mistake of hiring an attorney who did business in Chicago. The city is big but it's small at the same time. Most of the businessmen who do well there are able to make their fortunes because they work together. So, basically, my attorney took my money and then hung me out to dry. From the beginning he was telling me to take a plea deal. He was never on my side. When you have money and the right connections, you have all the power necessary to do whatever you want."

Those were things that I hadn't told anyone who didn't

know me when it all went down but there I was letting it all out for Sage. I hadn't even told Indie. She knew I'd been locked up before but she didn't know why. It wasn't like she couldn't find it if she went looking for it; I just never brought it up. For whatever reason, no blog had ever picked up the story and I think it was because the chick's father did all he could to keep her name out of the news. Because of that, my past was pretty much a secret.

I was shocked at how easily I could speak about it. In fact, I actually felt like, for the first time in a minute, I had someone that I could be real with. Kale was one of my closest friends, but I couldn't speak to him about no serious shit. We were close because of the history we'd forged in the streets; we did business together and became friends out of our loyalty for one another. Tami was who I used to share my innermost thoughts with but we hadn't been that way in over a decade. Now Sage seemed to be the one that could take that place.

"I made a mistake, too. A long time ago," she began, speaking in a low tone.

"You mean your ex, right? The one who was married."

She nodded but didn't continue. I went back to adding color to her tattoo and gave her time to decide if she wanted to tell me more. I was almost done, and the artwork looked nice on her skin. It would definitely earn her a place on my wall of tatted fame.

"I told you the part about me dating him, even after I found out he was married, but what I didn't say was I realized that from the beginning. He always wore a ring so it's not like I didn't know. I wanted him, so I believed him when he said that it was a marriage of convenience and he was leaving her. But, of course, he was lying and he never did. He never planned to."

She went silent. This time, I understood exactly what was on her mind.

"You don't have to worry about that with me. Yeah, I'm technically married, but Tami and I are never getting back together. I'm not playing you like that. The only reason I'm moving the way I am is because of my daughter. I want to make sure that, legally, I'll have the right to be in her life. Tamiyah isn't biologically mine and Tami can make it so I'll never see her again."

I was saying it but deep down I knew there was no way. I'd never let Tami take my daughter from me. That was something I was willing to die about. Until I had a real wife and family, my daughter was the only person that I had left to love in the world.

"That's not an option. I have friends in high places, too. I wouldn't let her do that to you. I fight for my friends."

"Your friends?" I grunted, playfully. "I don't have many friends. And the ones I do, I've been rockin' with them since we were wearing diapers. They proved they deserved their spots through their loyalty. They've proven that they will do whatever when it comes to having my back."

Sage snapped around to look at me. She would've fucked up the tattoo had I not been holding the iron steady in my hands. Her eyes shined as she looked at me a moment longer before speaking.

"I can be loyal," she battled back.

I shot a skeptical look her way.

"And how would I know that? Loyalty is something that has to be proven."

We stared into each other's eyes for what felt like the better half of forever. Before I realized it, I felt the urge to kiss her. The subtle pout her lips made as she tried to find a way to answer my question was so sexy to me.

"Well, I—"

Before Sage could answer, someone started beating hard on the front door of the shop. She flinched but my eyes went to the drawer in the desk next to me where I had my burner stashed. Being that I had served time and was technically a felon, I wasn't supposed to have it but I did anyway. In my experience, it was better to be caught with a gun than to be caught up in some bullshit without it. I was reaching out to grab it when a voice stopped me.

"Ink, I know you're in there! Open up this motherfuckin' door!"

I gritted my teeth.

Tami... the fuck she want?

"Is that the girl from the other day? Brisha?" I heard Sage ask as I pushed away from her and dropped my machine on the stand next to me.

"Nah, it's not," was all I said.

Taking steady strides, I walked to the front to open the door, knowing that, once again, Tami was up to her bullshit. After the club incident, she'd given me a good three days of peace but that was all coming to an end. Sage was right; my life would make a hell of a show. Or at least a banging ass book. I just wished I wasn't the unlucky motherfucka that was living it.

"Who's this bitch?" Tami roared as soon as I pulled open the door.

I couldn't even see her because she had her phone all up in my face, waving around a video of two people fuckin' on the screen. Sliding the door closed behind me to block her from another run-in with Sage, I took a closer look at her phone. My chest got tight as I narrowed my eyes. It was Brisha and me, a short clip from when I had dicked her down in the bathroom. From the angle of the video and the giggles in the background, it had been taken by one of her thotty ass friends who had been peeking in from outside.

I exhaled a short burst of air as my anger multiplied. I had been so wasted that night after dealing with Tami's bullshit that I hadn't even thought to lock the door. Truthfully, I hadn't been planning on being in there with Brisha all that long. As soon as I got my nut off, I tossed the condom and was on my way out.

"You know we ain't like that so why all the attitude? Ain't that the same line that you said to me the other night?" I gritted down on Tami as she cocked her neck to look at me sideways.

Her attitude increased with a quick suck of her teeth and dramatic show of rolling her neck.

"Oh, you mean that night when you *fucked* me? I guess you weren't able to catch up with this salty bitch so you decided to run up in me. Does the lil' green-eyed bitch you were with the other night know about that?"

Lifting her hand, she put her finger in my face. I bit down on the back of my teeth to stop myself from breaking it in half. She knew I hated when she put her hands in my face and that's why she did it. I kept my mouth shut to stop from saying some shit that would make her attitude even worse. There was no way that Sage hadn't heard what was said and that only meant I would have a lot to explain to her later.

"Yeah, that's what I thought, you cheating ass *nigga*!"

"Aye, Ink… you good, man?"

I didn't have to look to know exactly who it was. Jamal was a dude around my age who owned a small barbershop next door. We didn't kick it much, he was closer to Kale, but we still looked out for each other every now and then. Being that this wasn't the first time that Tami had showed her ass in front of my place of business, he knew my situation with her pretty well.

"He's good. Mind your own motherfuckin' business!" Tami snapped at him with her hands on her hips.

"Aye, calm that shit down," I told her. "I let you come up here and act a fuckin' fool but now it's time for you to go. You shouldn't have brought your ass up here anyway trying to check me on some shit that ain't your business. You're not my chick!"

"No, I'm actually your *wife* and I'm tired of this!" she shot back.

She wasn't the only one tired of the shit—so was I. How convenient was it that she could pull the 'wife' word out when it benefited her but didn't think about it at all when she was in the club rubbing her ass against the next nigga's dick.

"You need to take your dumb ass home." I turned to walk away but then something else occurred to me and I stopped.

Where the hell was Miyah?

Before I could even ask, Tami was in my face once again.

"Don't fuckin' walk away from me! I'm not about to have you out here disrespecting me like I ain't got no ring on my finger. Nobody made you do a damn thing you didn't want to do. I wasn't the one who put this shit on my finger or signed the papers at the courthouse. That was *you!* Now you out here wilding out, fuckin' bitches in the bathroom in some nasty ass club. You got them sending me this shit to fuck with me. Like I don't have enough misery in my life to deal with!"

The second I saw the tears in her eyes, her words hit me hard. At some point in my life, Tami was the woman that I loved but, not only that, she was one of my closest friends. Circumstances of life had pulled us apart, but I wasn't heartless. I wanted her to be happy and live a good life. I didn't know how to do that when she thought the only nigga for her was me and she continued to use my relationship with my daughter as bait. But, as was the norm, the second I started to feel sorry for Tami and guilty for the role I played in her unhappiness, she opened up her mouth to say something that made me want to strangle her to death.

"Soooo," she began, snaking her neck as she held out the word. "Since we both know that Miyah is the only reason you even fuckin' with me right now, I'm gonna make this shit easy for you."

Turning away, she walked to her car, parked curbside, and opened up the back door. When she pulled my daughter out of the backseat, heat built up around my collar. My rage grew even further when she grabbed her hand and yanked her towards the door so hard that Tamiyah screamed and almost fell forward.

"Yo, don't be grabbin' her like that!" I snarled.

Stepping forward, I lifted my child up in my arms. When I saw the fear and worry in her eyes, it crushed me in the worst way. Tami and I argued and fought all the time, but I always tried to make sure that Tamiyah never witnessed it. That meant I had to hold my tongue more times than I wanted when she was around, but my daughter was important to me, so I pushed through it.

"You don't have to worry about me grabbing her ever again if you don't want to," Tami snapped back, folding her arms over her chest. "I left her birth certificate, social security card, medical records and a notarized legal document on the kitchen counter stating that I'm signing full parental rights for Tamiyah over to you. Since you want her so bad and can't give a shit about me, you can cut me a check to start a new life and I'll get ghost. Consider this my parting gift to you."

My mouth almost dropped open at the audacity of her to say some shit like that right in front of Tamiyah like she was too dumb to understand that her own mother was giving her away. Something told me that Tami was only trying to get a reaction out of me and couldn't possibly mean what she was saying but it still didn't matter, especially not when I heard my baby start to cry. She had officially crossed the line.

Turning to Tamiyah, I kissed her forehead and then placed her down on her feet.

"Aye, Miyah, go walk inside and play with your coloring books for a second. You know where to find them."

Her sad eyes clouded with more tears and the shit broke my heart.

I can't keep letting her go through this shit, I thought.

My only responsibility as her father was to love her, provide for her and protect her. I never expected to have to protect her from her own mother but maybe it was time for me to accept that Tamiyah wouldn't have the upbringing that I wanted her to have.

"Okay, Daddy."

She nodded her head slowly and then walked through the door to do as I'd asked. I ran my hand over the bottom of my face, brooding internally as I watched her reach into the back of Indie's desk to get her books and crayons.

Sage, knowing that her assistance was needed, shot me a curious look before walking over to Tamiyah. She was fully dressed, which told me that she expected and was prepared for our night alone to be interrupted. Bending down, she smiled at Tamiyah as she spoke words that I couldn't hear. Whatever they were must have been impactful because the next thing Tamiyah did was hold her hand up for Sage, who led her to the back. Once I knew she was good, I closed the door and focused my attention back on Tami, who was staring at me with a smug-ass smirk spread across her face.

"You must be outta yo' fuckin' mind," I said in a low tone, as if speaking to myself. I chuckled as I ran my hand over the back of my head, thinking about how lucky Tami was that I had a daughter to think about. Tamiyah was the only thing keeping me from choking the life out of her mama's bum ass.

"No, *you* must be outta *your* mind," she replied, narrowing her eyes. "How long did you think I would sit around and be your pretend wife while you out here living your best life? I deserve better, Ink!"

"And what about your daughter?" I raged. My voice was loud and that wasn't even in me, but I was losing control. "What the fuck does *she* deserve? Doesn't she deserve to have her mother in her life?"

A sorrowful expression passed over Tami's face and, for

a second, I thought that maybe she was reconsidering her decision.

Then she opened up her mouth, shrugged and said, "She's better without me."

"That's some selfish shit and you know it."

Eyes flashing in rage, Tami ran up so fast that I thought she was going to barrel right into me until she stopped in front of my face.

"Selfish?" she spat. "Who are you to tell me what's selfish?

The headlights of a car illuminated the parking lot beside where we stood, instantly catching my attention. It was Kale.

"Well, look who it is," Tami said, singing her words with a taunting tune. "And just on time."

I didn't understand what the hell she was talking about, but I'd long ago stopped trying to figure out what craziness went through her mind. As soon as the engine died, Kale jumped out his whip, frowning as his eyes traveled back and forth between Tami and me. He was trying to figure out what was going on. The passenger door opened, and someone stepped out, a chick. I recognized her as Sage's friend from the first time I'd met her.

"What's good, Ink? Tami," he added, cutting his eyes at her briefly. Beside him, his girl was glaring first at Tami and then at me.

"I can't call it," I replied.

"We came here because I flew in and wanted to surprise *Sage*." She put extra emphasis on the name. "She texted me earlier and said she was here. Did she leave?"

The accusatory stare in her eyes matched her tone.

Obviously, she thought that Sage was gone and I was caught dipping out on her friend with my ex.

"Yo, chill. She's here." I nodded my head back towards the shop. "She's inside."

The tension in her face faded and she nodded to me before turning to walk inside. All of the negative energy that she left behind her was absorbed by Tami.

"Are you telling me that bitch is in there? You got her in there with *my* daughter?"

I looked at her like she'd lost her damn mind. "What? You mean the daughter you just said that you didn't want no more?"

"Nigga, I don't give a fuck if—"

She lunged forward and the only thing that stopped her from jumping on me was Kale, who moved just as fast and grabbed her around her middle.

"Yo, calm down," he told her, looking around at the people who were gathering around us. "This ain't the time or the place for this shit."

I heard Jamal in the background telling the crowd to get lost. After taking a few parting photos, the crowd began to disperse and Tami was right back on it.

"Why not?" She positioned her hands on her hips and rolled her neck. "Because you brought your little bitch up here with you? What happened to everything you said to me the other night—about being with me? That's not what you want no more?"

My temperature shot to the sky. What *the fuck* had she just said?

Chapter Sixteen

~ Ink ~

Right before my eyes, it looked as if all the blood drained from Kale's face.

"Tami, listen, don't do that shit." He put his hands up and took a step back. "Don't go there."

"Oh, now you wanna keep quiet because *she's* here, huh?" She pointed towards the shop. "Because you definitely weren't worried about all that when you were telling me that we needed to come clean to Ink!"

My frown deepened to the max as I watched the interaction between the two of them, trying to figure out what the hell was going on. Those days, Tami said all kinds of shit to get under my skin so I didn't know if she was playing around or not, but Kale's reaction would tell me.

Back before Tami and I got together officially, it was no secret that he had been crushing on her, but she wanted to be with me. I stepped to him about taking her out and he didn't object to it; he even had a girlfriend at the time. Sometimes I felt like he still had a thing for her, but he'd never stepped out of line with her after we got together. At least not from what I knew.

"Man, get the fuck outta here with this bullshit, Tami. You on some reckless shit and I ain't fuckin' with you right now." He batted at her with his hand before turning to me. "Yo, I'm about to grab Lola and get the fuck up out of here. If you want, I can grab Sage and Tamiyah, too."

"You aren't taking my daughter nowhere with either one of those bitches!"

"Yeah, whatever," Kale replied, not even bothering to look her way. "She doesn't even need to be with you right now and you and I both know why."

Something about how he said it felt like he was referring to a lot more than the ratchet shit that Tami had been on lately. Especially when I saw the shame-filled expression on Tami's face. For the first time since she showed up, she actually looked like she wished she were anywhere but there.

"Yo, what's that mean?" I spoke up finally, unable to stay out of the conversation for a second longer. "What do you mean, Miyah shouldn't be with her? Am I missing something?"

Stopping in his tracks, Kale paused for a few seconds before slowly turning around. When he did, he was looking at Tami.

"Do you want to tell him or should I?" he asked her, his eyes narrowing in. It was a threat and Tami never was one to react well to those. Instead of cowering under him, she stood tall and shot him a malicious glare right back.

"Oh so you wanna start telling secrets now, huh? Why don't you tell Ink who Tamiyah's *real* father is? It ain't Dolla and it damn sure ain't him. But *you* know who it is. Since we telling secrets, why don't we start with you?"

My nostrils flared. "Kale, what the *fuck* is she talking about?"

"I don't have a fuckin' clue," he replied, glaring so hard at Tami that she was forced to take a step back to create distance. "Then again, there is a lot a junkie does that I don't understand."

"Junkie?" I searched Tami's face, ready for her to refute what had been said but she was silent. Her bottom jaw had dropped, and her eyes were slightly bugged in utter panic and shock.

"Tami's right about one thing. I did tell her that we needed to come clean to you, but it had nothing to do with her fucking with me. I told her that we needed to come clean about her drug habit. She's been taking pills." He paused and blew out a sharp breath. "And God knows what else."

"Well, since you wanna talk, tell him who been giving them to me then!" she hissed.

"Answer my fuckin' question!" I yelled so loud that I caught the attention of a few people walking out of the bar across the street. "Is that true? Are you taking drugs? You been doing this shit around my daughter?"

"No I—I just—I didn't mean to…"

Her brows knitted across her forehead, but she left the rest of her sentence unsaid.

"I have to go."

She pivoted fast, trying to run away but I wasn't having that. Reaching out, I stopped her by grabbing her roughly by her wrist and whipped her back around to face me. With her eyes stretched wide in horror, she screamed like I had stabbed her in the chest.

"Get your hands off me, Ink! Let me go!"

"Aye, man, we need to handle this inside the shop," Kale said, looking behind him. He backed away from us and helped Jamal deal with the returning crowd. People from the barbershop, the bar and another small club on the corner started to walk out to watch our train wreck in action. In the back of my head, I knew I had to calm down but I couldn't.

"Stop! You're hurtin' me!" Tami howled and began to squirm. She was putting on for the crowd because I was barely touching her.

"Stop acting and tell me the fuckin' truth! Have you been on that shit around my daughter? And you better not fuckin' lie!"

When her lips didn't part, I was overcome with fury. I shook her so hard that her purse flung out of her hands and landed on the street, causing the contents to spill out on the asphalt near my feet. I didn't pay it any attention and kept my eyes on Tami until she dropped her head to look. The sight transformed her expression into one of sheer and utter terror.

"What the *fuck*?"

I blinked hard and then looked once again, knowing for sure that my eyes had to be deceiving me.

Pills and coke. How the hell had I missed this?

"Ink, I've been so miserable…so sad and so hurt."

She began to cry, spouting tears from her eyes like water from a faucet. With her thin, willowy arms out, she moved towards me, but I pushed her away. I wasn't moved by any of it. For the first time, I took a good look at her and noticed that she was noticeably thinner than before. She was still thick in all the places that used to matter to me, but it wasn't the same.

"I've loved you my entire life and, all this time, I thought I could find a way to make you love me back. I thought that Tamiyah would be enough and, when we got married, I kept hoping that one day things would go back to how they used to be. But nothing changed. I just wanted to be with you." She sniffed and batted away a tear that was sliding down her cheek. "If you help me, I will get clean."

Snickering, I shook my head. "Nah, not happening. I'll get a driver to take you wherever you need to go but you ain't staying with me anymore. That's a wrap."

"I—I made a mistake," she said as she began to move quickly forward. "I didn't know what I was sayin'. I still want to be a mother. I need Tamiyah."

Frowning, I swatted at her, nudging her away with force. She was in a state of panic—her eyes were rolling around in her head as she began to grasp the reality of what was happening. Then it was as if someone had turned on the crazy switch. She bolted back to me, crying out with tormented wails.

"Ink, move out of the way! I want to see my daughter! She's not yours; she's mine and you can't keep her from me!"

She was screaming at the top of her lungs, grabbing the attention of not only a group of drunk white fraternity boys stumbling out of the club, but other random people walking and driving down the street. She started to fight me, pushing, scratching and sobbing as she cried out for the same daughter that she had just said she didn't even want.

"Tami, stop!"

As soon as the words fell from my mouth, she reached up and raked her long fingernails across my cheek, cutting through my skin.

"You can't keep her from me! I won't let you!"

She was hysterical. With no other way to stop her, I grabbed her by her shoulders and shook the shit out of her until her head jerked back and forth like a ragdoll. With any hope, I had rattled some sense into her brain so she would get herself together and leave.

"The next time you think about coming anywhere near Miyah, you better go somewhere and snort acid instead of coke. Keep messing with that shit and then try to come around her again. You'd be better off dead."

When I released her, Tami was so shaken up that she could barely stand. She collapsed like a puppet; her legs crumbled from beneath her and she dropped to the ground. It wasn't until that moment that I looked up and noticed even more people standing around us, a couple of them with their cellphones in hand, documenting the entire incident.

Fuck, I thought as I straightened my clothes and ran my hand over my face in distress.

The shit was bad. And I halfway thought that was how Tami wanted it. She knew what she was doing when she came there with Tamiyah in the car, telling me that she was done being a mother. She could have told me that shit at home, but she'd wanted to cause a scene and she did. Maybe exposing herself as an addict hadn't been part of her plan but the headlines in the morning about us having a public fight definitely was. The video would hit the blogs soon and, by morning, I would be the leading story. I would be the monster and Tami would have all the sympathy she wanted from the public as the victim.

"Are you okay?" one of the drunk white guys asked. He held his hand out to help her up.

"No, I hurt everywhere," Tami cried.

Disgusted, I watched as she put on a show for her pity-party.

"I don't know why he hates me. I only want to be a good mother. I want my daughter to love me."

A chorus of "awws" erupted from the crowd. Before I was able to slip through the door to my shop, I glanced at Tami and saw an evil smirk form on her lips. She was playing and I'd allowed her to win.

On God, I *really* hated that fake-ass celebrity shit.

Chapter Seventeen

~

Sage

Somehow, and I wasn't quite sure when, I was able to fall asleep after the craziness that Tami had caused when she showed up at Official Ink. But I wasn't able to do it until after spending hours scrolling through the comment section under all of the viral video posts of Ink and Tami's fight. Interestingly enough, most people sided with him, although he appeared to be the more aggressive one. Tami's party life and antics in public weren't as reported about as the fight but that didn't mean people didn't know about it. Public opinion was that she deserved what Ink did to her.

The following day, I was swamped to my eyeballs in financial reports I'd been told that only I could go over. That part, I was skeptical about. Charles, the board member who had brought the paperwork over to me, was the one who had told me that I needed to sign off on their accuracy. There was no way that I was going to sign off on something I hadn't thoroughly reviewed—which I was sure he knew—so it was likely that my entire day would be spent tending to it.

"They are hazing you," Sherelle said as she walked into my office. She pointed her eyes to the pile of papers on my desk.

"The financial reports are checked nearly a million times before they leave the finance department. There is no way an error is in there. I've never seen the board ever check over that paperwork once it comes in. They lied to you."

I nodded. "Maybe. But I don't trust them to not have put something wrong in here to catch me being lazy. Especially Charles." I rolled my eyes. "He hates me."

"He does not!"

I gave her a pointed look and her shoulders dropped.

"Okay. Maybe he does…" she replied and then sat down in the chair on the opposite side of my desk. "Let me help you. As an executive assistant, I have a background in accounting, so I'll put it to use."

Placing the document I'd been scrutinizing flat on my desk, I looked up at her. I was truly thankful for Sherelle; I normally didn't gel well with people that I didn't know but we had clicked from the beginning. She was always looking out for me.

"Why are you so great?" I asked with sincerity.

She smiled. "For one, I've been happy as hell since the day I found out that you—a young, Black diva like me—was coming here to sit at the head of the table and run shit! There is no way that I'm going to let them old-ass white people, and I say that in the nicest way, bring you down. You can always count on me to dish it to you straight and help you when you need it."

That warmed my heart in ways that I couldn't even begin

to explain so I returned her smile. There weren't many people in my life, outside of Lola, who openly protected me. Even my own father didn't do that.

By the time we were almost finished going through everything, we had ordered and eaten lunch, dinner, and a late-night snack. It was a little after midnight when I decided to put my foot down and send Sherelle home. As I'd expected, she fought back some but gave in when I promised her that I would pack it up shortly after.

I was lying. As much as I hated to admit it, I didn't want to go home yet. Ink hadn't called or texted me all day and the only thing that stopped me from thinking about it was the fact that I was so busy. For the first time since he'd started taking me to lunch, he didn't show, and I had a million questions in my head as to why.

About thirty minutes after she left, I had swapped up my playlist and was tapping my foot to the beat of a hot new hit by Megan Thee Stallion when my office phone began to ring. With my eyes never leaving the document in my hand, I put the receiver to my ear.

"Sherelle, I promise that I am about to leave in a few minutes. I'm almost done."

"This is not Sherelle. Why the hell are you still at work and why haven't you been answering your phone?"

I frowned and placed the papers down on my desk. "Lola? What's wrong? I thought you and Kale were getting ready to catch a flight."

"That's what I have been trying to tell you all day! I've been calling your cell and your office line, but you weren't answering either one."

I'd complete forgotten that I'd forwarded my office line to voicemail. The only reason Lola was getting through now was because all forwarding settings reset after midnight.

"My phone is on silent and I'm still here because I've been swimming in paperwork all day. What's going on?"

"Tami's dumb ass is what's going on. Do you know that bitch showed up here three hours ago, high as fuck, asking Kale for drugs? And she had Tamiyah!"

"What?"

I was positive I hadn't heard her right. There was no way that Ink would have left his daughter with Tami so soon after their fight. He was serious about never letting her see Tamiyah again, even though I'd repeatedly told him that he couldn't say things like that. I'd grown up without a mother and, in many ways, I felt like it ruined my life.

"According to Tami, the daycare called her to pick up Tamiyah because Ink never showed up and that's why she had her. We didn't even know that she was there because she left her in the car to wait while she was begging Kale to give her drugs. She said Ink had cut off all her cards and she didn't have any money."

"Are you serious?"

"Yes! I heard the whole thing, even though Kale went outside to talk to her; you know I was eavesdropping. We have been trying to call Ink but he's still not answering and we have to catch a flight in a couple of hours. Have you heard anything from him?"

A lump formed in my throat. This wasn't like him at all.

There was no way he would disappear and leave his daughter hanging unless something had happened to him.

"No, I—I haven't," I said, scrolling through my missed calls. None were from Ink; however, someone had called me multiple times from a blocked number.

"Have you checked the hospitals? Or the jail website?" I asked suddenly.

"Yes, the hospitals but... no, I didn't even think about jail. Why would he be locked up?"

"I don't know." I sighed. "But the only time I've ever had this many blocked calls in my phone was the time you got arrested for drunk and disorderly conduct that one time. Hold on, I'm looking now."

I was already online searching for myself. The craziest thing was that I was actually hoping that he was in jail. At least then I would know he was alive. The only thing that would keep him from his daughter was if he physically couldn't get to her. My heart dropped when I found nothing. After even searching state-wide, there still was nothing about Ink.

I went to my missed calls again and then decided to check my voicemail while Lola talked on and on about how much she couldn't stand Tami and how much of a terrible mother she was. There were two visual voicemails available from the blocked line. I clicked on the first one that was left and read through it as fast as I could.

"He's at the jail," I said finally.

"What? So he was locked up?"

"No, he said he's in a holding cell, but he hasn't been charged with anything. They picked him up after he got in a fight with...

someone. I'll have to listen to the message to hear exactly what he said."

"Damn, that's crazy." Lola sighed. "Well, let me get off the phone so I can let Kale know. I need to see if we can push back our flight."

"No... you don't have to do that." I paused for a few moments to think. "I can keep Tamiyah until Ink can pick her up."

"Are you sure about that? What do you know about taking care of a child?"

I rolled my eyes. "About as much as you do. Besides, Ink was calling me to ask if I could watch her anyway so I'm sure he doesn't mind."

"Thank God! Because I really didn't want to have to push back my flight for somebody else's brat. I'm so ready to go!"

"Lola!"

"What? Girl, you know I ain't got no kids and that's for a reason. I'm selfish, shit!"

***

Tamiyah was the cutest little girl in the world. Though named after Tami, she only remotely looked like her. With spirals of honey-brown hair dancing around her head and milk chocolate skin, she was an absolute dream.

When I picked her up from Kale's, she was already asleep. The next morning, I woke up to her standing by my bed, staring at me so hard that I'd opened my eyes after feeling like I wasn't alone. Once she saw that I was awake, her inquisition began immediately.

"Where are we and where is my daddy and Uncle Kale?"

Rubbing the sleep out of my eyes, I sat up, yawned wide and stretched my arms up to the sky.

"Your Uncle Kale had a flight to catch so he asked me to watch you until your daddy is able to pick you up from here. And we are in my apartment."

"*This* is an apartment?" she asked with her hands up as if she were shocked. "But it's so big!"

I laughed. She was so cute. "Yes, it's pretty big but it's technically still an apartment. Having a house requires too much maintenance but I still need allllll the space."

"Wellllll..." She jumped up and joined me on the bed. "What are we going to do today until my daddy comes?"

That was a good question. Since we weren't at Ink's house, I didn't have anything around to entertain a child.

"How about I paint your nails and..." I looked around. "And we can play in my makeup, if you want."

Those were obviously the magic words because her face lit up like a lightbulb.

"Yes!"

She stood to her feet and began jumping up and down on the bed with all the energy of a five-year-old child at eight o'clock in the morning. On the other hand, I didn't function at full potential without a shower and at least one cup of coffee.

"First, I'm going to make you a bowl of cereal so you can eat and watch T.V. while I take a shower and then we will get started."

She cocked her head to the side and gave me a sideways look.

"What kind of cereal?"

Another good question. I was a health nut and didn't have anything that any normal kid would eat.

"Uh… how about waffles instead?"

"Deal!" She squealed and commenced to jumping once again. Laughing, I slid from under the sheets and grabbed my robe to pull it on.

"I want one, too!" she said and then tumbled off my bed to help herself to a pink silk robe that I had lying on the end of the bed.

Once she'd secured it around her small, short frame, she took off in a Beyoncé-style strut towards the door.

Shaking my head, I laughed a little to myself and then followed behind her. The little girl was a whole trip.

***

It was a rainy, wet and all-out miserable day in Atlanta but Tamiyah made it a beautiful day for me. Most kids annoyed me because they demanded a lot and I valued time to myself but she wasn't like that. I truly enjoyed her company and, though only five, she handled herself like she was much older. It was crazy how I could actually have conversations with her. In the end, I felt like I could pat myself on the back. I had absolutely no experience with handling a child but so far, so good.

"My daddy hates my mommy."

Okay, maybe I had spoken too soon.

Looking into Tamiyah's pretty face and peering into her sad eyes, I balled up my nose and shook my head.

"I don't think that's true. Why would you say that?"

She paused to stop coloring and scrunched up her face to look up at the ceiling. "Well… my mommy told me that. She said he didn't want her to be around anymore."

Hmm, I couldn't say that I was sad to hear it.

"Does that make you sad?" I asked, picking up a crayon of my own. With it in hand, I began to color in the image on the other side of the book. As a child, I had a therapist who used to color with me when she wanted me to talk and open up to her about my feelings. I had become withdrawn and my father thought it had something to do with me not having a mother in my life.

"I don't know," she whispered, as if she knew it was wrong to speak truthfully. "But I know my daddy is only sad when mommy's around. He doesn't think I know it because he tries to fake it, but I know his sad face."

"What does his sad face look like?" I asked, trying to find a way to change the subject. "Let's see how good an actress you are."

Still holding her crayon, she lifted her head and gave me her best impression of a 'sad Ink.' It was so cute; I couldn't help but laugh.

"And what does your sad face look like?"

She was so pretty, like one of the dolls that I would pretend were my babies when I was a little girl. Only someone as evil as Tami would abandon that child. I would've jumped in with both feet at the opportunity to be her mother.

"This is *my* sad face."

She made a pitiful puppy dog face with her bottom lip poked out and I laughed even harder. She joined in and then happily asked me to make my sad face. I used my pointer fingers to pull the ends of my eyes down and pushed my lips out as if I were crying. She thought it was hilarious and erupted with giggles.

After completing our picture, we were about to go on to the next when there was a knock on the front door. I had an idea who it was. Though Ink hadn't called back, I'd left a message for him letting him know that I had Tamiyah and gave him my address.

"Is that Daddy?" Tamiyah asked, observing the expression on my face.

I nodded. "I think so. Stay here."

At the door, I checked the peephole and the first thing I noticed were Ink's slumped shoulders and sunken eyes. He seemed completely depleted of energy, devastated about whatever had gone on since the last time I'd seen him. It tugged at my heartstrings.

The only thing I wanted to do was figure out how to make him feel better.

Chapter Eighteen

Sage

"Thanks again for this."

I looked up from a magazine that I'd been flipping through in time to see Ink emerge from the hall leading to the spare bedroom that I'd made up for Tamiyah to sleep in. After he'd gotten in, I made him a shower, washed his clothes and then started dinner since it was almost that time. After we finished eating, we watched a movie together and Tamiyah fell asleep in his arms. He didn't seem ready to leave and I didn't want him to, so I offered up my place for another night and told him that he could leave in the morning.

"Don't mention it," I said, sitting up on the sofa. "I'm happy that I was able to help… and that you trusted me enough to let me."

Letting out a breath, Ink sat on the other end from me and pressed his elbow on the arm of it before running his forefinger across his perfectly trimmed goatee.

"I trust you more than you know. It may sound crazy, being that we haven't known each other all that long but…"

He let his words hang in the air and then shrugged to complete his thought. It didn't matter that he didn't finish; I understood what he was saying.

"I've never been able to click with anyone this way either. I don't know, it just feels right. Like fate."

Nervous, I pressed my feet down into the shag rug and then teetered back and forth from the tips of my toes to the balls of my feet. For some reason, I couldn't look Ink in the eyes.

Turning to me, he lifted his brows. "You believe in fate?"

That was a no-brainer for me. "I do. Not in totality but when it comes to the grand scheme of things, I do. I definitely think that certain parts of our lives are meant to be, but we have free will in how we get there. Some people take the easy road and some take the hard road but, in the end, we get where we are supposed to be."

There was something so boyishly attractive about the way that Ink looked at me in that moment, like my logic fascinated him.

"You're perfect," he said then. "My mind was totally fucked up when I got here but you have a way of making a nigga feel like new."

My body responded to him and I swallowed hard, feeling my nipples harden through the thin material of my shirt. It was late, the candles I'd lit in the living room were setting the mood and I hadn't had sex in God knew how long. I was horny as hell and the sexy way that his hooded eyes drooped lustfully as he stared into mine said that if I pushed the issue, he was game.

"I have other ways of making you feel like new."

The connection between us was so strong, it was clear that we were made for each other. Without words, our eyes spoke to each other, our bodies yearned to be together. We had chemistry on a different level from anything I'd ever experienced before.

"Oh yeah?" he asked, one side of his lips slowly rising. "Show me."

Before I knew it, I was scooting over to closer to him. He didn't stop me when I leaned over and pressed my lips against his, kissing him gently. For a moment, it was like he'd lost himself. He deepened our kiss, pushing his tongue past my lips. I sucked on it and then moaned into his mouth when I felt his hands on my breasts. Excitement filled my belly. I just knew I was about to get what I'd been wanting for so long... Until he suddenly stopped.

"Sage, I want to do this and you don't know how much I do but I don't wanna do it like this. The first time we take it to that point, I want to be able to call you my woman officially. I want to be able to get mad if another nigga even looks at you in a way that I don't approve. I want to feel like I can stake claim on you because you're mine. You deserve that."

On one hand, I fell deeper for him because of what he was saying but, on the other hand, I wished he didn't respect me quite as much. I wanted a man to know my worth and treat me accordingly, but I also wanted to be fucked.

"We don't have to go the whole way if you don't want but there is still something that I want to do."

My eyes never left his as I began to pull at the buckle of his belt. He breathed evenly, with a lust-filled gaze, allowing me to take control until he then shook his head.

"Nah, I can't let you—"

With my finger pressed against his lips, I stopped him before he said something neither one of us wanted to hear. He could play the respectable gentleman another day. We both knew that he wanted it. I was willing to be patient because I knew that if he got a taste of me before he made up his mind that he was ready, he would have regrets. He was a man who liked to be in control when it came to things that he considered were important and I wanted to give him that. Regret was something that I didn't want involved in the equation when it came to Ink and me. However, when it came to other things, I couldn't wait.

"You've made me cum a few times and never asked for anything in return," I told him, whispering my words against his neck. "At least let me do you this once."

As I said those last words, I dropped my hand into his lap and began massaging his dick through his jeans. It was hard already, bulging through the material, begging for my touch before it had even had the chance to feel me. Ink didn't object and when I felt his length swell even further under my touch, I applied more pressure as I nestled my face into his neck. I heard him suck in a deep breath, inhaling my scent.

"Damn, you smell so good," he whispered, and I felt my pussy gush warm honey. He hadn't even touched me, but I already was ready to come.

With expertise and quick movements, I unzipped his pants and slipped my fingers inside the opening to grab his girth. He responded by reclining back on the soft suede sofa and that was all the permission I needed.

Once I was able to release his massive manhood through the opening in his designer boxers, I lowered myself down until I was face to dick.

God, he's so big, I thought, my mouth moistening as I eagerly observed his length. More than anything, I wanted to take him in between my jaws but I delayed, knowing that the anticipation of it all would only turn him on even more. Using my hands, I manipulated his muscle between my fingers, running my thumb over the mushroom head with expertise until he let out a low, guttural moan.

He didn't speak and I didn't either. I didn't want to put words to our actions because I knew that his body was at war with his mind. I preferred it to be that way than for his mind to be at war with me.

Opening my mouth into a large O-shape, I blew hot air on the tip of his dick and watched him squirm in response, as I expected. No man could resist the promise of good head when it was offered, and Ink didn't show me anything differently. Like the tip of an ice cream cone, I licked the slit of his opening a few times, dick-teasing him for a few moments before lowering my mouth on top of him, trying my hardest to swallow him whole. It was a miraculous feat. Though I hadn't been with many men before, Ink was by far the largest and I had to squeeze my eyes tightly shut as I forced myself not to gag as I took him in. I had to put on my grown-woman shit.

He tastes so damn good.

I sucked and licked on him as if I were trying to reach the center of a Tootsie Roll pop. My clit thumped to the rhythm of my tongue as I beat it across the head of his pole, beckoning him into that happy place where he could release all worries, angst and fury into me so I could swallow it down my throat.

His hips began to move, and he placed his hand on the back of my head, forcing himself deeper down my throat. Like a champ, I rolled with it, clamping my lips hard on his pole. I sucked that dick like it gave me life, like my oxygen came from it. In my mind, it did. Cupping my breasts in my hands, I played with my nipples, pinching them hard as he jerked into my mouth, pushing past my tonsils. I felt his dick began to throb as the nut in his balls made its way further south. My pussy leaked with anticipation for that moment. I couldn't wait to swallow him down. I imagined that his semen tasted like rich vanilla cream and I sucked even harder, impatient for the moment when I would be able to see if it were true.

"Fuck."

Ink talked dirty while I fucked him with my mouth and it only made me want to get even nastier in response. I spit on the dick and then rolled my saliva around over the top of his head all the way down to his balls, working him so good that he grew nearly another whole inch more. While jacking him off, I clamped my lips around the head and thrashed my tongue against it while sucking hard like I was trying to pull slurp a smoothie through a mini-straw. His body went rigid as he came, shooting warm, thick liquid between my jaws. I didn't miss a beat and swallowed over and over, not spilling a single drop. With my hand, I gave him a squeeze and pushed upward like one would do when trying to get the last bit of toothpaste out the tube. I wanted to empty him completely, I was hungry for him and, even after he was done, I still craved more.

"Got damn." He sighed and leaned his head all the way back, his eyes closed with his face pointed towards the ceiling.

"I ain't never in my life experienced no shit like that."

With a smile, I ran a finger over my lips, swiping up any leftovers that remained there and then dipped it into my mouth to suck them off.

"Do you feel relaxed?" I asked, leaning into him.

"Like a motherfucka," he replied, his eyes still closed.

I fixed up his clothes, staring at his dick longingly before forcing myself to push it back into his boxers and zip up his jeans. I could tell that he was only seconds away from going to sleep.

"I'm going to bed. If you still want to sleep out here, the linen is in the closet in the hall."

Without opening his eyes, he nodded his head. I paused and stared at him for a moment, admiring how incredibly breathtakingly sexy of a man he was right then. When I rolled around on my heels to head to my room, the sound of him calling my name stopped me in my tracks.

"Sage?"

"Yes?" I answered, turning around.

His head was up, and his eyes were open, pointed directly at me. He appeared completely relaxed, almost in a state of bliss.

"You know I want to come in there with you, right? If I can't control this shit… don't be surprised if you find me slipping up under those covers. What you just did was mind-blowing," he added with a light chuckle. "But thanks again for putting up with this shit. This ain't yo' drama but you really came through for me in a way that I can't remember anyone else doing in my entire life."

With a smirk, I clasped my hands behind my back and twisted playfully back and forth while shooting him goo-goo eyes.

"I'm supposed to. Aren't I your friend?"

His face went serious all of a sudden; the small hint of a smile immediately disappeared from his lips.

"Yes, you're definitely my friend," he replied. "And I don't take that shit lightly. When I consider someone a friend, to me, that bond is the same as being bound by blood. Like family... and, soon, something more."

That last part sent flutters of excited energy coursing through my belly.

"Goodnight. I guess I'll see you in the morning," I told him, giving him one last smile before making my exit. I made sure to walk slowly, winding my hips seductively, because I was absolutely positive that he was watching me go.

"Maybe in the morning," he called out. "Maybe later tonight."

Chapter Nineteen

Ink

Sage had my mind fucked up.

The shit was crazy when I thought about it because I'd been so used to dealing with empty headed females who weren't about shit but hooking up with a nigga with cash. I never considered I would ever find someone real. But the more I spent time with her and the more I saw her interactions with my daughter, the more I could see us together. I still wanted to take it slow, though. We were vibing heavy, but I wanted to have something lasting with her; a real relationship for once in my life.

And then there was Tami...

An entire month had passed since the night Tami left Tamiyah at Kale's and I hadn't seen or heard from her since. I wasn't complaining about it, though, and Tamiyah hadn't said much about her either. Although I never thought I would feel right having another woman around my daughter, after the morning we both spent the night at Sage's place, she'd been asking about her and begging for her to be around ever since.

At first, I didn't know how she'd made such an impression on Tamiyah that she would ask about Sage before her own mother but when I really thought about it, it made sense. Sage spent time with her, brushing her hair, coloring with her, playing with toys, and reading to her. Whereas Tami had always treated her daughter like an obligation she *had* to deal with, Sage enjoyed having her company, taking her on shopping trips and to the nail shop whenever she went; all kinds of girly shit.

"Daddy?" Tamiyah said, squinting as we pulled up in the circular driveway of my crib. "Is that Mommy? Sitting in front of the door?"

I looked up and suppressed my groan.

Fuck.

So much about her was different from the last time I'd seen her, but I could make out Tami anywhere. As my ride crept to a complete stop, she stood to her feet, my eyes on her and hers on mine. It was easy to see that she had been living the not-so-fabulous life of a junkie during the time she was gone. She was emaciated beyond the point of what was natural. Not only was she sitting there with the Mercedes Benz I'd bought her nowhere in sight, her clothes were dirty and soiled, her hair looked like a bird's nest, her once perfectly manicured nails were broken and sporting traces of chipped polish and, though she tried to hide it, the way she fidgeted and scratched at her arms was more than enough evidence of her most recent activities.

I don't have time for this shit.

"Miyah, let's get out. I'll unlock the door. You go on in the house and let me talk to Mommy outside," I told her, trying not to clench my teeth as I spoke, though my jaw was so tight.

"Okay," she answered, her voice barely audible.

When I stepped out of the car, Tami refused to meet my eyes as she continued to scratch and looked anywhere but where I stood. After the blogs finally cooled down from the story of our public argument in front of my shop, I saw a few bloggers post photos and videos of her on Instagram. In each one, she was 'living her best life' in multiple night clubs all around town. There were videos of her popping bottles, ordering shitloads of food for random broads and dancing with niggas who couldn't keep their hands to themselves but most likely weren't paying for shit. Evidently, the money she had stashed had run out and now she was back to beg for more.

"Miyah!" Tami spoke with a cracked voice, the second that I pulled her from the back seat.

She spread her arms wide and her lips followed suit, forming a smile. I winced at the sight of her dark yellow teeth and cracked lips. Never in life had I seen Tami look that bad but the image gave me déjà vu. This was exactly how I remembered her mama looking before she overdosed. It was a sight that I tried hard to forget.

"Come here! Give me a hug, baby."

Holding my hand in her tiny one, Tamiyah paused for a moment to observe her mother and then turned her head up to look at me, as if for permission. With my lips in a straight line, I nodded to tell her that she could go ahead. No matter what I'd said before, I would never keep her from her mother. I would never let her be with her outside of my presence, though. Not until I was certain she would be safe.

Tamiyah walked slowly forward and when she was close

enough, Tami bent down to give her a hug, pulling her in tight as if she hadn't been the one to make the decision to abandon her in the first place. Tamiyah's arms wrapped around her mother's neck but there was an awkward expression on her face throughout the embrace. Like she was confused about her emotions or Tami's appearance… maybe both.

"Let me get you in the house, Miyah," I told her when I couldn't take anymore. The shit was hard as hell to watch.

With my keys in my hand, I began walking towards the door to unlock it with Tamiyah dragging her legs behind me. When Tami tried to follow, I put my hand up to stop her. Thankfully, she didn't give me no shit about it.

"Why are you here?" I gritted on her as soon as I walked back out. "You're a fuckin' fiend, Tami. Damn… look at you! This shit is pitiful as hell. You been hitting that dope hard and there ain't no way that you this bad after one damn month. When did you first start using that shit?"

She opened her mouth to say something but couldn't get anything out. It was a disturbing sight and, as much as I wanted to hate Tami for what she'd done to herself, it was all too pathetic to even get mad. I felt sorry for her and partly to blame for what was going in her life. If I'd never married her, knowing I didn't love her, and then moved her across the country to a place where she knew no one, maybe she wouldn't have turned out that way.

"Ink… I need your help," she said. Tears spilled from your cheeks. "I'm disgusted with myself. And when I saw the look in my baby's eyes when she came over to me…" She began to cry even harder and lifted her arm to wipe snot from her nose. "She was afraid of me. I don't want that and… if you'll let me come back home so I can get clean, I can get better. I can be the mother that she wants me to be."

"There is no way I can allow you to be alone with Miyah while you're dealing with this shit, Tami. You won't be in the right frame of mind and I have to protect her."

She threw her hands up. "So, have someone here with us! A therapist or somebody to help me get through this and also look after her. I just—I want my life back. I want to be clean and I can't do this without you, Ink."

Watching her, I shook my head, not believing what I was about to say. Still, it had to be done. I'd spent a lot of time trying to help Tami get her shit together and, in the end, that's all it was: time wasted.

"I can't do that this time. You need to go."

Her eyes swelled with tears and when she looked in my face, I knew that she was just as surprised as I was to hear my words. She'd had a lot of people come and go out of her life but, from the beginning, she always knew that she could count on me. Even when I told myself that I was done with her, Tami always found a way to weasel herself back into my life. Not that time.

The streets said I was heartless and cold because that's the side I showed to them. But Tami was one of the rare people who'd had the privilege of seeing the other side of me. When someone stuck their neck out for me or was there when I needed them, it created a bond between us that wasn't easily broken. Throughout my life, Tami had done that on more than one occasion, but, like Sage once told me, I couldn't think about our past when I was trying to make sure my daughter had a chance at a future.

"Ink, don't do this."

I sighed and placed both hands on top of my head, interlocking my fingers together. It wasn't going to end well for either one of us. I couldn't do what she wanted me to, and she wouldn't do what I wanted unless I did something to hurt her feelings. Tami was stubborn; she never let go that easily.

I didn't know how but I had a sudden feeling that the situation that I was finding myself in was going to quickly go from bad to worse. When I saw a car turn around the corner towards my house, I was proven to be right.

A sparkling cream Bentley coupe pulled up, the top down, as the premium paint job glistened in the sunlight. Sage had her long hair flowing in the wind, dark glasses on her face as she pulled into the driveway. She was so beautiful that she brightened up the entire street, until she got close enough to see Tami in front of me. I couldn't see her eyes, but from the way her face seemed to tense under the dark-tined shades, she was not happy in the least.

"This bitch is still in the picture?" I heard Tami snarl, curling her lips in disgust and fury before turning to me. "Ink, listen to me, I know we got problems, but please trust me when I say you need to leave her alone."

I shook my head. "How can you be jealous of her when you were trying to fuck with Kale behind my back? And what about all the other niggas you been around here being a hoe with? Get da fuck outta here. You must still be getting high."

Stepping to the side, I was about to head over to Sage when Tami reached out and grabbed my arm. I turned to her and, even though I wanted nothing to do with her, I couldn't avoid seeing the desperation in her eyes.

"Send her away!" Licking her lips, she glanced over her shoulder to make sure that Sage wasn't near before continuing. "Don't go to her. She's not the one for you."

I snatched my arm away. "How would you know what's for me? You've spent the last few years trying to prove it's you and now look."

Tami dropped her head, her shoulders slumping over as she realized that her words no longer held weight when it came to me.

"You don't even know her."

I snorted out a burst of air through my nostrils.

"Well, turns out, I don't know you either. You need to leave."

"Just talk to me for a minute, Ink, so I can explain. For Miyah's sake—"

I narrowed my eyes at her, trying to hold back my rage.

"For *Miyah's* sake? You mean the daughter you don't want? You should be done using my daughter to get what you want by now. That's some pathetic shit."

Brushing by Tami, I met Sage at her car and pulled the driver's door open. She smiled but when she pulled the shades off her face, I could see the worry in her eyes.

"Everything okay?" she asked.

"Everything is how it should be. Let's go inside. Tami was just leaving," I added the last part for Tami's benefit, hoping that she would take the hint and see that I was serious. She had made her decisions about her life and now she had to live with them.

Turning to lead Sage to the house, I tried to avoid it but

couldn't resist glancing at Tami again. She was standing alone, her arms wrapped around her frail body and her head down. It was clear that she was crying from how she would occasionally brush a hand across her cheek. I couldn't leave her like that.

"Let me get you situated in the house and then I'm going to give her a ride wherever she wants to go," I told Sage.

Her face paled and she hesitated to respond, swallowing hard. "Do you really think that's a good idea?"

I frowned. "What am I supposed to do? Make her walk?"

"Well, how else did she get here?"

For someone who had been so giving of herself, her resources and her time, Sage's callous response was confusing, but I chucked it up to her being on some territorial female shit. She felt threatened by Tami because of our history and couldn't see that there was no need for her to be.

"Let me just get you inside."

With her lips pressed tightly together, Sage returned her shades to her eyes, most likely to hide the fact that she was pouting, as I walked her to my front door. Once inside, I grabbed my keys and let Tamiyah know that I would be back soon, and that Sage would be watching after her. She was excited to hear it and I was grateful to Sage for being someone who could distract from her mother showing up looking like a crackhead.

"Alright, I'll be back. Y'all don't blow up the place before I return," I said, smiling when I heard Tamiyah giggle.

Turning back, I gave one last look at the two new women in my life before walking out the front door, exhaling heavily as I mentally prepared myself to deal with the old one I couldn't get rid of. But when I stepped down the walkway, looking for her, she was nowhere to be found.

Tami was gone.

Chapter Twenty

~

Ink

I woke up in the complete dark, my head pounding. I winced and then groaned, running my hand over the top of my head in anguish. It felt like I had been attacked with a sledgehammer.

Opening my eyes, I blinked a few times, waiting for them to adjust to the dark. I was in the basement, sitting in the most uncomfortable chair on Earth. It was a small, leather chair that went to a small desk I'd put down there. Wasn't cheap but definitely wasn't something you wanted to fall asleep in. Groaning once more, I stood, feeling my bones ache. My muscles were sore.

What the hell happened?

I tried to recall the night before, but I couldn't. The last thing I remembered was playing Monopoly with Tamiyah and Sage. Then I put Tamiyah to sleep and Sage left a little after that. The last mental image I could bring to mind was me kissing her on her lips right before she walked away. I closed the door behind her and everything else was blank after that.

Moving to the wall, I frowned, realizing I had shoes on. In fact, I was fully clothed. My hands grazed across my middle and my brows dipped even further when I felt something wet.

The fuck is going on? I was even more confused and somewhat panicked as every one of my senses told me that something wasn't right.

Reaching out, I felt along the wall for the light switch and then cut it on. My eyes squinted and then blinked rapidly, quickly adjusting to the light before I dropped my head to look at my hand.

"What the fuck?"

My jaw dropped as I gawked at it, mortified. From there, I lowered my gaze to my clothes and that was when I nearly lost it. They were covered in blood. Blood that wasn't mine.

"Fuck!"

Gripping the sides of my head with both of my hands, I left a bloody smear on my skin as I paced the room, trying to recall anything that happened after Sage left. Or did she leave? I looked back down at my clothes. Did something happen? An accident that I didn't remember witnessing? Was this Sage's blood?

"Ink? Is that you?"

The sound of her voice at that exact moment when I was wondering if she was somewhere dying or dead, made me freeze.

"Yeah," I heard myself say.

"Oh! I didn't hear you come in. I'm about to make breakfast for Tamiyah since she'll be awake soon. Come on up and I'll make some for you."

My thoughts merged. I turned slightly to glance into a mirror across from where I stood, and flinched at my appearance.

I was dressed in all black; black sweatpants, black hoodie and black shoes. Blood was on all three. I lifted my blood-stained hand and turned it over. My nails were dirty, like I'd been digging outside.

"Ink? Did you hear me?"

I flinched. Her voice was coming from the top of the basement stairs. There was a rattling sound that followed as she twisted the locked handle on the door.

"Is something wrong?"

"Nah," I replied. I closed my eyes and tried to keep my voice tempered and natural. "I'm going to take a shower and then I'll be up soon."

Sage paused and I hoped that she wasn't going to ask me any questions. From the looks of it, I had killed somebody or something the night before. I couldn't remember shit! I didn't even know how, why or when Sage had come back.

"Okay, that's fine. Just... let me know if you need anything."

"Yeah, I will."

I needed a lot right then but there was nothing that she could give me.

Then again...

I carefully pulled the hoodie from around my neck and then paused to think. Maybe talking with her could give me some recollection of the night. I thought about what she'd said.

"I didn't hear you get in..."

I left? Where the hell did I go?

Placing my hand to my head, I tried to force away the questions in my mind and focus on what was going on. There was no telling what I'd done but I knew one thing for sure. I had to get the hell out of those bloody clothes, hide them and burn them as soon as I had a chance. I didn't know much but experience had taught me that when it came to being Black in America, more important than being innocent was knowing how to cover your own ass.

Chapter Twenty-One

~
Sage

"Did you *sleep* here?" Tamiyah asked, giving me a stern look of suspicion.

Her question caught me off-guard and I almost choked on a thick piece of the pancake in my mouth. Coughing into my closed fist, I reached out and grabbed my glass of orange juice to help me get myself together.

"No," I managed to get out in between sips.

"You didn't?" She raised an eyebrow and focused a pointed eye at the pajama shirt I was wearing. I'd planned on showering and changing after I'd finished breakfast but she woke up before I got the chance.

"No, I didn't. Um, well... I kinda did but not really because..."

Sighing, I rolled my eyes and took the time to get my words together.

"I left to go home after you went to sleep. I was in bed when your daddy asked me to come back so I could watch you because he had to go out. I fell asleep a few times while I was waiting for him to come back but I didn't *sleep over* if that's what you mean."

She scrunched up her nose in confusion. I couldn't blame her. I was trying to explain to a child how 'sleeping over' was different from 'falling asleep overnight while babysitting.' It was only a big deal to me because I cared about Tamiyah not thinking I was hugged up on her daddy in his bed when he was still married to her mom.

"Smells good as hell in here."

My heart lifted as Ink made his appearance at just the right time.

"Ms. Sage made pancakes and sausage!" Tamiyah exclaimed, speaking with her mouth full of both as she chewed. "I like when she stays over."

My cheeks went warm. "I was trying to explain to Tamiyah that I didn't stay over and that I actually went home until you called me to come back here."

"Oh?" Ink's brows jumped as he stuck a piece of sausage into his mouth. "I did?"

I frowned. "Um, yeah. You did."

"And why did I do that?"

Pausing, I cocked my head to the side.

"Because you said you had to go out. So technically, I was just babysitting. I was here for a few hours and ended up falling asleep."

"Sounds like you slept over to me." He stuck a sausage link in his mouth and chewed it. "And I agree with Tamiyah. I like when you sleep over, too."

I nearly gasped at him and then raked my eyes over to Tamiyah. There was a satisfied grin on her face.

"See? I knew it!" She giggled. "Next time you stay over, you can sleep in my bed. It's more comfy than the couch."

I smiled. She was such a beautiful girl and I couldn't resist her automatic charm. She was the kind of child that made your ovaries flutter. She could make a woman who didn't possess one maternal instinct decide to give motherhood a try. Intelligent, beautiful and packed with more than a little charisma, Tamiyah was everything I wanted a daughter of mine to be.

"I'll keep that in mind. If there is a next time." I added the last part for Ink's benefit.

He winked and it made me smile.

"Miyah, if you're done, go ahead and get up. Brush your teeth and change. I need to talk to Ms. Sage."

"Yes, Daddy," she said and then jumped out of her seat. Midway between running off, she turned around and doubled back over to Ink. Jumping up into his lap, she gave him a kiss on his cheek before yelling "Bye!" over her shoulder as she ran off again.

"She's an angel," I said once she was down the hall. "I love spending time with her but I wasn't comfortable with her thinking that I was staying over. I mean, we haven't even talked about our relationship like that. And... I didn't want to overstep."

Ink watched me carefully as I spoke, his eyes scanning every part of my face as if he were trying to read something behind the words that I was saying.

"You didn't. My daughter is smart. She can tell that I'm feeling you and whether or not you slept over last night has nothing to do with that."

My body felt warm and nervous jitters filled my stomach. It was the feeling of new love blossoming inside of me. I was going to respond but before I could, Ink spoke up once again.

"By the way, I need to ask you some things about last night."

The good-natured and carefree disposition that was normal for him was gone. He appeared tensed, bothered and conflicted. I sat in silence with my hands clasped in my lap, waiting for him to continue.

"Maybe it was the drinks, even though I didn't have all that much, but I can't remember too much of what happened after you left. It's like..." He sighed and ran his hand over the top of his head. "I don't know. Like I lost time. Can you fill me in?"

I nodded and then lifted my eyes to the ceiling as I thought back to that night.

"You only had one drink while I was here and you didn't seem drunk when I got here or else I wouldn't have let you leave."

"I left?" He looked shocked.

Frowning, I let a nervous smile curve my lips and then nodded again.

"Yeah, that's why you asked me to come. You texted me about coming to watch Tamiyah and I called you. You said that you got some message from Tami and you had to handle something for yourself." I stopped talking right then to set something straight really quickly. "Now, normally, I would have told you to go fuck yourself had you been any other man telling me to come watch his child while he went to meet his ex at two in the morning but you told me to trust you so... I did. I got here around two-thirty and you left right after. You seemed mad, distracted and it seemed like something serious. I don't know when you got in because I didn't hear you in the basement until I woke up this morning."

The more I spoke, the more Ink's expression shifted. His brown skin seemed to ashen, like the blood was being drained from his face. My mouth went dry and my palms felt clammy. I was nervous as well.

"Is everything okay?" My voice came out in a whisper.

"I don't know," he said, not meeting my eyes. His head was down, elbows on the table and his hands clasped together behind his neck.

"Why don't you let me take Tamiyah to—"

My words were interrupted by loud knocking at the front door.

"Let me get that," Ink said, his brows knitting into a frown across his forehead.

I watched him as he stood and walked to the door, looking like he had the weight of the world on his shoulders. He didn't tell me anything about what happened the night before and I didn't ask. I didn't need to. My only concern at the moment was being able to be there for him.

Damn, girl, you got it bad.

I almost couldn't believe how hard I'd fallen for him so fast. It wasn't like me. Or, actually, maybe it was... I was the type to always go full-speed towards anything that I wanted. At some point, I'd decided that I wanted him and my emotions and behavior had fallen in-line with that. Months ago, I couldn't picture myself being domestic for anyone but, there I was, making breakfast and taking care of his daughter like she was mine. It was insane how quickly life had changed.

"Sage, it's the police."

My thoughts stalled when I heard the tension in Ink's voice. I lifted my eyes to him and frowned.

"The police? Why?"

He shook his head. "Shit, I don't know."

A bewildered expression spread over his face. Lifting his hand, he ran it over the top of his head, silent as he thought to himself. Behind him, the loud pounding on the door sounded off once again.

"Um... you want me to get it?" I offered, feeling anxious.

My concern increased the more that I watched him. The police showing up was never a good sign but for Black folks, especially Black men, that reigned especially true.

"Nah," he said and then turned away. "I got it."

As he walked away to the door again, I sat unmoving until the moment that he was out of sight. But the second I heard him begin to unlock the front door, I jumped up from my chair and crept closer towards the front of the house until I was within earshot.

Chapter Twenty-Two

Ink

I opened the door with a tight expression on my face, feeling on edge.

Being a street nigga, my personal thoughts about the police were anything but good. The fact that I had no recollection of what happened the night before and woke up in my basement wearing bloody clothes only made the moment that much worse. Every run-in that I'd had with the police in my life ended with me being taken away in handcuffs. I opened my clenched fist and tried to appear relaxed.

Two officers stood side-by-side, staring back at me. From their poker faces, I couldn't tell one way or another what to expect.

"Can I help you with anything?"

My tone was tapered and unaggressive, not at all matching my body language. The taller officer, a lean white man with a buzz cut took a step forward, appearing to be the more senior to the shorter black woman standing by his side.

"I'm Officer Louis and this here is Officer Meeks." He paused and the woman nodded her head before he continued. "And... actually, you may be able to help us. Are you Dom Richardson, the husband of Tami Richardson?"

I nodded, feeling the onslaught of panic as I anticipated what would come next.

"Yeah. Why?"

Officer Louis opened his mouth to say something but then closed it again, thinking quickly to himself before he spoke again. "Actually, can we come in? We need to speak to you for a moment and it may be better if you can have a seat."

I shook my head. "Nothing personal but nah, I can't do that. Not until y'all tell me what's going on. Why are you asking about her?"

Both officers exchanged glances before Officer Louis cleared his throat.

"Mr. Richardson, when is the last time you saw your... Tami?"

I shrugged. "Early afternoon yesterday. She was here when I brought my daughter home. We talked and then she left. Why?"

The more they delayed, the more agitated I became.

"Did the two of you argue?"

The way he asked the question, like he was already suspecting me of something that I had no idea about, rubbed me the wrong way. Straightening my spine, I held his glare, not backing down in any way.

"Why are you asking?"

"Is there a reason why you can't answer the—"

Before he could finish, the Black woman, Officer Meeks stepped up, shooting him a look before placing her attention on me.

"Excuse my partner for his… eagerness." She spoke with an air of confidence that made me rethink my assumption that she was the rookie of the two.

"The reason why we are asking about your wife is because we were called to a motel today after a maid went in to service a room and found a great amount of blood. Based on the amount found, if it belongs to one person, it's impossible that the person in question could still be alive. We are asking you about Mrs. Richardson because, though we have not tested the blood, the room was registered under her name and her belongings, along with her identification, were found inside."

I froze, my entire body growing cold. My chest seemed to cave in as if my heart was plunging to the pit of my stomach.

"Damn…" I said finally, exhaling heavily.

I heard what they were saying but the feeling in my soul spoke loudest. There was no need for any tests, no investigation… something told me that it belonged to her. Tami was dead.

"Of course we will be launching a full investigation to figure out if it is Mrs. Richardson's blood or someone else's. There was no body found so it could quite possibly be that she's still alive. If you hear from her, please let us know. And, in the meantime, we will keep you alerted on the results of our investigation."

"What motel was she at?" I was asking the question, but I already felt like I knew the answer and the reason why further unsettled me.

In my pocket at that exact moment was the key card to a motel. I'd found it in the pocket of my sweatpants when I took them off and had been hoping that after speaking with Sage, I would know why it was there.

"A rundown spot near Riverdale. Do you know if she knows anyone there?"

"I don't. I don't even know why she would be there. The Tami I knew wouldn't be caught dead in no rundown place anywhere."

"The Tami you *know*, is what I'm sure you mean." Officer Louis looked at me suspiciously. "Like we said, we can't verify that the blood was hers. But that's an interesting pun you said... about her not being caught dead."

Taking out a pen and pad, he jotted something down, wearing a smirk on his face. Watching him closely, I clenched my jaw to keep from speaking.

"A full investigation has been launched," Officer Meeks continued. "Our office will definitely keep you updated."

A nod was all I chose to give her. There were too many thoughts going through my head right then. Both officers turned as if to leave but then Louis suddenly turned back to face me.

"Just one quick question. Did you go anywhere between two and six this morning?"

The question didn't catch me off-guard. Based off his obvious suspicions of me, I expected it.

"No, I've been here all night. With my daughter. She's inside."

Sliding a small pad and pen out of his pocket, he scribbled something down before lifting his head.

"Can anyone verify this?"

My eyes narrowed. "Should anyone have to?"

"I don't mean to offend you, Mr. Richardson. I'm simply trying to get to the bottom of all this. As I'm sure you want me to." He said the last part with a more than necessary amount of sarcasm. "So… can anyone verify what you said?"

"I can," a voice spoke up behind me.

I watched as both officers' attention went behind me. I didn't turn but I could hear Sage's steps echoing on the tile floor behind me as she walked my way. She'd been listening and now she was lying to cover for me, something I didn't want her to do. I didn't even know what the hell I'd done the night before and now she was putting herself out on a limb and lying to the police.

"I arrived while Tami was here yesterday and I stayed the night. I can verify everything that Ink said." She took my side. "Now, from what I've heard, Ink has to figure out a way to tell his daughter that her mother is missing and could possibly be harmed. Please allow him the time to wrap his head around what you've told him and to be with his child."

As Sage spoke, Officer Louis looked her up and down with a sly grin on his face and then, every now and then, cut his eyes over to me. His unspoken thoughts were easily assumed. He was already putting two and two together as to my relationship with Sage.

"We will do just that." Officer Meeks spoke up and then reached her hand out towards me to extend a card. "Here is my card. If you hear anything, please give me a call. At the moment, this is being called *a missing person's* case. Should anything change, I'll let you know."

Before they left, I gave the officers my number and Sage gave them her contact info as someone that could be reached if they couldn't get to me. Like a boss, she took charge, no questions asked.

"You told me that I left out last night," I said once we were back inside.

She nodded. "I know. But I can tell where that conversation was going and I knew you needed my help."

From there, she gave me a pointed stare that spoke so clearly, I wasn't even surprised about what she said next.

"Maybe you should look into hiring a lawyer."

Chapter Twenty-Three

Ink

"So this isn't you in the video saying that you were going to kill Mrs. Richardson?"

"No, what Mr. Richardson has stated is that, though that is him in the video speaking to his wife, Tami, who he had just found out had been taking illegal drugs around their daughter, led him to make a remark that he did not intend on being taken literally."

Officer Louis raised his hands. "I can't tell! It doesn't look like he doesn't mean it to me. He's obviously angry and he already put his hands on Mrs. Richardson once—"

"He tried to hold her back once she began to assault him. You can't be serious, Frank."

"I only mention that as evidence that Mr. Richardson wasn't in a joking mood and that this was a serious situation. A serious situation in which he spoke, with sincerity, when he stated that if Mrs. Richardson came near him or his daughter again, he would kill her. Now, here we are some weeks later and Tami *did* come back near Mr. Richardson and his—excuse me—*her* daughter, and it was on the afternoon of the same day that we received the call about her motel room being covered in blood. Blood that we know now was hers. That doesn't seem suspicious to you?"

Silence filled the room as Officer Louis leaned over, boring his eyes into Elshire, my attorney. I glanced at him. His expression hadn't faltered a bit and he seemed calm and absolutely in control. I most definitely wasn't. I already knew from the first time that I met him that Louis wanted nothing more than for my ass to be locked up for Tammy's murder, but I thought it may have been on some 'racist cop' bullshit. The more he began to lay out his case, questioning about events that led up to that moment, the more I began to see why he was so arrogant and aggressive in his pursuit. It wasn't looking good for me at all.

"What seems suspicious to me is that you are only focused on my client when the real murderer could be getting away. Mrs. Richardson has been using drugs and she was staying in a cheap motel located in an area where crime, drugs and violence are incredibly high. That leaves a lot of alternatives open for you to pursue. As stated, my client has an alibi for the night in question. He was home with his daughter and Ms. McMillian—"

"Oh, I forgot about his *girlfriend*," Louis chimed in. "She's the one who gave you your alibi, right?"

"She's a friend," I corrected him with an even tone.

"Only a friend?" His tone was covered in sarcasm. "Well, I'm sure she would do *anything* to be something more. From what I hear, you're some kind of celebrity with the ladies."

I frowned at the suggestive way in which he spoke, like I was using Sage to lie for me. Though she was covering for me, it wasn't because I'd done anything wrong and I hadn't asked her to do it anyway.

"Unless you have any additional questions, we are finished here." Elshire stood sharply.

With my eyes still on Louis and his on me, I did the same.

"You will hear from me again soon." Louis issued the threat with a scowl on his face, like he hated me. It was beyond just a cop wanting to nail a suspect. It was too personal.

As I walked out of the police department, I tried to ignore the way people looked at me while trying to pretend they weren't. In only a few days, I'd gone from being a local celebrity that was somewhat known to being discussed nationally.

The news story about the missing wife of the celebrity tattoo artist who was later on found to be dead had gone viral. The old videos taken of me and Tami arguing in the weeks leading up to her disappearance had almost as many views as a new music video dropped by Beyoncé. People were obsessed with what would happen next. There were articles all over the web of people proclaiming my guilt while others fought in favor of my innocence. Every news station across the globe was reporting any little new discovery as breaking news. In other words... I was the new O.J.

I hadn't been officially charged yet and that's what made it that much better. Everyone was on edge, waiting for whether or not the police would be able to bring a case against me based on what they already knew.

"Wayne is about to bring the car around now," Kale said to

me once Elshire and I were at the main entrance of the police department.

Someone in there had leaked it to the public that I would be called in to be questioned today. For that reason, media was camped out in front of all of the exits, ready to swarm me with questions. Reporters were armed with microphones to shove in my face and photographers would be snapping pics.

All the attention made it so that I couldn't even move around the way I normally did. Just to come in to be questioned, I had to get a driver and ask Kale to come along because he had a license to carry a concealed weapon. When you were like me and from the streets, having someone close to you that wasn't a felon was priceless for that exact reason. Although I couldn't carry a gun, he could.

"Yeah, I appreciate you getting him to bring me here. I ain't think it was going to be thick like that when I got out," I told him, looking out the glass doors at the crowd of reporters out front.

Kale chuckled a little and shook his head. "Yeah, man, I know you been avoiding the news and shit but you been on damn near every station and blog. White folks keeping up with this shit. So I knew you would be able to get here without people knowing but it would be insane when you got ready to leave."

I nodded my head with my lips firmly pressed together but didn't say anything in response. Being that Tami was gone, I was overlooking some of the questions I still had about him and Tami until everything died down. But something still wasn't right with me when it came to Kale; I just couldn't place it.

"He's pulling up now; I see him," Kale said, staring out the front entrance. "C'mon."

I followed behind Elshire with Kale to my back and took a deep breath before we all walked out the front door. That was the part that pissed me off because I couldn't say shit but everyone around me could say whatever the hell they wanted to say.

"Again, remember, let me do all the talking," Elshire reminded me.

"You tell me that shit every time," I snapped at him, even though I knew it wasn't his fault. He was there to help me but I was pissed off that I even had to deal with the bullshit.

"Ink, why did you kill your wife?"

"Ink, do you think that you'll be arrested for killing your wife?"

"Mr. Richardson, how did it feel being asked to come in for questioning about your wife's murder case?"

"Ink, did they tell you that you're a suspect?"

The few seconds I had to wait before we made it to the doors of Wayne's black Cadillac SUV felt like an eternity. The second I was able to get in, Kale closed the door behind me, cutting off the noise. With my eyes closed, I exhaled out a long breath while dropping my head onto the back headrest.

"Ink, I gotta tell you, this doesn't look good," Elshire told me once Wayne started to drive away.

A partition was lifted, cutting off Wayne from being able to hear our conversation; one custom addition of many that he'd had done to his whip. Kale said that Wayne used to be the driver to some major rapper who also was still running work in the streets and that's how he knew he should be the one to drive me around. His Cadillac was bulletproof, where Elshire and I sat was a soundproof room and Wayne was also licensed to carry.

"Officer Louis handed me this on our way out." He handed me a piece of paper.

"It's log from the week that Tami was killed. She wrote her name down saying that she was coming to apply for a restraining order. Now I haven't been able to look yet into whether it was actually filed but... did she ever mention wanting to get one taken out on you?"

With a frown, I shook my head. "No! *Hell,* no, I never put my hands on Tami and never would, no matter how mad she'd made me. If she went down there for a restraining order, it wasn't for me."

"Well, I'm thinking that has something to do with the reason Louis is so confident. With whatever this is, the videos, your background and the amount of noise being made about this case, any time now they will officially be pressing charges against you."

Lying back against the seat, I pushed a 'whoosh' of air through my lips and turned my attention out the window. There was nothing I could say because he was right. Hell, if I were any other nigga, I would think I did it, too.

To be honest, I didn't even really know for sure that I wasn't the one who killed Tami. I couldn't remember a thing about what happened that night that would lead to me having blood all over my clothes.

Beyond that, there was shit that the police didn't even know yet that had me feeling like I was losing my mind. They hadn't been able to find Tami's phone at the scene but there was one thing I knew for sure. According to what the police told me, she was murdered around four o'clock in the morning. One of the last texts in her phone, possibly the very last, came from me.

At three forty-six, a few minutes before the time that she was murdered, I had sent her a text that I didn't even remember sending; words that had me thinking I was losing my mind. The text read, *Open up. I'm outside.*

"Can you think of anything else... anything that they may have to try to pin this on you? We really need to be talking about a strategy right now. We already know that we need to look into Tami and whether or not she made any enemies you aren't aware of, but I need to be sure they don't have anything else they can use."

I paused for a moment to think. "No, there isn't anything. I mean, Tami and I had issues, but nothing more than any other couple."

"There is also the matter of Sage."

I piped up at the way his tenor slid, like Sage was a handicap of mine in some way.

"What about her?"

Elshire gave me a pointed look. "She was photographed playing in the park with your daughter. It's not exactly in your favor to have her around. At least not publicly."

"She's a friend who I was seeing before all this happened. She's the only thing that keeps Tamiyah's mind off her mother." I tossed my hands in the air. "I can't help what it looks like but we are just friends."

Elshire shrugged. "I mean, I like her and all but having her around doesn't look good for you. The media is painting you out to be some heartless, heavily tattooed, arrogant celebrity who was married to a woman that he publicly disrespected by having open affairs with other women. They even have some law-school student crying on *TMZ* about how she didn't know you were married when she had a relationship with you before you tossed her to the side like garbage."

Brisha's lying ass strikes again.

I gritted my teeth. "I didn't have a relationship with her. I fucked her one time in the bathroom at a club."

"It doesn't matter. Right now, she's a hurt little college girl who wants to be a lawyer and you're the thug who breaks hearts. And sometimes kills."

Lifting a brow, I gave Elshire a hard look. He was lucky that he was so good at his job because the more it went on, the more I felt like breaking his ass.

He must have felt my anger building because the next thing he did was sit back a little, clear his throat and then continue in a much less aggressive voice.

"Anyway, I merely mean to illustrate to you the severity of everything and how public opinion affects you. The more eyes on this case, the least likely they are to give leniency."

Frustrated, I blew out a breath and turned to the window, watching the outside scenery pass me by. Elshire was saying that things didn't look too good already, but something was telling me that was only the beginning.

Chapter Twenty-Four

~
Sage

I drummed my hand across my desk, a habit that I was doing now more than ever, and sighed. My anxiety was at an all-time high those days and in more ways than one.

With the case regarding Tami's murder receiving so much coverage, every day that I went to work, I had to mentally prepare myself for the shit to hit the fan.

The public attention was affecting business and McMillian Enterprises was losing clients. People had me pegged as the evil side bitch who had broken up Ink's marriage and was responsible for Tami's death. Most people were split on their opinions of Ink; they either thought he was innocent and felt sorry for him or they thought he was guilty and hated him. No one was split on their opinions of me. The ones who cried guilty said he murdered his wife and my Jezebel ways drove him to it and the ones who thought him innocent said that if weren't for me, Tami would have been home with her man instead of the seedy motel where she'd died. I couldn't win for losing.

"Sage? The board is meeting... I know you told me to tell you if they were seen meeting without alerting you." Her eyes dimmed and she looked away from my face. "So, I wanted to let you know."

My chest throbbed. Though I knew it was coming, it still hurt to know that it was finally being done.

"Thank you for telling me," I replied as I let out a huff of air.

"I'm sorry that this is happening," she added in a quiet voice. "I know that this is a hard time for you and... I'm sorry the board isn't standing by your side. Your father would've wanted them to."

Emotions were lodged in my throat, so I only nodded a response. She left, and I was finally alone and able to retreat into my thoughts.

The board was trying to get rid of me. They never wanted me there to begin with, so I wasn't shocked that my connection to Ink was being used to start conversations around making me a silent member who had no real power or connection to the company. Their argument would be that I was bad for business.

Right then, there was a woman's group protesting outside, WAH... Women Against Homewreckers or Women Against Hoes—one of the two, depending on who you asked. The group was led by a woman who had made it her personal mission to destroy me. She said she was a friend of Tami's and wouldn't let her killer go free without a fight, so she'd made it her business to terrorize both Ink and me. She did protests, called for people to strike our businesses, and had arranged for her supporters to yell and shout at me from outside my home. It was driving my neighbors crazy and the homeowners association was trying to file claims to force me to move. In a matter of a week, my whole life had completely changed.

My cell phone began to vibrate and I grabbed it quickly. It was almost noon so I knew exactly who it was.

Wish I could take you to lunch.

I smiled—the first of the day—and then replied back.

So do I.

It had only been two days since I'd last seen Ink, but I was missing him a lot. I could understand why he had to keep his distance, but it was hard always being home alone. Besides work, I couldn't go anywhere without being harassed.

How are things at the office?

I rolled my eyes. "You want the long version or the short version?" I muttered, picking the phone up into my hands.

Me: *Not too good. Protestors outside and the board is having secret meetings.*

Ink: *Damn. I can't stand that humpback bitch.*

Me: *That's not nice!*

I stifled a laugh. She did have a hump in her back. Actually, she kinda reminded me of a penguin in the way she was built. She was heavyset and hobbled over when she walked. The fact that she looked like that and had all those stories about how nice the beautiful Tami was to her only made them love Tami even more. Thanks to Cindy, people were acting like Tami was Mother Theresa.

The phone in my hands began to ring and I answered it after seeing that it was Ink.

"Now you know that wasn't nice," I said as soon as I got on the line.

"Yeah, and I don't care. I can't stand the bitch. She asked Tamiyah this morning if she felt like she was safe living with me."

"What?" I almost shouted. "She's trying to strike a nerve. She wants you to act violent or upset so that she can catch your reaction."

"And she almost got that shit. I don't mind what she says to me but my daughter is off-limits."

"Did she get to Chicago safely?" I asked.

"Yeah, she called me about an hour ago, having the time of her life at Kale's mom's house..."

His voice died and a few seconds of silence passed. I assumed he was probably thinking of Tamiyah. He hadn't wanted to send her away but keeping her around the craziness in Atlanta didn't seem like a good idea, especially with it looking like he would be charged with murder at any moment.

"It's the right thing to do," I assured him. "I know you probably feel like she's losing both parents, with Tami gone and you having to deal with this, but it's only for a moment. Plus, it's not bad for her to get away from this. Being around other kids and away from things that remind her of Tami will be good for a little while."

"These motherfuckas wanna lock me up for this... what if it's longer than just a little while?"

I swallowed hard. The way he said it let me know that he was believing it could be a real possibility.

"You didn't do this so you won't go down for it, Ink. You'll see."

He didn't respond and every second that passed increased my anxiety even further.

"I hope you're right," he finally said. His voice was so low that I wasn't even sure I'd heard it.

I could hear the doubt.

"Do you need me to come over?" I asked. "I mean, I can slip in through the garage around back so I'm not seen. I'll drive one of my other cars."

He hesitated for a moment. "You still want to be around me?"

"Yeah." My brows bent. "Why wouldn't I want to be?"

The sound of him sighing gave me the answer.

"Because of the stuff in the news? Ink, if you don't want me to come, I won't but I don't care about if I'm seen. There isn't much more they can say about me than they have already."

"That's not what I mean." He paused. "I mean, there is a lot of shit being said and—I just thought you would be cutting ties with me soon."

"Ink, there isn't much that I'm sure of right now but one thing I do know is that you did not kill Tami, nor did you have anything to do with it. And I'm not saying that because I'm your friend. I'm saying it because I know. You can trust me."

Holding the phone to my ear, I stood up from my desk when I heard voices from outside my office.

"Damn, that's what's up," Ink said. I could practically hear him smiling through the other end. "You don't know how good it is to hear that from you. A lot of people been acting weird around me lately."

Taking a glimpse outside my office, I saw Sherelle talking with another assistant who worked for Charles. She was most likely filling her in on their meeting.

"Yeah, I know what you mean," I said, turning back to my desk. "I haven't heard from Lola in a little while and that's not like her."

"She still been fucking with Kale? That nigga been acting funny, too."

"Not too much, from the last I spoke to her. Classes started and she doesn't have a lot of time."

Ink and I continued speaking for a short while but the conversation was strained. It was hard to talk about anything that didn't involve the case because everything about it weighed so heavily on our minds, but we definitely couldn't discuss it over the phone.

I was sure that he thought I was supporting him because it was the right thing to do but he was wrong. No matter what the circumstances looked like, I knew in my heart that Ink didn't murder Tami. He wasn't a killer and, even though he had problems with her, the love he had for his daughter was to the point that he could've never harmed her mother. In Ink's mind, even with all of her faults, Tamiyah was better off with Tami in her life than not at all. He understood how much a young girl needed her mother and I could tell that by the things he said when I spoke about being abandoned by mine.

"You're right. They are trying to invoke a special vote for your removal on the basis that your involvement with the company is greatly impacting revenue negatively."

I looked up at Sherelle as she burst into my office, holding a paper in her hand. She then held it out to me.

"These are the minutes from the meeting they had. I'm friends with someone who got them for me."

She stood over me as I briefly read it over.

"They want me to make a public statement, distancing myself from any and everything concerned with Ink," I said aloud. "I can't do that. He's a friend."

"Yes." She nodded. "A friend that they are going to use against you. You might want to think on if he's worth it."

Why did everyone keep saying that?

Chapter Twenty-Five

Sage

"Hello?"

"Damn, stranger! Med school got you to the point where you can't return phone calls anymore?"

"Of course not, Sage," Lola replied before releasing a long sigh. "It's just... crazy these days."

I snorted. "That's definitely an understatement."

Lola and I hadn't spoken much in the past few days and it wasn't normal for us at all.

"Yeah, my parents called me about it a few times."

My gut twisted. Now I was thinking that there was another reason why I hadn't heard from Lola recently.

"What did they say?"

"They don't believe anything the news is saying about you." She put extra emphasis on the 'you.'

"But they think Ink is guilty."

Her hesitation was a dead giveaway. "They just think you're making a mistake by still hanging with him."

"He says he's innocent and I believe him."

"Of *course* he did, Sage. Do you expect him to say, 'hey, I killed my wife,' right to your face?"

My teeth ground together and the muscles in my body tensed as I sped through a red light and made a left hand turn, narrowly escaping oncoming traffic. I was on my way to Ink's house after having a terrible day and only called Lola because I needed a friend, but the conversation wasn't going the way I thought it would be.

"Lola, what if it were you? What if everyone believed you did something bad just because coincidence made it look that way? Wouldn't you want me to be there for you?"

"Yeah, but you've got to admit, it looks *really* bad."

"Don't you remember when Erica thought you slept with her boyfriend because she found some panties in his apartment and he said they belonged to you?"

"Yeah, with his lying ass. He was sleeping with her sister and we both had the same Gucci cheerleading bags. When she found the bag at his apartment, he didn't want to tell her that he was fuckin' her own sister so he said it was me. You were the only one who didn't betray me."

I nodded as I turned into Ink's neighborhood, driving slowly. I didn't want to bring any attention to myself.

"Right. Erica was your best friend at the time. She turned against you and everyone else did too until she later on found them fucking in her bed. Sometimes things look one way but it's not the truth. Ink didn't do this."

I pulled slowly past Ink's house, hiding behind my illegally tinted windows as they chanted with signs in their hands. With any luck, I could ease behind, pretending I was going to someone else's house and then slide around to the back.

"But that's the thing, Sage. In my case, I was innocent but when it comes to Ink, I don't think it's true."

Sucking my teeth, I groaned.

"But how can you know that, Lola? You don't even know him—"

"Kale told me. He thinks he did it, too. He won't tell me exactly how but he said he has proof."

My heart stalled. Thankfully, I had already made it to the back and was in front of Ink's garage. I jammed my finger against a button to kill the engine and sighed.

"What proof?"

"He said that he was talking on the phone with Tami that night. She got off the phone around a quarter to four, after telling him that Ink was outside. Then the next thing he knew, she was dead."

My breaths were elevated as I stared ahead at the closed garage door with the phone in my hands.

"I'm sure there is an explanation for that."

"Sage, don't be crazy."

"Lola, I have to go. I have another call coming in."

I ended the call before she could call me out on my lies.

People would say that I was crazy but isn't that how they describe all the best loves ever known? In the moment, right when tragedy strikes, people always pass judgment, but once it was all over, I would be the epitome of what it meant to be a ride or die chick; the kind who loves a man enough to stay by his side.

The garage door suddenly began to open and I felt my body go warm when I saw Ink staring back at me. The excitement in his eyes was almost boyish. Like how a child looks when they run to the door and see that Mama is back home.

"I heard a car pull up," he explained. "You made it."

I smiled and grabbed my duffle bag from the passenger seat before stepping out the car.

"Of course I did."

Chapter Twenty-Six

Ink

Spending time with Sage had me living the best moments that I'd experienced in a long time. With Tamiyah gone, I had fallen back on old habits and started drinking more than I normally did. Being that I knew how it was for me as a child the brief time when I had my father around, it was a habit I'd fought to shake loose when I became a parent. However, with everything going on, I was more stressed than I'd ever been and couldn't do anything but sit home alone. The pressure of it all was killing me.

"I'm going to head out to work. I got a schedule full of clients today."

Leaning over, I kissed Sage lightly on her forehead. She groaned and snuggled in close to me with her eyes closed.

"No, I don't want you to leave," she said. "We need to stay here and avoid everything outside. It's perfect here."

"Yeah, it is perfect," I had to agree. "But the one upside to all this shit is that my work schedule has been packed. The few people who still believe in my innocence have been going hard to show their support. I've got clients back to back."

"I've always believed in your innocence. Can I have a time-slot reserved for me on your full schedule?"

She wrapped her arms around my neck and laid her head on my chest.

"You can have all the time you want for however long you want it."

"How about forever?" she questioned back.

I dropped my head and buried my nose in her hair, loving the way that her presence made me feel so content; a sharp change from how I'd felt all the days before.

The timing couldn't be worse but I'd thought about marriage more than a couple times since the moment she had shown up. Having her around felt so natural, like it was supposed to be that way. Even when Tamiyah was home, that's how it had been. We both made space for Sage in our lives without even knowing that's what we were doing. She fit like the perfect piece to our puzzle.

"Forever sounds nice," I told her, speaking honestly.

Lifting her hand to my lips, I placed a kiss on top of the finger where I would slide an engagement ring, when it was time. In some crazy way, Tami's death had made me want to move faster with my intentions with Sage. If anything, it had taught me how quickly life could change for the worse.

There was so much that I regretted when it came to how I'd handled my relationship with Tami. There was so much that I wished I had done to help her have a happy life while she was alive, things that could have changed her fate, but there was nothing I could do about that then.

"Stay here until I get back. Spend the night with me again," I said to Sage as I moved to slide out of the bed. "I want to talk to you about something when I get home."

"Ohhh, sounds serious."

She lifted up, holding the covers around her naked body to cover her chest as if I hadn't been sucking all over her nipples all night long. There was a devilish smirk on her lips that said she had a few suspicions regarding what I had in mind to discuss.

"Maybe. But it's a much needed talk."

She fell back onto the bed and I left to take a shower and get ready to leave. By the time I was all dressed and ready to go, she was sleeping again. Before leaving, I kissed her once more on her forehead and then made my way to the garage to leave. For the first time in my life, I had a woman in my bed that made me hate having to go to work. Going to the shop had always been my reprieve away from dealing with Tami but when it came to Sage, it felt more like punishment being away from her.

***

"El, what's up?" I said as I jumped on the interstate. Atlanta traffic was notoriously terrible but it was the perfect time for me to speak with Elshire about my case.

"Not too much. Everything is quiet but that's a little what I'm afraid of. When things are like this, it makes me feel like Louis and his crew are cooking up something. You know he used to be at sergeant level, slated to be captain, but he fucked up big on a case. So, he has a personal reason for going so hard with this. He's trying to capitalize off of all the attention."

"I was wondering why he was working overtime like they were paying him time-and-a-half," I mumbled. "He's been coming for me since the first time I saw him. Did you get any word on the restraining order?"

"Yeah, about that. I have a source that says Tami never actually filed for one. She walked in and put her information down but, by the time Louis got to her, she'd left. There is no telling who she was getting a restraining order for. It could have been anyone. Louis is trying to use it to scare you."

I snorted air through my nostrils and shook my head.

"That's bullshit."

"Well, hopefully, this quiet time is for good reason and not because he's about to try to come at you from another angle."

I pulled into the parking garage of my building, thankful that I'd at least dropped the extra couple stacks to make sure that I had a private way into the building and a designated parking space. Kale had been telling me to use it for months and I was finally listening. It made it easy to slip in and out unnoticed. I decided to lock my shop down and close it to the public, meaning that the only ones who could come in were the people who had made an appointment in advance.

"He can't come at me from no angle because I haven't done shit."

"I understand," he replied, but I wasn't sure if he did. The whole situation was stressful as hell and I didn't like the fact that it seemed like all I was doing was reacting to what was happening to me instead of taking some kind of action.

"I'm about to head into work, man," I said, feeling exasperated. After only being away from Sage for a few moments, I was already back to being stressed out.

"Work? Do you think that's a good idea?"

"Aren't you the one who told me to continue to live my life as normally as possible?"

"Yes, but I meant at home, out of the public's eye. You need to be grieving about how you lost a wife, not looking like you're perfectly fine with her gone."

I let out a sharp breath. There was nothing I hated more about being in the spotlight than always having to worry about what a motherfucka thought about me.

"Working to pass the time is the way I grieve. Call me once you hear something."

Without giving him a chance to respond, I hung up the line and grabbed my things. I had a long day ahead of me with more than my normal load of clients to take care of.

Walking at a fast pace with the hood of my jacket pulled over my head, I made my way through the parking garage towards the back door to my shop. I unlocked the door and had to kick boxes and mailed packages out of the way before I could get in. With everything going on, Elshire was having a service do a security check on all of my mail before it could be opened.

Indie had already opened up, prepped my station and, from the conversation I heard once I walked in, she had let my client in, too.

"I've wanted to get Ink to do a piece for me for a while now. I never had the chance to come and get it. But with everything I keep hearing, I couldn't wait to schedule an appointment to show my support. Ink is a really good man and anyone who pays any attention to him knows it."

"Yeah, he is," Indie was saying, but something about her tone seemed like she had more to say behind that statement.

"Aye, what's up?" I walked in from the back, nodded my head at Indie and then looked over to my client, an older white woman who looked like she could be well into her 70s. Definitely not my normal type.

"You ready?" I asked. I was unable to hide the half-smile on my lips.

"You bet I am," the woman replied and, with Indie's help, stood to her feet. "I've been wanting to get a tattoo for a long time but never did. I've been watching the news since the beginning and wanted to let you know that people like me support you."

The old lady had my heart already.

"What you tryin' to get?"

"My husband's name. Over my heart." She paused to slide her thick bifocal glasses off her face, wiped them and then continued. "I told him that I would get it when he got mine. He put my name here." She pointed to her neck. "But I didn't. I guess I was scared. Then last year, he died and... I guess I felt guilty that I had waited so long and now he would never see it. But I think it's the right time now."

I nodded my head. "This is the perfect time. Let's get started."

***

Ten minutes later, I had the sketch done and was about to add ink when she began to talk about her former life again.

"You need to marry her while y'all are both young. If you don't, and you lose her, you'll be like me. Full of regrets."

I lifted my eyes and looked at her from under a raised brow. "Marry who?"

I hoped she wasn't one of those people trying to get me to speak on personal things.

"The young lady up front. Indie." She smiled brightly. "I can see how you are around her. She's so nice and helpful, too."

"That is true. And she's also not my girl."

"Oh?" Her brows bent. "Well, I can tell that she likes you a lot. You should give her a chance."

The sound of my phone ringing saved me from having to respond.

"Just a minute. Let me take this right quick."

"You do what you gotta do, honey," she told me with a wink.

I stepped into the back to take the call. It was Sage and she normally didn't hit me while I was at work so it must've been something important.

"Hey, what's up?"

"Ink! The police are here. They said they have a search warrant!"

My thoughts merged and for a minute, I felt like I couldn't possibly have heard her right.

"The fuck? Why did you open the door? Don't let them in!"

"I didn't!" she screamed, sounding near tears. "They broke down the door and came in. They gave me some paper from a judge and…"

Her words faded out. I could tell she was panicked and even though I was still trying to wrap my head around why the police were in my house, I tried to calm her down.

"Aye, I need you to stay calm. Find somewhere to sit and stay there until I get back. I need to call Elshire."

She whimpered something that sounded like agreement and I ended the call so I could get my lawyer on the line. The bloody clothes were long gone. I'd burned that shit the first chance I got but I couldn't get over the feeling that something still wasn't right.

"Yo, El—"

"I'm already on the way. I got the notice about the search warrant. Is there anything there that you think they will find?"

I stopped dead in my tracks. Until that moment, I didn't even realize that I had been pacing. To be honest, I didn't know what they would find. There was a whole night that I couldn't remember.

"I got some guns there that I shouldn't have but I think that's it."

"You think? What do you mean, you think?"

I couldn't answer that question, so I didn't say anything.

"I'm pulling up at your house. When you get here, we need to talk."

Elshire didn't wait for me to answer before he hung up the line. I felt someone else's presence in the room and when I looked up, Indie was standing at my office door. Her eyes were clouded with tears and her bottom lip was trembling.

"I saw it on the news... the police at your house. They are saying that you could be arrested today."

There was a sharp pain in my chest. Without saying

anything right away, I walked forward and wrapped my arms around her. She laid her head on my chest.

"Dav got in a fight the other day. Some boys at school were saying you were a murderer and deserved to be in prison. I know you didn't do this but, Ink... I'm so scared for you."

I buried my nose in Indie's hair and rubbed her back as she held onto me sobbing quietly.

"Mr. Ink?"

It was my client, calling for me from down the hall.

"I'm here," I told her.

"I wanted to say that I'll be back another day for the tattoo. I know now isn't a good time. I'll make an appointment for when you come back." She walked up so that I could see her and gave me a pointed look. "And you will come back."

After giving me another warm smile, she took a minute to admire the sight of me standing there with Indie in my arms. Her smile widened further and then she gave me a kind wink.

"Remember what I told you. No regrets," she said before walking away to let herself out. My mind was too much of a wreck to even give her words much thought.

"I gotta get to the house. El is there and so is Sage, but—"

Indie snatched away from me and frowned. "Sage? Sage is at your house? She's the one who let the police in?"

Her sudden anger as she asked the question wasn't at all what I expected.

"Yeah, she's there. Is that a problem?"

Her eyes narrowed. "I guess not. I would think your girl would know not to let them search your crib without you.

Someone from the streets would have known better."

Now wasn't the time for that fight.

"Not if she knows I ain't got shit to hide."

I was more aggressive than I should've been, but it was the stress of the moment, combined with the fact that she was copping an attitude with me over some jealous shit.

"I find it funny that you are all caught up in her so fast. You don't even answer texts anymore, but you have time to be around that bitch. Every time I call, you send me straight to voicemail. You don't even come and hang out with Dav anymore. Kale's right... you've changed."

"*I've* changed?"

Taking a step forward, I jabbed a finger into the center of my chest.

"I haven't changed shit! You're the motherfucka who is changing around here. I'm going through all this bullshit and you're more worried about what female that I stick my dick in than anything else. You talking about Kale being right about me, but maybe he's right about you, too! Maybe you're so worried about who I'm with because it ain't you."

Her body jerked back as if my words had physically hit her and, once again, her eyes filled with tears. I was dead wrong for what I was saying because since moving to the A, Indie was someone who had always looked out for me. She was like a sister, but she could have been my girl. I was always attracted to her, but my track record with women at the time was fucked up. I made up my mind not to take it further with her because I valued her as a friend.

"You're an asshole," she said as a tear slid down her cheek.

She quickly brushed it off and sniffed the rest away.

"You'll realize that you're making a mistake, but I hope by then you'll be able to change it. I hope it won't be too late. Now have a good life."

She turned around to leave and I didn't stop her or walk her out like I normally did. She was in her feelings, but I had to deal with that later. My freedom was on the line.

Chapter Twenty-Seven

Sage

"*Atlanta tattoo artist and owner of Official Ink, Dom Richardson, has been arrested and charged with the murder of his late wife, Tami Richardson. Earlier today, the Atlanta Police Department conducted a search on his home where they found evidence linking him to the murder weapon found on the scene. Toxicology reports have also confirmed that semen found on a dress in a motel belonging to the deceased belonged to him, further connecting him to the scene of the crime. Now, we have received updates on this story.*"

On the television, the head of the Atlanta Police Department, Captain Short, stood at a podium. Behind him were several other officers and in front of him was a crowd of reporters and people hidden behind flashing camera lenses. Reaching in front of me, I grabbed a half-empty glass of wine and held it firmly in my hands as I listened with all attention on the screen.

"At the moment, we are confident that we have more than enough evidence to substantiate our belief that Dom Richardson is responsible for his wife's murder. Multiple witnesses have stated that they were present when the suspect threatened the victim's life, assaulted her, and we have witnesses who also state they saw a man, who appeared to look like the suspect, leaving her motel room shortly after the time that our experts have stated the victim was killed. Our investigation is still in progress and we hope to bring justice for Mrs. Richardson and her family very soon."

My phone rang for the hundredth time and I reached out to silence it, but stopped when I saw who was calling. Reluctantly, I grabbed it and answered on the second ring.

"I already know what you're about to say."

The sound of Lola exhaling heavily came through on the other line and I closed my eyes tight. I wasn't ready to have the conversation. As it was, my phone was already ringing back to back and when it wasn't, I was getting hit with text after text.

Even my stepmother had called. After not hearing from her since my dad's death, I was curious of what she had to say and checked the voicemail.

"Sage, I know we haven't spoken in a while and I don't really like to insert myself into your personal life but, for the sake of your father's business, you need to distance yourself from that man. He's a murderer. I can read people very well. Trust what I'm telling you."

I scoffed and quickly erased the message as soon as it ended. My father had been having an affair with my mother for years before she found out. She never suspected a thing until I was left outside their home. And she said she could read people? Yeah, right.

"Sage, you can't still believe that Ink didn't do this," Lola said in a way that made me feel stupid for what I was about to say next.

"Yes, I actually do believe that."

Lola clicked her teeth in that way that women do when they are trying to seem empathetic but really want to say, "You're one stupid-ass bitch."

"How can you say that? Like, how can you *possibly* say that? You barely even know him."

Letting her words hang in the air, I fell back onto my bed and held the phone to my ear. There was a secret that I had held every day of my life.

"Because I know when a man is lying. I can tell when someone is saying something they don't mean and I know when they aren't."

Sometime when I was in middle school, I found a letter from my mother saying that she regretted giving me away and was going to fight to get me back. It was buried in one of my father's things and I'd only found it because I had been snooping. My birthday was in a few days and I wanted to see what he had bought me. For so long, I had wondered about my mother and what had become of her life. I wondered if she had missed me, or had even thought about me after giving me away. Now I knew for a fact that she had.

Also with the letter was another piece of paper, a news article. The article said that a woman, with the same name as the one who had written the letter, had been killed in a hit and run. The date on the article was less than a week after the one on the letter.

I remember feeling a chilling sensation traveling up my spine when I read the line saying that witnesses had stated a black Lincoln Town Car had run her over before speeding away.

They said the windows were too tinted for them to make out who was behind the wheel, but I had an idea. My stepmother had a car just like it but she had recently gotten rid of it for something newer. I thought back to the day when she had texted me a picture of her new ride. I'd been taking final exams so it had to have been in May. Right around the time my mother was killed.

When I brought the papers to my father, I raised all natural hell. For the first time in my life I screamed at him about the hateful woman that he had in his life and how I always knew she never liked me. I told him that she was a murderer and when she walked in on me shouting at him, I pointed my finger in her face and told her, too.

The problem was, when I looked in her eyes, the shock that I saw there silenced me. She looked down and plucked the papers from my hand, her eyes tearing up with emotion as she read every line.

That's when it dawned on me. She hadn't seen the letter from my mother. I had assumed that my father had shared it with her, but he hadn't. As my stepmother broke down into sobs behind me, I trembled and stepped towards my father and looked him straight in the eyes.

"Tell me you didn't do this," I'd asked him. "Was it you? Did you have anything to do with this?"

With his head lifted, shoulders squared and his jawline tight, he looked right back at me and lied.

"No," he said. "I didn't have anything to do with it."

When he saw my doubt, his face crumbled under the pressure and I could see the guilt in his eyes.

"I swear, Sage. I didn't," he lied some more.

Although I was the victim, I was still born as a result of the ultimate betrayal a man could inflict on his wife. So my pain from knowing my mother was dead came second to my stepmother's pain of being reminded of the woman who had been behind the worst moments of her life. All through the night, my stepmother cried, howled and carried on to the point that my father spent the rest of the night consoling her until she fell asleep.

"I saw the way that Ink looked at his daughter when he had to tell her that her mommy was never coming home. He was broken. He held her in his arms as she cried and didn't leave her side until she was asleep. There was nothing he would do to bring her that kind of pain. If he had caused it, he wouldn't have been able to stand seeing her like that."

After I found out about what my father had done, he sent me away to spend the rest of the summer at a prestigious camp before going back to school. My entire birthday was wasted at the airport, on the plane, and then with me unpacking my things at a camp full of people I didn't know.

I'd asked him about going to the camp before school ended for the summer, but it was full and he told me that he'd rather I was home. Then, all of a sudden, a spot opened up the day after I found the papers in his shoebox. Of course, my daddy told me that he had to pull favors to get it for me so I had to leave immediately. He made it seem like he was only sending me away because it was what I wanted, but that wasn't true. When he told me goodbye, he couldn't even look at me.

It was a long time before I was able to come back home after that. I noticed that every time I spoke to him in a way that made him have to face his guilt about what he'd done, the more he would find excuses as to why I shouldn't come home over breaks. When I finally gave up, buried the thoughts in the back of my mind, and tried to move on, he once again began to request for me to come home. Eventually, we went on like it never happened.

"Sage, you know that I love you and I will always support you but—"

"Then do it," I said, cutting her off. "If you're going to love me and support me always, then you can start now."

"But, Sage, I…" She sighed. "I don't want you to get hurt."

"Ink would never hurt me. He would never hurt anyone that he loves. I'll call you a little later."

Before she could respond, I hung up the phone.

The next day, I was sitting at my desk, trying to work although my mind was too distracted, when I saw the headline pop up in my phone notifications. Ink's bond was denied by the judge.

"What?"

My lips mouthed the words as I quickly scanned through the article. It was the first time I realized how strongly other people felt about his guilt. There was no reason that he shouldn't have been released; no one else with his background, ties to the community and celebrity would have been. Even with his prior record, it didn't add up.

"Sherelle, please get Dyano on the line, please," I said, holding the button to the intercom.

"Yes, ma'am. I'm on it now."

Dyano, my father's attorney, was also his best friend and I suspected that he was the one to help him cover up his crime. It took a little digging, but I eventually found out that how my father even got my mother's letter was because of him. Since we no longer lived at the same address where she'd left me, she contacted Dyano for my address. He didn't give it and told her that he would pass the letter to me himself, but he never did.

I counted on his own guilt, and loyalty to my father, to pressure him into lending me his help.

"Sage," he said right after answering the line. "Is this you?"

"Yes," I replied. "I need a favor."

There was a long pause before he answered.

"Anything you need, all you have to do is ask."

Chapter Twenty-Eight

Ink

Returning to jail, even for only a short amount of time, made me think about what was really important to me in my life. Once I was out, I wanted nothing more than to spend whatever free time I had left with the people who mattered most to me. I closed down the shop for the time being and arranged for Tamiyah to return home. I didn't care that there was a circus outside of reporters, paparazzi and protestors. I just wanted my daughter by my side.

Sage took a leave from her job to support me. I was hoping that it would be enough to satisfy the board, so they'd stop pressuring her to step down for good. Although I told her to do what was best for her, she refused. She was determined to be there for me.

"Aye, we here. Coming up now."

With the phone in my hand, I stood and looked out the front window at Kale's car pulling to the front of my house.

"Nah, don't pull up front. Come around back."

"Dyano called and told us to pull up front. He said it would look good for the press."

I gritted my teeth. "I don't give a fuck about the press," was what I wanted to say but, at the same time, Dyano knew his shit. His track record was proven so I had to fall in line with his plan. After he was able to petition the judge for a bond and get me out when Elshire basically told me there wasn't nothing he could do, I brought him on as my new attorney. So far, he hadn't failed me yet.

"I'm coming out there to her myself."

"Yeah, he told me that you'd say that, too."

Somehow, I felt like I was being set up. Unlike Elshire, Dyano said that it was better for me to be seen as long as it was planned out before in a way that would draw sympathy through the press. He wanted to stage shit; like a video of me giving money to the poor or pushing my daughter in a swing. I wasn't for being fake. If I was at the park with Tamiyah, it would be because I wanted to be and not so that I could pose for a photo op.

Pulling on a hoodie, I groaned as I slid the fabric over my head and prepared to face the crowd outside. I hated to have to deal with them, but I didn't want anyone talking sideways to my daughter.

"Daddy!" Tamiyah squealed when I opened the back door of Kale's car.

"Hey, baby girl," I quickly replied before grabbing onto her. "Put your hood on and lay on my shoulder. I want to get you in the house fast."

She did as I requested, and I tried to ignore the loud shouting behind me as I jogged back to the house. Kale was right behind me and closed the door once we made it in.

"That shit out there is crazy, yo," he said. "It's worse than the last time I was over here."

"Daddy, why are all those people here?" Tamiyah asked me. "Is it because of Mommy?"

For a moment, I didn't know what to say but then I finally settled on the truth.

"Yes, baby. It is."

Her eyes widened. "Are the police going to find out who hurt her?"

My lungs felt constricted. "I hope so."

Behind me, Kale made a sound, like grunting. I cut my eyes in his direction and saw skepticism, loud and clear. In that moment, I wasn't sure whether it was because he doubted that the police would find Tami's killer or if he doubted me saying that I hoped they would.

"Tamiyah, go check out the surprise I got you. It's in your room. You can go play with it for a little bit while I talk to Uncle Kale."

She ripped out of my arms and flew down the hallway at top speed. When I heard her screaming, I knew she'd found it.

"What did you get her?" Kale asked, taking a seat in the living room.

"A cat. She's wanted one for a minute, but Tami was allergic."

Kale snickered in a way that said he didn't find a thing funny. "And since she's dead, I guess it seems like the perfect time to get one."

My eyes narrowed in on him. "Damn, man, I sense a little hostility in your tone."

"My bad," he said with a shrug. "Not my intent."

He couldn't look me in his eyes as he said it. I'd always been taught that a man who didn't look in your eyes when he spoke to you was either a coward or had something to hide. At that moment, something occurred to me. Not once through all of it had Kale ever said that he thought I was innocent. He had never once told me that he believed I didn't kill Tami.

"You sure?" I questioned, leaning in. "You think I did it?"

There was a short delay before his eyes finally met mine. From his bewildered expression, he hadn't expected me to ask.

"Man, Ink, don't ask me no bullshit like that. As it is, you and Indie done already fell out."

"What's that got to do with anything? Indie and I started arguing because she got some personal issue with Sage that she can't get over. What's that got to do with you?"

Kale shrugged. "Nothing. I just think that since she's popped up, shit been crazy for us all. You ain't even been acting the same. I don't ever remember a time when Tami came to you for help and you pushed her away, except when you started fucking with Sage. She's got your mind gone and the rest of us gotta take a back seat. To be honest, these days, I don't know what you would or wouldn't do."

And there it was. Finally, it was out in the open.

"Then you *do* think I did this," I said. My tone was firm, but it really felt like all of the air was expelling out of my lungs.

"This shit reminds me a lot about the case when you got locked up. For what happened to that white girl."

I felt my muscles tighten. "What about her?"

"You told me that you didn't do it but we both know you did. Everybody knew she was on pills hard; that's why she was so loose. She was a little rich girl who liked to get high and fuck niggas. Everybody was slipping bitches pills to get their dick wet. It was the norm; we ain't know that was considered rape. The only problem was you fucked around and didn't use a condom, so she caught you up."

That was the craziest thing I'd ever heard coming from him. But not only that, it wasn't true. If that was what everyone else was doing, I didn't know it. I'd never slipped any woman a pill for sex; never had to.

"I didn't lie about that shit. If somebody drugged her, it wasn't me."

Kale leveled with me, his chin high, and he spoke his words with grit.

"I think that you'll do whatever the fuck you have to in order to get what you want. Don't forget, I was there when niggas was calling you 'Infamous Ink.' That's who you were in the streets and it was for a reason. People out here know a lot but none know all that I do about you. We've done a lot of shit together. We ain't never been innocent."

That was enough for me. He'd stated his case, told me where he stood, and it was clear. In the background, behind the sound of Tamiyah singing to her new pet, I could hear shouting outside. The protesters were back. I already couldn't go outside the house without people accusing me of things I hadn't done.

There was no way I was going to listen to it inside.

I stood to my feet. "You need to leave. Thanks for bringing my daughter to me."

Kale's eyes remained fixed on mine as he stood as well. His boldness was renewed now that he'd come clean with how he really felt.

"Don't mention it. I'll always look out for my niece."

Without waiting for me to let him out, he did the honors himself. Hearing the door close behind him, I ran a hand over my face and blew out a burst of hot air.

I was at the loneliest point in my life. Everyone I knew, the ones I thought I could depend on, had abandoned me. Outside of my daughter, I had no one.

Well… no one but Sage.

Chapter Twenty-Nine

~ Sage

Someone leaked the address to my house, and I woke to the sound of protests calling for a week straight before the homeowners' association finally got rid of them for me. They took their time because they wanted me gone, too. I wasn't working and because Ink was spending quality time with Tamiyah, I hadn't seen the outside of my apartment in a while. However, I didn't mind because I felt like shit. I had no idea what it was, but I was coming down with something and it made me feel miserable.

The only thing that bothered me more than whatever infection I'd contracted was Cindy Conway, the leader of the group of protesters. How lucky was I that she had decided every morning to use her precious time screeching to the top of her lungs about how I was a homewrecking whore with no morals or values. You would think that she was related to Tami for how hard she went for her. She'd rallied a crowd of people just as miserable as she was to help destroy my life.

I couldn't help but be disgusted by it all. Yes, a life was lost but Tami had been a junkie, a terrible mother and an even sorrier excuse for a wife. Now she had people who wouldn't have given a damn about her when she was alive, crying out for justice in her death.

"Ugh!" I rolled over in the bed, my head ringing to the point that I could almost feel it in my ears. Suddenly, my stomach jumped, and a sour taste settled on my tongue. With the speed of an Olympic sprinter, I was on my feet and rushing to the bathroom again.

For the fourth day in a row, I was starting my day with my head in a toilet bowl. I didn't know what stomach virus or flu that I'd caught but I was so ready to get over it.

"Oh god, it hurts!" I whined with one hand on my head and the other on my stomach. I wasn't sure which I was referring to because they both hurt just as bad.

It wasn't until my head was once again hovering over the toilet bowl that I thought about something else…When was the last time I'd had a period?

Mentally, I ran through the past few weeks, trying hard to remember when it last began and ended. I couldn't recall anything more recent than over a month ago.

Oh. My. God.

I stood and almost tripped over my own feet as I hurried to the mirror to look at myself. Outside of looking and feeling like I had caught the flu, there was nothing different about me. I hadn't gained any weight. In fact, it actually looked like I'd lost some. Turning to the side, I pulled the fabric of my robe tighter around my frame and stared at my belly.

Could I be pregnant?

***

"You are most definitely pregnant. I would estimate... about seven or eight weeks."

My lips parted in awe as I stared into my doctor's face. Although she was smiling, I could also see that she was also a little worried at the same time.

"You can go ahead and ask," I groaned, dropping my head in my hands. "I know what you're thinking. I can see it all in your eyes."

"So it's what I think? This is Ink's baby?"

With my head still hanging low, I nodded.

"Yes."

"Well, are you going to keep it?"

"Yes."

She expelled a breath. "This is going to be a long and hard road for you. You might want to consider leaving the city for a while. Just to get away from it all. It's important that you have a healthy pregnancy."

I understood what she was asking but there was no way I could do that. Even though I was giving Ink his space for now, I knew how much he needed me. We talked, texted, and video-called each other almost every moment of the day. The only reason I hadn't been over recently was because of Tamiyah and then I got sick. Even so, he begged me to come and told me every night that he missed me.

We finally had that talk that he wanted to have the night he was arrested. He said he wanted me to marry him—fuck being a girlfriend. He didn't want me to tell him what I felt about that until after he beat his case because he didn't want me to feel pressured. But I already knew what I would say. I would jump at any opportunity to be Ink's wife. I knew it the moment that I first laid eyes on him. No matter how much I wanted to play it tough, being with him felt right.

"I won't be leaving. Not any time soon anyway."

She gave me an even but careful look, one you would give someone if you thought they'd lost their mind but wanted to be careful not to offend them.

"I understand," she replied. "Well, in that case, I'll be your obstetrician instead of just your GYN and we will journey through this together."

She forced herself to smile and, again, I felt stupid as hell.

Chapter Thirty

Ink

"I really miss Mommy."

Dropping my head, I looked into Tamiyah's tear-filled eyes and had to swallow down my own emotions. I wasn't a bitch but there was something about seeing my daughter about to cry over her mother's death that cut me to the core. Especially with over half of the country convinced that I was the one who killed her.

If I went down for that, Tamiyah would lose both of her parents. Sometimes I wondered if she would grow to hate me. Or was the man I'd shown her that I was in the first five years of her life enough to show her that I couldn't have possibly done anything to destroy her life? No matter what evidence popped up, that was what I held onto. Drunk or not, there is no way I would've killed my daughter's mother. Never.

"Come here, Miyah," I said and patted my lap.

She sniffed back her tears and slowly walked over before

sliding onto my lap. I grabbed her around her waist to steady her and then gave her a hard look as we locked eyes.

"You're still young but I want to be real with you because a lot is happening that you don't understand and I don't know how long we have until our lives change again."

Her eyes rounded with worry and I wanted to stop but I had to get it out.

"Mommy is gone because someone hurt her. We don't know who did it, but we do know who didn't. Daddy would never do anything to hurt you and Mommy was an extension of you. I loved her, she was one of my closest friends, and I've almost known her my whole life. No matter what you may hear from anyone, know that I would never have hurt Mommy in any way."

Her bottom lip began to tremble, and she dropped her head. I couldn't see her eyes but when I saw tears drop and darken the edge of her pale blue shorts as they landed, I hated that we even had to have that conversation.

"I heard Uncle Kale talking and he said that he thought you *did* hurt Mommy. It was when he came to pick me up. He said that he talked to Mommy before she died and that's how he knows."

My body tensed and, though I'd been trying to hold a blank expression, I could tell by how hard my jaw was clenched that I was failing at that. Kale was talking reckless as hell in front of my daughter and I didn't appreciate it. It was bad enough that he'd said the shit at all but to say it in front of Tamiyah was more than fucked up.

"A lot of people are like Uncle Kale, unfortunately. They

believe that because they don't really know me. Not like how you know me. When you hear people say things like that, remember that you know me better than anyone. Your heart will tell you what is true."

She took some time and thought about that while nodding her head.

"I feel sad because I didn't get to say goodbye." Her eyes filled with tears again. "People say goodbye at funerals, but Mommy never had one. Why couldn't I say goodbye?"

Tamiyah wasn't the normal child and even at only five, she was very advanced for her age and could comprehend a lot. That made it hard sometimes to remember that she was still so young and the way she processed her grief was so much different from how I did mine.

"We can have one of our own. Just me and you. We can do something for Mommy so that we can both say goodbye. That sound good?"

She smiled through her tears and nodded.

We spent the rest of the morning getting things ready for our memorial service for Tami. I took Tamiyah to the floral shop and let her pick out the flowers that she wanted for her mother. She decided on blue hydrangeas and asked for some real ones along with another bouquet of artificial flowers so that they wouldn't go bad. Afterwards, we went to another store where I gathered wood, nails and a nail gun to create a sign. Tamiyah found a glue gun, glitter and some sparkly stuff that she wanted to use to decorate the wood.

We were in the car heading back to the house when Sage called me. Since I'd been spending the day with Tamiyah, who obviously needed me, I hadn't hit her up since the day before, but I couldn't say that I wasn't excited to see her name light up on car's touchscreen.

"Daddy, it's Ms. Sage!" Tamiyah exclaimed, reading her name. "Can I say hi?"

I was smiling and didn't even know it when I nodded 'yes' and answered the call.

"Hey, I got Miyah in the—"

"Hi, Ms. Sage!" she interrupted.

Sage laughed. "Hey, Miyah. How are you doing today?"

"I'm good! Me and Daddy are buying stuff for my mommy's memorial."

There was a short moment of silence before she spoke up again. In that time, I was wondering what she was thinking but I was positive that she understood the reason why we were doing that.

"That's really nice. And very necessary," she added. I was sure that part was for me.

"Did you want to come?" Tamiyah asked but, before I could say anything, Sage answered.

"No, babes, I can't this time. I think that is a very special moment that you and Daddy should share together."

"Aw, man!"

I chuckled at that. Sage had no idea but the effect she had on my daughter only made me even more certain that she was the one for me.

"How about this? You pay your respect to Mommy and I'll come over later on so we can make cookies."

In no time, Tamiyah had dropped the sulking and was hooting and hollering loudly in celebration.

"I think you won somebody over," I said, laughing to myself as I watched Tamiyah fist-pumping in the back seat.

"Just trying to make the princess happy."

"And I'll think on how I can satisfy the queen," I replied with all seriousness.

"Sounds like a plan," was her only response but I could hear the smile in her tone.

She was always close-lipped when Tamiyah was in listening range. That was another thing that I liked about her. She was more worried about the well-being of my child than she was about me sometimes.

"I'll see you later on tonight. But you can always hit me up whenever," I told her, hoping that she would.

"Well, I didn't want anything else really. Was just calling to see what you were up to. I didn't realize how much work was taking up my time. Now that I don't have that to worry about, I hope I'm not becoming a bugaboo."

"Aye, I've had a few chicks bugging me in the past. None quite as awesome as you though, so feel free to bug me at any time."

The laughter that followed on the other end almost made me forget what I was going through. Sage was the type of woman who knew how to make a man feel like a man. She was the softer, more compassionate side that I needed; she completed me in so many ways. I was happy to finally be able to call her mine, but I needed more than that. I wanted to deepen our bond. She was riding with me through the worst time of my life and not once did she allow the opinions of others to sway her. In so little time, she had become my best friend and the only person in the world I could depend on. Indie and Kale were pretty much gone but Sage still remained. If nothing else told me that she was the one, her dedication did.

***

"Can you talk?"

"Hell yeah, I can talk when it comes to you. What's happening with my case?"

"A lot."

Standing a few yards behind her to give her some privacy, I watched my daughter pay her respects to her mother. She was sitting down in front of the memorial that we constructed, with her legs up and her arms wrapped around her knees, talking to Tami as if she were sitting right in front of her. It was therapeutic, even for me. I had only said a few things just to make sure that Tamiyah was comfortable, but I was surprised at how saying those few things gave me some sort of peace. Not much because I still had no idea where her body was or who killed her, but at least I'd allowed myself to say goodbye.

"So, what's happening now?" I asked, feeling on edge. I knew Elshire to the point that I could pick up his vibe, especially when it came to bad news. Dyano wasn't as easily read.

"I know you're not going to like this but I'm going to file for a speedy trial. I want to get your case settled ASAP and, from what I've heard, the judge is more than ready to try your case. Election year is coming up and, depending on the outcome, your case could work in his favor."

Exhaling, I rubbed at one end of my brow and took my time

replying back.

"I don't know about speeding this up. It's not looking too good for me right now and—"

"Trust me," he said, interrupting. "I know my stuff and I'm very connected here in this city. Your prosecutor is playing to the media, holding interviews and such every chance he gets in hopes that he can sway public opinion against you, but it's all circumstantial evidence. There is no body and it's hard as hell to pin a murder charge on anyone without one. They found a butcher knife at your house that they are claiming to have been the murder weapon, but they can't prove how she was killed other than some specialist who claims he saw a blade print in the blood. It was found under a bush—anyone could've put it there. The videos of you arguing could describe any couple in America on the verge of divorce. The sperm on the dress, it's yours, but who can say for certain that it was from that day?"

I sighed and ran my hand over my head as I listened. What he was saying sounded good, but I still wasn't completely convinced.

"You're a loving father and you were fighting on video about maintaining custody of a child who isn't even yours biologically. That in itself shows character. You have a past but you're not a killer. I even pulled your file from when you served time in prison. Your record was impeccable. Plus, the girl who accused you of assault, I looked her up. She is married to a Black teacher now and her father disowned her once she got engaged. If it comes to it, which it won't, I can probably get her to testify on your behalf."

I had to give it to him, Dyano really did know his shit.

"Man, listen, I still haven't gotten a bill, so I don't know how much you charge but I have a feeling it's expensive as hell and for good reason. So, I'm going to go ahead and trust that you know what you're talking about. How soon do you think I could go to trial?"

This time, he was the one to exhale. "Well, I hope you meant what you said about trust because I'm about to make you prove it. I was invited to a dinner party that Judge Carmichael, the one assigned to your case, is also attending. If all goes well, I'm hoping to get the trial slated to begin in a couple of weeks, a month at most."

"Weeks?"

Snapping my head up, I looked over at Tamiyah who was now skipping around the memorial, while giggling and singing as loud as she could. She was having more fun with Tami now than when she was alive.

"Yes, weeks. The prosecutor is using the media to poison the pool of jurors against you the longer that we delay. If we have any hopes of having an unbiased and impartial jury, we have to act fast. I'm going to try for getting it on the docket for the first of next month."

I squeezed the bridge of my nose, took another look at my daughter, and then nodded. The faster I could get the over with, the better my chances at getting her back to living a normal life.

"Okay, I'll be ready."

And just like that the timer for my freedom was officially set.

***

"Breaking news: This has just come in not even an hour ago. In what appears to be a freak accident, Cindy Conway has died. According to police reports, Ms. Conway was found dead in her home by a neighbor who came to check on her after not seeing her for a few days. The cause of death is carbon monoxide poisoning. It seems that the gas on Ms. Conway's stove wasn't properly shut off and she died in her sleep. No foul play is suspected. The City of Atlanta mourns for Cindy Conway, who was known as the 'Voice of the Voiceless'"...

As the reporter continued covering the story, I listened intently. Of course, they took the opportunity to mention me in their coverage since my case was the last thing that she'd had all of her attention on. The last thing I wanted was my name to be said in connection with another story about some dead woman.

"Damn," I said, looking at a photo of Cindy on the screen. "You see this?"

"Yeah." Sage nodded her head and looked up from her book. "Yeah, I heard that she was dead earlier today."

"You couldn't have. They just found her body less than an hour ago. Her neighbor checked on her after not seeing her for a while and said that her door was unlocked. She went in and found her."

I looked over at Sage who didn't seem at all surprised, but I didn't think anything of it. Like me, Cindy had been also making her life hell, putting pressure on her executive board members to remove her and her homeowner's association to kick her out of her neighborhood. She was a nightmare that was finally over.

"Oh," she replied, looking up at me from over her glasses.

"Maybe it was something else I'd heard. But wow... that's kinda crazy, huh?"

I nodded. "Yeah, it is. But I can't say I'm mad. I wanted to kill her ass when she was over here talking sideways to Tamiyah that one day. The old me would've snuffed her ass out on the spot."

"Snuffed her out? You mean like kill her?"

I almost wanted to laugh at the way she asked, like she was excited at the thought. It was a natural thing: good girls always wanted a little thug in their lives.

"I did a lot of shit back in my day, especially when it came to earning my reputation in the streets. I don't know anyone who has been able to make a name for themselves in the dope game without ever taking a life. It's part of the game; how a lot of niggas earn their respect. Or to protect the ones you love."

Those were things that I didn't want to dive too deeply into. It wasn't that I was running from my past; it just wasn't me anymore. There was a lot that I did in my old life because I thought there wasn't another way to make it. Now, I knew better.

"That's pretty dope. Knowing that you'd do anything to protect your loved ones... including me."

Her lips spread into a sneaky smile, then she dipped her eyes back into the pages of her book. For years after that moment, I would replay the conversation over and over in my mind.

"What's that book you're reading?"

"It's called *Innocent*, about a man who is wrongly accused for a crime. He's a twin, his brother is in the streets, but he's a college kid who was in the wrong place at the wrong time."

My brows raised and I leaned over, slipping the book from

her hands.

"Hey!" Reaching forward, she tried to snatch back her book, but I moved out of her way.

"Yo, this sounds too much like my life right now. Minus the twin. I might need to read it."

"It's a good book," Sage said, leaning over to extend her reach. I pulled the book back and she lost her balance, falling into my lap.

"Aye, come here. Let me hold you for a minute."

Placing the book on the end table on my other side, I wrapped my hands around her waist and pulled her onto my lap. She was facing me, straddling her legs over mine, and I swore that I could feel the heat of her sex. My dick began to get hard.

"You sure that holding me is all you want to do?" She eyed me suggestively and then lifted her hips to reach underneath. She ran her hand lightly over my erection, applying just enough pressure to make me lose my train of thought.

"Hell nah, it ain't all I want to do." I licked my lips. "But fuck it, I don't even wanna do that anymore. Not *just* that anyway."

Holding her steady, I rose up and carried her in my arms the entire way to the guest room. It was where I had been sleeping instead of the basement. I couldn't sleep in Tami's room and hadn't been inside of it since she was living in it, and probably wouldn't ever make it mine. If everything went right with my trial, the first thing I would do was move.

"I hope you ain't gotta go somewhere in the morning. I have a feeling that tonight is gonna be a long night."

"Oh yeah?" She smiled and cocked her head to the right

to look at me sideways. Her energy was so addicting that I couldn't understand how the hell I'd lucked up and met her while she was still single. Women like her rarely didn't have a man trying to soak up their time. Unless they didn't want one which, based on her success, was possible. Relationships took time and ambitious women didn't have a lot of that to give to anyone. For whatever reason, she was willing to put her work and life on hold to spend time with me and it happened to be at the moment when I needed someone the most.

Taking her in the room, I lay her down on the bed and then pulled away. Suddenly, I had a thought about doing some romantic shit, like lighting candles, pouring wine, and running bubble baths. However, when she dropped her knees on opposite ends, spreading her legs wide to tease me with a sight of her pussy, I caved.

With her skirt pooled around her hips and her red panties sporting a dark red pussy stain that showed just how wet she was for me; I was unable to hold back from being inside her. I slipped my fingers inside of the moist material and grazed her exposed clit with the back of my fingers. Pinching the rounded tip of it between two fingers, I squeezed lightly on her sensitive spot and felt my dick throb when she opened her mouth and let out a gasp. Within seconds my fingers were drenched in her juices as she wound her hips against me, indulging herself. I allowed her to do it for a little bit but then pulled away. I was a pleaser and I wanted to take charge when it came to her desires.

"Pleassseee," she whined, writhing her body sexily on the bed. "I don't want to wait any longer."

"I won't make you wait," was the last thing I said before I dropped my mouth down over her lower lips.

Chapter Thirty-One

~

Sage

"Where do you think we should go after all of this is over? Like, for vacation. I think we owe it to ourselves."

Turning, Ink took a moment to look at me, not speaking for a second. I guess it was a weird thing to ask something like that the day before his trial was set to begin.

We had been avoiding the topic all day but, in the end, there was no escaping it. Every time I looked at him, I could see it in his eyes. And in the moments where I caught him gazing off into the distance at some unseen place, I knew that the thoughts he wouldn't voice to me ran rampant in his mind. Depending on how this trial went, his life could change forever—all of ours could. In every moment of happiness that we had, any laugh and with every embrace, the thought at the forefront of his mind was that those moments could be the last ones for a long time.

Ink didn't want to spend the time that he had making us feel sorry for him or sad, so he avoided the topic altogether and

I understood that. But I wasn't hesitant at all when it came to speaking about our future because I knew we would have one. Together.

"I can't really think about all that right now. I don't know if I'll even make it to that point. If it were up to Stanson, I'll be taking an extended vacation at the pen," he replied with a sigh, referencing the State's Attorney and lead prosecutor.

I rolled over in the bed onto my stomach so that I could look him right in the eyes.

"It's not up to him. I'm not going to let you be taken away from me for something you didn't do."

For the first time that day, I was able to get a smile out of him that didn't look like it was being hindered by some competing thought in his head.

"I can dig your confidence," he said.

I smiled and then flipped back around on the bed, joining him with my arms positioned behind my head and my eyes to the ceiling.

"It's easy to be confident when I know what I know."

We fell into a thoughtful and comfortable silence, wrapped in our own separate thoughts.

"Do you ever think about who did it? I've been so caught up trying to prove I'm innocent that I never really took the time to think about it. She was murdered... but by who?" He shrugged his shoulders and sighed.

"What about Dyano's theory about Kale? He had a motive, too. He was in love with Tami for a long time. They had a secret relationship going on behind your back and he lied about it."

He blew out a breath and waved his hand, as if to bat the thought away.

"Nah, I don't believe that shit. He's done a lot of foul shit, but he cared about Tami. Fucking her is one thing but killing her is another. And to be honest, I can't even say I'm completely surprised about that. There were always signs about how he felt about her."

"It's not for us to believe it. The jury just has to. All you need is to give them a shred of doubt. What's wrong with that?"

Ink sat up on one elbow and pierced his eyes into mine.

"Because it's stupid and I ain't 'bout to flip this on Kale just to get off. I look guilty as hell and I can't provide any kind of explanation about what actually happened because I don't remember shit. For the first couple of weeks, I actually thought that maybe there was some way I murdered her and didn't know it. When I woke up that morning in the basement, I had blood on my hands. My fuckin' clothes had blood on them, and I don't know why. That's how bad this shit is, Sage. What person in their right mind wouldn't say I murdered her after all of that?"

Another response began to bubble up in my mind but as soon as I opened my mouth, I closed it back shut. He was right; I couldn't argue with that.

"It'll all work out fine. You'll see," I said, wrapping my arms around him.

For the rest of the night, that's how we were; my head on his chest and our bodies fully touching as we lay in each other's arms.

***

"*Hello, this is Shine Moore with WSB-TV, reporting live from the courthouse here in Atlanta where the trial to determine whether Dom 'Ink' Richardson is innocent or guilty of the murder of his late wife, Tami Richardson, will take place. We will be live tweeting as well as giving you the latest developments as soon as they come in. Now, I want to turn to the crowd behind me and get their opinions and hopeful outcome as it concerns this case...*"

"Don't listen to that," I said to Ink and covered the screen of his phone with my hand. "You should try to keep your mind clear. It's hard enough as it is without paying attention to what other people have to say. They don't matter. You had a lot of people show you love today... focus on that."

The day had been a whirlwind and, to be truthful about it, my head was still spinning. The coverage of Ink's trial was insane but, surprisingly, he'd received a lot of support from celebrities, both major and up-and-coming. His fans had flooded his Instagram page and his name was the #1 trending topic on Twitter.

Thanks to Dyano, a lot of public opinion had swayed in Ink's favor. Clips of Tami's behavior prior to her murder had 'all of a sudden' shown up online, including a video of her grinding up on more than a couple men at the club as they felt her up. Ink had suspicions that Dyano was behind the leaks, but he denied it every time because he knew that Ink wouldn't go for it. I, on the other hand, knew that there was no limit on what Dyano would do to look out for his client and win his case, especially one as big as that one, so I had no doubts that he was instrumental in the leaks.

"Damn, there are a lot of people out there," I absentmindedly spoke, staring at the crowd through the dark tints of the SUV that we were in. We had rolled up in front of the courthouse and the crowd was huge. I sucked in a breath, feeling a little anxious about having to walk through. Even with security, the thought of it was intimidating.

"Yeah..." Ink agreed, and I turned towards him. He'd been quiet the whole morning and completely silent the entire way there until now. The most I had heard him speak was when he was kissing Tamiyah goodbye.

Regardless to which way things went, he would see her again and be able to handle his affairs before he was made to serve time, if it came to that. Per Ink's request, Dyano was able to work it out that he would have a few weeks between his sentence date and when he'd have to report to serve time so that he could tie up any loose ends regarding custody of his daughter and his business.

With the fate of one child weighing heavily on his mind, the last thing I wanted was to give him another one to worry about it. I was only a little over three months pregnant and, thankfully, not showing much at all outside of the tiny bulge that Ink referred to as my 'baby fat.' He didn't know how accurate that was. I couldn't wait until the trial was over so that I could give him the news I'd been waiting to share. It had been so hard to keep it in that he was going to be a father again.

"Dyano said to wait here until he comes to get us. He said he would text my phone when he was on the way."

Ink nodded and then caught my eyes, cradling them in his. I felt my cheeks go warm.

"Are you okay to walk in with me?"

I gave him a pressed smile and nodded before slipping my hand into his.

"Of course. I'm by your side the entire way."

Lifting my hand, he pressed the back of it against his lips and gave me a sweet kiss.

"You've been there for me in a way that no one else has ever been," he whispered against my skin before staring into my face. The emotions inside of him were so raw and intense that I could feel them as well.

"I love you in a way that I've never loved any other woman and, somehow, I know that I never will love any woman quite the same. I can't possibly ask you to put your life on hold for me if this shit goes wrong but I do want you to know that, regardless to what happens, I will always be there for you in any way that I can. I'll never let another woman come before you or take your place. I love you, Sage."

He leaned over and pressed his lips against mine, giving me such a gentle kiss so packed full of love that it brought tears to my eyes. They rolled down my cheeks as he deepened our embrace, kneading my ass with his hands and gripping my thighs. When he moved between my thighs, I didn't resist to spread my legs so that he could slip a few fingers into my panties.

My pussy gushed honey for him. Our tongues were intertwined as he slipped first one finger, then another into my hole, using his thumb to massage my clit. The partition was up and the space was soundproof so I didn't think twice about moaning out my pure ecstasy when he softly pinched my nub.

"I gotta taste her. I need her right now."

His voice was raw, almost pleading. There was no way I could tell him no.

With a press of a button, he made a secondary shield rise to cover the windows, blocking us off from everything happening outside. The tints were too dark for them to see in but the shield made it so that we couldn't see out. The chaos outside was immediately a non-factor and all we had to focus on was each other.

Ink pressed me back and spread my legs as he lowered down to his knees and positioned his face in front of my mound. He was staring at it hungrily, as if in anticipation, and I could feel his hot breath on my clit. It swelled and throbbed as I waited for what was going to come next.

Almost as if he were savoring the moment, Ink slowing dipped his head and sucked the center. My back arched and I yelped out a scream as he increasingly became rougher and more savage. The more aggressive he got, the more I fed him my pussy, trying to satisfy his hunger. He sucked and expertly ran his tongue through my folds, bringing me to a climax. I screamed through gnashed teeth when he suckled the spot that brought me over the edge. My river flowed and he rode the wave of it with the tip of his tongue, thrashing against my sensitive clit until I calmed down.

"Now I'm ready for whatever," he said with a grin, licking his lips. I fixed my clothes and used a wet wipe to clean as much as I could between my legs. When Ink handed it to me along with a small bag to dispose of it, I wondered for a quick moment if I'd been set up.

"Did you plan to do this before going in?"

A look of mischief crossed over his face. "Nah, I don't know what you're talkin' about."

With perfect timing, Dyano sent me a text and then followed up with a call.

"I'm on the way now. I've got security with me but be ready to move quickly and make sure to remind Ink to let me do all of the talking," he said. I cut my eyes to Ink before answering. He had his eyes closed and his head back, lying on the headrest.

"Okay. We'll be ready when you get here."

Chapter Thirty-Two

Ink

I never was the type of nigga to do drugs, not even weed.

It was a rule in the game that you never got high on your own supply and I'd always held fast to that. In my time on the streets, I saw a lot of people who were balling self-destruct because they started using their own shit. For that reason, I vowed not to be one of them. I was a businessman who didn't even try out my own product. It was virtually unheard of, but I'd made my own path to success.

I said all that to say that then was the first time in my life that I wished I were high. It wasn't my first time sitting in a courthouse so I understood how it all went down, but that didn't make the process any easier. There was a whirlwind of noise, people, and chaos outside that Sage and I had to fight through to make it in. Hand in hand, we walked, surrounded by security, up the steps leading to the courthouse doors. Reporters yelled questions above the sound of the protesters and fans who were either shouting for my prosecution or for my defense.

With my head down, I did as Dyano said and made sure not to make eye contact with anyone. By then, I knew how the click of a camera's lens at the right moment could catch me making a face that could easily become the next headline. Keeping my head down made it less likely they would get a shot of the sour expression I was making as I heard their questions.

The inside of the courtroom was packed to max capacity. I wanted the proceedings to be private but Dyano somehow thought the extra publicity would work in my favor.

"All rise for the Honorable Judge Carmichael, presiding," the bailiff announced, immediately gathering everyone's attention.

We all stood to our feet as the judge, an older Black man with a bald head and salt-and-pepper beard, walked in. He was tall and muscular with broad shoulders. Even in his old age, you could see that he was a man of real strength.

"Thank you. Everyone but the jury may have a seat. Bailiff Johnson, please swear in the jury."

"Yes, your honor," the bailiff said and moved to do just that.

The constant churr of chatter that had been ongoing since the moment I'd walked into the room all of a sudden died down to near silence. I took a quick look around at everyone who was either waiting intently, scribbling something on a notepad, or staring back at me, until my eyes found Sage's. She gave me a calming smile and I returned her show of love with a subtle nod. Some ways behind her, I caught a glimpse of Indie and Kale sitting together. It was odd seeing them. The last time I spoke to Indie was when we argued at the shop and I hadn't seen or heard from Kale since he dropped Tamiyah off at my house. We weren't on the best of terms, so I really hadn't expected them to come.

"Members of the jury," Judge Carmichael began after the bailiff finished swearing them in. "Your duty will be to determine whether the defendant is guilty or not guilty based only on the facts and the evidence provided in this case. The prosecution has the burden of proving the guilt of the defendant *beyond a reasonable doubt.*"

He paused for a moment to let that sink in. On the other end, Attorney Stanson looked more than pissed at the judge's emphasis on that.

"This burden remains on the prosecution throughout the trial. The prosecution must prove that a crime was committed and that the defendant is the one who committed the crime. If you are not completely satisfied of the defendant's guilt to that extent, then reasonable doubt exists, and the defendant must be found *not* guilty."

A ripple-effect of sound erupted throughout the room as people shifted, rustled papers, and adjusted their equipment. Out of the corner of my eye, I glanced at Dyano who seemed especially chill as he sat by my side. His confidence was on point, but I didn't see where it came from. Since he hadn't shared much about his angle of defense, I felt like I was going in blind.

"Trust him," Sage had told me when I told her how frustrated I was at his lack of sharing information. "He doesn't share because he's confident that he has enough to prove you're innocent. You should be worried if he was asking a lot of questions. That would mean he's searching. You don't want him to have to search."

"Is the prosecution ready?" Judge Carmichael asked.

"Yes, your honor," Stanson stood and replied. The judge nodded as he took his seat and then turned to Dyano.

"Is the defense ready?"

Dyano nodded and then stood to his feet.

"Yes, your honor but, before we get started, I want to make it known that my office discovered that the prosecution was withholding evidence."

Murmurs erupted around the courtroom. My brows jumped; I was shocked as well.

"What?" Stanson snapped. "That's preposterous! Judge, I—"

Judge Carmichael banged his gavel and Stanson's mouth snapped shut. With a brief nod at Dyano to continue, he folded his hands and waited to hear the rest.

"I was given a statement here by a source that I will not name at the moment—" He waved a stack of papers in the air. "—stating that another set of fingerprints, bloody, was found at the scene of the crime. I was told that those prints didn't match the defendant or the victim. My source said that his discovery was deemed unimportant."

"What!" Stanson piped up again. "Lies! We were not aware of any relevant fingerprints outside of the victim's left at the scene of the crime."

"Well, there it is." Dyano chuckled sarcastically. "He found them; he just didn't find them relevant."

"That is *not* true!"

What in the hell was going on? I was sitting at the defense table as confused as everybody else in the room. The judge looked over the thick black frame of his glasses and peered first at Stanson before turning back to Dyano. Not a single sound was heard as we all waited on edge for what would be said next.

"Mr. Dyano, is this witness prepared to testify to the declarations you have stated today?"

He nodded his head. "Yes, your honor. He would like to have his identity hidden, if possible, because he fears retaliation. However, he's prepared to give you his testimony. He also has photos to prove his claims."

From there Carmichael nodded and then cut his eyes to Stanson, a flash of annoyance showing clearly on his face.

"Is there *anything else* that your team may have *forgotten* or neglected to include in discovery?"

Stanson's cheeks were slightly red when he muttered an unenthused, "No, your honor," and took his seat. There was some chatter between the judge and the bailiff before he turned around to address the prosecution again.

"You may begin your opening arguments."

Stanson stood, his body tight and his frustration vividly apparent. "Thank you, your honor."

"You didn't tell me about the fingerprints," I whispered to Dyano as Stanson began to gather his materials to prepare his speech.

"The least you know, the better you'll be."

I squinted at him, wondering what the hell he meant by that and why he seemed reluctant to look at me. I decided to let it go and address it later.

Stanson made his opening argument and, though I tried to

remain calm, I began to get heated before he was even halfway through. There was nothing new coming from him, I'd heard it all and so had most of the people in the room, thanks to his constant interviews and briefings with the press. However, watching him in person as he spoke and jabbed his fat ass fingers in my direction, incensed me.

"He's putting on for the cameras," Dyano whispered at one point. "Don't get upset; it's all a show. But you see how Carmichael is looking. He knows it and he doesn't like it."

I glanced over at the judge and the expression on his face was almost comical as he watched Stanson put on a performance. He was watching with his head resting on his hand and his eyes clouded with what seemed like an equal dose of boredom and annoyance. In fact, it looked like he might have been on the verge of falling asleep until it was time for Dyano to begin his opening argument.

"Wonderful citizens of Atlanta and devoted members of the jury, I thank you for your time today. It's a shame that you have to spend these precious moments listening to us argue the details of this witch-hunt that has been launched against my client." Dyano turned and held his hand out to me for a moment before continuing. The jurors' eyes followed his hand and I watched them all scrutinize my face; more than a few expressions appeared sympathetic to my cause. When I saw the subtle smirk on his face, I realized he saw them as well.

"As Judge Carmichael has been gracious enough to remind us, the prosecution must prove beyond a reasonable doubt that Mr. Richardson is responsible for the murder of his wife. However, the only evidence they can bring to you to support that is circumstantial. My client is a loving father, and he was a devoted husband until the couple decided to part ways, only living together to be parents to their only child. He lives his life in the public eye and has managed to remain free of any legal issues or scandal until this point."

The sound of camera shutters clicking was the only other sound in the room. The judge had allowed one photographer in the room and, from the sound of it, he was working overtime to get all the shots that he possibly could.

"During this trial, you will be presented with evidence showing that, not only is my client innocent, but he is actually a victim as well. Tami, his former love and his child's mother, was senselessly murdered and taken away from their family, leaving his daughter without a mother and him without a friend. Not only this, but the fact that Tami was murdered after telling him that she was a few weeks pregnant with their child, one which would have been Mr. Richardson's *biological* child, further shows how much he's lost."

What?

I had to duck my head to hide my frown. What the hell was Dyano getting at? Tami hadn't told me shit about being pregnant and, even if she was, it damn sure wasn't my kid. I hadn't touched her in over six months. Keeping my head low, I clasped my hands together on top of the table as he continued.

"The defendant didn't kill Mrs. Richardson. He's not that type of man. However, as this case draws on, you'll find that there is, in fact, someone else who had reason and motive to want Mrs. Richardson dead. Someone who loved her for a very long time and had been hoping that she would leave her husband to be with him. Someone who, as evidence will prove, was also present the night when Mrs. Richardson was killed.

Thank you."

Dyano returned to his seat as I fought to keep myself in check. My mind was reeling with all kinds of questions but beyond anything else I felt, there was an immense amount of anger. I had said that this was not the kind of defense I wanted. I wasn't no snitch and there was no way that I could blame Kale for something he didn't do.

Stanson brought on his first witness, Officer Louis, who was first on the scene at the motel. Louis answered each question with confidence and an obvious bias against me, as Dyano had already warned me that he would. At some point, I turned around to check on Sage, but she was gone.

My eyes instead fell on Indie, who caught me looking. She gave me a small smile and then wiggled her fingers in a half-wave. I hadn't seen her since the day we argued at the shop but she was there to show her support.

"Defense, you may cross."

"Thank you, your honor."

Buttoning his jacket, Dyano stood, looking completely calm and in control. He was expertly dressed in a custom-made suit that easily cost a grip and his short fade and manicured beard were so on point that I halfway wanted to ask him who his barber was.

"Officer Louis, according to your report, the motel where Mrs. Richardson was found is known for... how should I say this... being used for many illegal activities?"

The officer nodded. "Yes, it has been known to be a hot spot for those things."

"Things like what?" Dyano pressed.

"Um, well, prostitution, drugs—both sales and use—primarily. However, Mrs. Richardson did not have drugs in her system at the time of death."

"Correct but she was a drug user in the past?"

"We saw some drug residue as well as drug paraphernalia in the room. I can't say for sure whether it belonged to her."

"So there was evidence that someone other than Mrs. Richardson had been staying there?"

The officer paused and allowed his eyes to travel upwards as he thought. "There was evidence that she may not have *always* been alone in the room. However, being that it was a motel, it's hard to say exactly."

"Because the room wasn't very clean," Dyano stated. "Which means, you didn't have a very clean crime scene to work with from the beginning. Could this be why you missed the bloody fingerprints that didn't belong to the defendant or Mrs. Richardson?"

"Objection, your honor!" Stanson shouted, jumping up.

"Sustained," Judge Carmichael replied and gave Dyano a look of warning before prompting him to continue.

For the next couple of hours, I sat through testimony after testimony of expert witnesses Stanson had gathered to prove that a murder had been committed. Forensic experts testified that the blood found at the scene belonged to Tami, that there were no traces of drugs in the blood tested, and that there was no way she could possibly be alive after the amount found.

Dyano only crossed to ask a few simple questions but otherwise allowed the prosecution to have their way. As he'd told me earlier, his task wasn't to prove that a murder hadn't taken place, but that I didn't do it. Even when the expert came on the stand to speak about the murder weapon, a butcher knife covered in dried blood that had been found near the scene and was the missing knife to a set in my kitchen, Dyano didn't say much about it.

Once Stanson was finished, Judge Carmichael called for a brief recess for lunch. I checked my watch. It was only a little after noon, but I felt like I'd been there all day long.

"One of my assistants is going to grab you a sandwich from the shop next door. There is a room outside and down the hall that they've reserved for you to relax and eat."

"Hell nah." I shook my head. "I can't eat shit right now."

"You don't have to," he replied as he gathered his things. "But it's the best place for you to be for the moment. Grab all of your things because I doubt you'll be back into this room. I'm going to petition the judge to throw out this case based on some new evidence."

"What evidence?"

He pressed his lips into a straight line and once again kept his eyes low so they didn't meet mine. "I really can't say but it'll all become clear soon."

Running my hand over my jaw, I followed Dyano out of the courtroom with the bailiff trailing behind me. Still, Sage was nowhere to be found.

"She's in the room already," Dyano told me as if he already knew what I was thinking.

"Thanks," I said. When I looked up at him, he wasn't paying attention to me.

"I'll be right back."

Before I could respond, he took off in one direction and I began to walk in another, making my way to the room he'd pointed me towards.

"Excuse me, Mr. Richardson, can I get a quote for my magazine? It's a small, independently run Black magazine that outlines the injustices that we, Black Americans, have to—"

"Damn, man, you wanna watch where you're going?" someone snapped, not loud but aggressive enough to seem as though it were.

I recognized the voice. It was Kale. I turned around in time to see him glaring into Dyano as he looked him up and down with suspicion.

"My apologies. I'm in a hurry and didn't see you there. Thank you so much for coming out to support Mr. Richardson today during his trial."

"I'm here to support a friend," Kale replied, and I caught his drift. He purposely didn't specify a name, so I wasn't sure whether he was referring to Tami or me.

"Mr. Richardson, can I—"

"I can't give you a comment right now but give me a call after all this is over and I promise that I'll give you the first exclusive interview," I said and then turned around to walk over to where Kale stood.

"Yo, Kale, let me speak with you for a minute."

Before I could close the distance between us, he frowned, turned his back to me, and then walked away. Clearly, he had picked up on Dyano's theory for my defense. I felt someone staring at me and I wasn't surprised when I turned around and realized it was Indie. She looked uncomfortable by my presence, swaying from leg-to-leg once our eyes connected.

"What's up, Indie? You good?"

She ducked her head, pressed her lips in a firm line before nodding.

"Yes, but—" She lifted her eyes to mine. "I hope you don't mind me being here."

"What?" I frowned and took another step closer to her. We were surrounded by people who, though they were pretending to mind their business, were definitely paying attention.

"Why would you say something like that?"

Now Indie looked even more confused than I was.

"Because of your last text. The one where you told me not to text you anymore and that my number was going to be blocked. I thought you were kidding, and I called you right after but when it went straight to voicemail, so it was obvious you weren't. I know you don't want anything to do with me but I didn't feel right not supporting you."

Running my hand over the top of my head, I blew out a harsh breath and then looked right at her, directly in her eyes.

"Listen, Indie, there is no way I would've ever said some shit like that. You know what you mean to me. We got into it a while back but that doesn't change shit. You and Dav are family to me. I would never do something like that to you."

"But you did," she cut in. "The text came to me from your phone and..."

Her words died as she paused, her eyes raking around us

as she searched the area for someone. Suddenly, they zeroed in on a subject and she narrowed her eyes, glaring hard. I followed her line of sight until I found who she was focused on. It was Sage.

"Nah, don't even go there. She didn't send you no text from my phone. She doesn't even have the code to unlock it."

"Well, who did?" Indie countered.

When I didn't say anything, she pulled her phone out and began going through it, scrolling through her messages most likely.

"Look at this," she said and then pressed the screen of her phone in front of my face. The message was there, clear as day, from my number to hers.

"Yo, I don't know who sent that, but I didn't."

"I believe you," she said, cutting her eyes towards Sage once more. "These days, there is a lot that you didn't do, even though it looks like you did."

"And what's that supposed to mean?"

The fury on Indie's face melted away and was replaced with something that looked more like worry and concern. Reaching out, she placed her hand on my arm as tears filled her eyes.

"It means that you need to be careful who you allow around you. Maybe my feelings for you got in the way of what I thought about the women you dealt with, but I have nothing but love for you and I want you to be happy with anyone you choose to be with. I want you to know that, no matter what, I'm always here for you. I've loved you for a long time, Ink, and I always will."

In that moment, something felt different for me. There

was always a spark between Indie and me but we both chose to ignore it for a long time. Now, as I looked at her, especially when I saw the fear in her eyes, I was reminded of how much I'd failed her in the past few months. She hadn't contacted me, but she had a reason not to. According to what she knew, I had pushed her away. But what was my excuse?

"How's Dav?" I asked, feeling guilty about referencing someone that I'd been a father figure to but hadn't seen in over a month.

Indie smiled as she began to update me on her son.

"He's good. His grades are up and—"

"Ink? You don't have a lot of time. There is food in the breakroom for you."

I watched as Indie's entire body visibly tensed at the sound of Sage's voice. I couldn't understand why she was so bothered by her, more than any other woman that I'd ever been with.

"You go ahead," I said, looking over at her. "I'll catch up."

There was a moment of hesitation and I thought Sage would fight me on it but, in the end, she turned to leave, doing as I asked. However, she wore her displeasure all over her face before she stalked away, walking harder than usual.

"You shouldn't have done that. She's going to be pissed." Indie laughed a little, showing that she was more than happy to see Sage so upset. Women were a trip.

"Let me worry about that later. I don't have a lot of time and I've wasted enough already by forgetting to be there for the ones who have always been around for me. I can't tell you how this thing will end but I can't get locked up for the rest of my life with you thinking that I would write you off like that."

The more I spoke, the more Indie's smile spread up her face. I wasn't sure about what I was going to say next, but it seemed like the perfect time to say it.

"Do you want to come by for dinner tonight? Tamiyah would be happy to see you and it's been too long since I've seen Dav. He's probably tall as hell now."

She lifted one brow. "And *Sage?*"

I ran a hand over my face and chuckled a little at the way she said her name. Lots of judgment and attitude, something I was used to when it came to Indie. It was at that moment that I realized Sage and I never argued, she never challenged me and never disagreed with what I said. The moment that I had told her that arguing was what ruined Tami and me, her confrontational side disappeared. It made things peaceful, but a little spice of a good debate didn't hurt from time to time.

"I think she'll understand me wanting to spend some time with an old friend, especially with what's happening. And if she doesn't, fuck it. I'm calling an audible."

Indie laughed so hard that people around us began to take notice, more than a few raising their brows. After a while, even I realized that something was wrong, and that thought was confirmed when I saw tears in her eyes.

"I'm sorry, I'm just..." She paused and dabbed at the teardrops in the corner of her eyes. "It's been a while and I didn't really expect us to be friends again, so I'd kinda already gotten used to not having you in my life. We were so close and then, in the next moment, we weren't even friends. And now, you have a girlfriend but you're inviting me to dinner and I'm actually wondering if I want to go because... What will come of it? I just finally got my feelings in check when it comes to you and—"

She was rambling and I figured I should take her out of her own misery. Grabbing onto her arms, I held her until she lifted her head to look in my face.

"Aye, calm down. It's only dinner, alright? We just eating. Let's take this shit one day at a time. That's how I've been doing it. It'll work for you, too."

"Okay," she said, nodding. "You're right. Thanks."

At that exact moment, a sudden whirr of activity began to build as everyone around us was either looking at their phones or tablets, or staring at someone else's. A few people were running back and forth, holding their cell phones to their ears talking excitedly about something that I couldn't hear. Next to us, a woman dressed in a black suit was watching something on her phone with her hand over her mouth in shock.

"What is it?" Indie said to the woman. Walking closer to her, she placed her hand on her arm to catch her attention and then asked again.

"What is it? What's everyone looking at?"

Chapter Thirty-Three

~ Sage

"It's a video," I said, answering Indie's question. "Someone uploaded an anonymous video from the night that Tami was killed. It shows Kale leaving her motel room with blood all over his clothes."

"What?"

Holding out my phone, I passed it over to Ink so that he could see for himself. With my arms folded over my chest, I looked from him over to Indie who was probably trying to find the video on her phone. My irritation with her presence couldn't be denied. Anyone with eyes and half a brain could see that she had a thing for Ink. And it was also obvious how much she didn't like me. From the very first time I'd seen her after Ink and I had become somewhat serious, I'd tried to be nice to her but all she'd ever given me was attitude. I understood that I was yet another woman coming in and attracting the man she wanted but it wasn't my fault that she'd had all the time in the world to lock Ink down and failed.

After watching the clip, Ink lifted his head and stood straight as a board, his expression stony and cold.

"Here," he said and handed over my phone.

I took it and slipped it into my purse. "I've already texted Dyano. He's with Stanson in the Judge's chambers, trying to get the case thrown out."

Even though he was processing what I was saying, there was no show of relief.

Indie was frowning as she shook her head and stood in front of Ink. I tried not to glare at her as she took her place.

"This can't be true. Kale didn't do this. Something isn't right."

I snapped. "You've got to be kidding, right?"

At that exact moment, Kale walked back through the doors of the courthouse and locked eyes with Ink as he proceeded through security. As soon as he was spotted, every single person inside the front entrance ignored the judge's order of no cell phone videos and photos and lifted up their devices.

With one hand on Ink's arm as if it would be enough to hold him back, I watched Kale maneuver through the metal detector.

"I thought he was gone."

"This motherfucka..." I heard Ink sneer under his breath. With one quick motion, he nudged my hand away and, in the next instance, he was charging towards Kale.

"Ink, don't!" Indie and I both yelled at the same time. It was too late.

Ink lifted his hand and delivered a right hook straight to Kale's chin, dropping him instantly. A team of officers swarmed in and grabbed Ink by his arms, pulling him away before he could continue his assault. Another officer grabbed onto Kale who struggled against them as they tried to keep control. Not only was he strong but his strength was magnified by the fact that he was mad as hell. Ink had got one up on him and he was eager to settle the score.

"Ink! What are you doing?" That was Dyano.

"What in the world!" That was Judge Carmichael.

"This shit is *insane!*" And, that was Stanson.

Apparently, their meeting was over, and they now had a front row seat to what would be the next breaking headline of newspapers around the world.

"Yo, I'm good. Let me go," Ink said, pulling away from the officers. They released him; however, they stayed in close proximity in case he decided to charge again.

"Get da fuck off me!"

Kale, on the other hand, was still fighting with the officers holding on to him. One had his hand on his taser, primed and ready to use it if and when it came to it.

"Cuff him!" one of the officers yelled once it became clear that he wasn't going to cooperate.

"For what? That motherfucka jumped on me!"

"Oh my god!" Indie cried out. "They are hurting him."

I wanted to slap her ass. Had she not watched the same video that everyone else had?

With Kale's face pressed to the ground and his body pinned under the weight of four officers, they were finally able to get his arms behind his back.

"You killed her!" someone screamed. "Why did you kill Tami?"

"I didn't do shit!" Kale shouted through his teeth and then looked from Indie to Ink. "How y'all gon' let them do this to me?"

No one moved as one officer pulled out his cuffs and secured one and then the other on his wrists. Next they began to pull him up from the ground and that's when something shiny slipped out of his jacket pocket. The sound of metal hitting the floor and ricocheting across the tile caught nearly everyone's attention and we all followed the object to where it stopped right at Ink's feet.

"The fuck?" Ink almost shouted as he knelt down to grab what appeared to be a ring. A flawless, platinum diamond ring.

"This was Tami's. I bought it for her to replace her old ring when we first moved here. How *the fuck* do you have it?"

Nearly half the people, including me, seemed to gasp in unison. I covered my mouth with my hand and joined everyone as we waited for Kale's reply. His eyes were stretched wide in sheer horror; his usually glowing chocolate skin looked like it had gone pale. He squinted at the ring in Ink's hand and then shook his head.

"Ink, listen. On God, that ain't come from me. Somebody is setting me up. You gotta listen to me, man."

"This is her ring, Kale!" Ink's eyes were narrowed into slits as he spoke in a cold and low tone. "She had it on the last time I saw her alive. How you gon' explain this shit?"

Behind where he stood, I saw Stanson's head droop low. He knew that the case he'd built was over and the media was going to tear him alive for trying to put away an innocent man.

"Ink, it was him!" Kale yelled suddenly.

His head was lifted, and he had his eyes narrowed in and pointed directly at where Dyano stood.

"He did this shit! You saw it; he bumped into me. That was when he did it!"

Dyano's brows jumped and he chuckled incredulously. "Judge, clearly he's delusional so I won't address his accusation. We've already discussed the video that was anonymously sent to my email during this morning's proceedings but, in light of this additional evidence, I think it's even more obvious that you made the right choice in deciding to dismiss this case."

Kale looked like a maniac as he stood in the middle of the courthouse, surrounded and held up by officers while accusing a celebrated and highly awarded attorney for setting him up for murder. A few people tried to hold in their chuckles or covered them behind various objects they were holding in their hands. None were on his side. Kale noticed and cast helpless eyes in Indie's direction. She was his only ally.

"Indie, you know I wouldn't do this shit. Remember what I said... what I told you that night. I can't prove it but what I told you was true. This isn't me."

When I looked over at her, wondering what in the world Kale was talking about, the first thing I noticed was that she couldn't meet my eyes.

"What is he talking about, Indie? What did he say?" Ink asked.

She kept her head bowed. She couldn't meet his eyes either.

"He said enough for me to know that... he didn't do this."

I eyed her hard, feeling like I had lasers coming from my skull. What could Kale possibly have told her to make her believe that he wasn't responsible for it? Especially after video evidence?

"Alright folks," Judge Carmichael began, lifting his hands up as he addressed the crowd. "Now, let's get back into the courtroom so we can officially end this thing. Obviously, the State will need a little more time to collect these new details in their case."

Although Ink's attention was no longer on her, I wasn't able to let Indie out of my sight. Only a few minutes ago, she was all in his face seemingly torn up by the thought of him being locked up for murder. Now that he was free, you would've thought she would be excited, happy and relieved. However, she was even more disturbed than before. Dyano ushered him inside the courtroom but I hung back with Indie, telling him that I wanted to make sure that she was okay before I came inside.

"This is for your nose." My tone was flat as I handed her a napkin from my purse.

"Thank you."

She lifted it from my hand and wiped first at her eyes and then her nose.

"Can you let Ink know that I had to leave? I'm sure his case will be thrown out and... I can't deal with all of this right now."

Unmoved by her emotion, I watched her wipe tears from her eyes as she spoke.

Weak.

That was the word that came to mind when I looked at her. She wanted to be Ink's woman, but she didn't have the backbone for the job. He was lucky to have found me.

"I'll let him know," I said with a smile.

Thinking twice, I leaned over and decided to seal the deal with a hug. Even though she didn't pull away, her body went rigid, like she didn't want me touching her.

She sniffed and pulled away, seemingly uncomfortable. "Thank you… again."

I didn't reply right away, deciding only to hold my smile. When she began to leave, I reached out and touched her arm.

"Can you keep a secret?"

Her lips parted and a frown bent her brows. "Uhh…. Yes?"

Giggling, I rolled my eyes and bounced back and forth from foot-to-foot. I was probably overselling my excitement, but… oh well.

"I haven't told Ink yet because of the case but… I'm pregnant!" I giggled after delivering the news and then stopped short.

"Pregnant?" she repeated, swallowing hard. "Um… well, congratulations. Ink has always wanted a child—"

"He has a child," I corrected her. "A daughter. Tamiyah."

She lifted sad eyes up to me and tried to fake a smile.

"Yes, I know but… you know what I mean."

I didn't respond to affirm or deny either way.

"I'll let him know that you won't be back in," I said. She nodded her head and then turned to walk away. I was on my way towards the courtroom when I remembered that I had forgotten my manners.

"Oh, and Indie?" I called, turning around.

"Yes?"

I took a moment to observe her, noticing that she was barely keeping it together. Her eyes were filling with tears that she was trying to sniff away, and the edges of her lips were turned down at the ends.

"Since Ink isn't here, I'm speaking for both of us when I say this," I spoke with sincerity. "Goodbye."

With that, I turned back around and didn't break my stride towards the courtroom.

Chapter Thirty-Four

Ink

The first morning in our new home and I was waking up to the smell of bacon. Opening my eyes, I took a moment to lie in silence with my eyes to the ceiling and my ears listening to the joyful sounds of giggles and laughter coming from downstairs.

Life was perfect. As perfect as it could be.

Kale's trial and subsequent sentencing moved so fast that it was all a blur. Although he proclaimed his innocence until the very end, the State had an open and shut case that Elshire was helpless to fight. As much as I hated the judicial system and hated the fact that I wasn't able to avenge Tami's murder on my own, I sat through the entire trial. The amount of evidence they'd been able to discover in such a small amount of time was incredible. If they hadn't been so focused on me from the beginning, they would have known that Kale was behind her murder all along.

Tami's cellphone was found in the glove compartment of Kale's car and it pretty much sealed the deal. There were text messages between the two of them where he was trying to urge Tami to be with him and she refused. She told him that she wanted her family together but then he told her about Sage and tried to use my relationship to push Tami to be with him. The night that she showed up to the club and divorce papers were served, I'd thought Brisha was behind it but once the man who served the papers was on the stand, he pointed Kale out as the one who had paid him to deliver them. The bloody fingerprint, proven to be his, tied him to the scene.

Then there was the night in question, the one I still was unable to remember. The night that she was killed. This was where shit got crazy.

According to the texts, once I left her, Tami texted Kale accusing him of telling me that she was pregnant, but the baby wasn't mine. In her text, she accused him of trying to ruin her life. When he ignored her, she sent another text and said she was going to kill herself if he didn't bring her crack. That got him to respond, but what he said was what fucked up my head.

This isn't Tami.

What bothered me most about it was that it was the same exact thing I had been thinking when they went through her texts. We were from the streets; all of us grew up together. Niggas in the street didn't call dope crack.

Even still, at some point, Tami sent an address and Kale said he was on the way. She'd told him that she was fiending for a hit and if he didn't bring her what she needed, she'd have to find it. I didn't need Kale to explain in order for me to know why he'd gone to the motel at that point because I would've done the same. Whether he believed it was Tami texting him or not, at that point, he wasn't going to chance her getting hurt looking for shit.

Truthfully, I didn't know how to feel about the entire thing.

In the back of my mind, I'd always felt like he was responsible for me getting locked up the first time. We were in the streets; I was the head of it all and he was my right-hand man. The problem was, Kale never seemed satisfied being my right hand and, though I could tell, he held it in. When I got locked up, he took my place at the top and hadn't stopped running shit ever since. I thought that when we moved to Atlanta, both of us were keeping our hands clean, but that wasn't true. He was still moving weight.

When I first got with Tami, I knew he had a thing for her, but Tami was never the type of woman to go for the sidekick when she had a chance to be with a boss. She didn't want him; she wanted me. When I thought back to all of the fights that we had concerning other women that she thought I was sleeping with, one thing I couldn't help but remember was how much Kale was always pushing me to cheat on her whenever I was kicking it with my crew.

In fact, the time that actually led to the breakup where she ended up getting with Dolla was because of him. We were at a club and Kale saw a chick he wanted to fuck so he asked me to distract her best friend. I was buying her drinks and talking to her about bullshit when Tami stormed in and caused a big-ass scene. I dropped her after that because I couldn't take it anymore. Her jealousy was getting to me and I couldn't deal with it. We called it quits and the next thing I knew, Kale was telling me about how he'd heard that she was Dolla's new chick.

Kale had to be in love with her. What other man would go to those lengths to be with a woman? Especially to the point of moving across the country to be near her. When I moved Tami to Atlanta, I thought it was loyal of Kale to move with me and help get my shop up and going. Now I couldn't help but wonder if he'd come there for Tami or for me. There was one point in my life when I thought all was good as long as I had Tami and Kale by my side. At one time, they were all I needed and the only family I had in my life. But time changes things and now they were both gone.

But if Kale was the one who killed her, how the fuck did I get blood on my clothes?

***

"It smells good down here," I said, smiling as I walked down the stairs.

Boxes filled every room in the house, except the kitchen. Sage had unpacked all of the kitchenware before anything else. We had spent about a month looking for a new house after the charges against me were thrown out, but we couldn't find anything that we all liked. Then, we took a break and spent a week at Sage's father's home in the mountains and the week was so perfect that we didn't want to leave. That's when it dawned on us that it was the perfect house to make our home.

"Daddy, me and Mimi Sage made pancakes, eggs and bacon!" Tamiyah shrieked, running straight at me.

I leaned down and scooped her up into my arms, then planted a kiss against her hairline. She gave me about two seconds of affection before she heard the theme song to her favorite cartoon. Then she was squirming out of my arms towards the living room. Just that easily, I'd been swapped out for a sponge that lived in the bottom of the ocean.

"If you're ready to eat, I'll make your plate," Sage said, turning towards me.

My eyes dropped to the apron that she had stretched across her bulging stomach and I smiled. Every day that passed, I was getting closer and closer to the birth of my baby boy. Part of me felt like Sage and I weren't ready to make that step; things were moving so fast. But then, after thinking about it, I realized that I would never feel absolutely ready for the life that I was stepping into. In three months, I would be a father again and, as of last night, I was engaged and would soon have a wife. Sage was wearing my ring and had accepted my request that she take my last name. Not bad for a Chi-Town nigga from the streets.

"How about I make your breakfast and we eat together since you cooked?" I countered, slipping the plate from Sage's hand.

I leaned over and kissed her lips, simultaneously rubbing her belly. She smelled like heaven. Like warm lavender and vanilla mixed. When she giggled against my mouth, I pulled back and kissed her smile then reached behind her to grab a handful of ass. It was always fat, just like I liked it, but pregnancy had made her even thicker in all the right places.

"Do you have to go to work?" Sage whined, rubbing her hand over her stomach.

I stared at it in wonder, amazed that it was able to contain everything necessary to give my child life as well as the three pancakes, four pieces of bacon, and three handfuls of scrambled eggs she'd stuffed in it.

"Yeah, you know I gotta go but I'll be back tonight. I need to interview some new artists and get back in the game. It's been a while since somebody got inked, know what I mean?"

Laughing, Sage rolled her eyes. "You're corny."

"Yeah and?"

"And..." She stood to her feet, making her chair screech across the wood floor as it slid back to give her room. "I have something for you."

I leaned back and clasped my hands together over the top of my head, watching her as she made her way over to her purse and pulled out an envelope. Sage was a classic beauty. Pregnancy hormones were working in her favor, her skin glowed and her hair, which had grown more than a few inches, was in smooth and shiny ringlets down her back.

Sometimes I felt like she was too good for me. What did I do to deserve a woman so sexy, accomplished, devoted and all around perfect? We never argued because she never chastised me and always followed my lead. Being called on my shit was something that I liked about the relationship that I had with Indie, but Sage avoided confrontations.

"I wrote you this letter," Sage said, walking back over to me. She handed the envelope out to me and I grabbed it in my hands and looked at the outside.

To my husband and love for life. From your wife, is what it said.

I smirked. Being called someone's husband again was crazy to see.

"Don't read it until you leave for work," she said. "I want you to be alone so you can read it without distractions. I want you to know how much I really love you."

With a nod, I folded the envelope, stuffed it in my pocket, and then joined Tamiyah in the living room to say my goodbyes. Although Sage was still a member of the board, after everything that happened and with her pregnancy so far along, she had decided to give them what they wanted. She was a silent member and left them to do the work and make all the major decisions while she reaped the rewards. In other words, shit was smooth as gravy on her end and all she did was collect a check.

"Drive safely," Sage said as I gathered my things and prepared to leave. "And come back to me soon, love."

I kissed her and then grabbed my backpack and keys. She'd bought me a gift; a custom-made, gold plated tattoo gun with my name engraved on it. It was sick as hell and I couldn't wait to put it to use.

"I'll call you a little later to see how things are going with you two. Lock up for me."

She closed the door behind me and I stepped out onto the front porch, all of a sudden feeling not at ease for some reason. It was almost Christmas, so the winter weather was in full swing. Flurries of snow had fallen in the days before and every now and then more came until the point that little patches of snow covered the tops of the hedges, trees, and some of the grass. It wasn't enough to pull Tamiyah into a snowball fight, but it was enough to appreciate the Georgia winter for what it was. In Chicago, snow fell in blizzards to the point that I got sick of seeing it.

In fact, it was snowing the night that I met Amber and caught my first charge. She walked into the club looking like a 'snow bunny' for real, dressed in a white turtleneck, some jeans, and those fuzzy construction boots that while girls loved to wear. I think they call them Uggs. She had a skully on her head and when she pulled it off, red, amber curls flowed out from beneath, catching my eye.

Tami was my girl and I loved her, but she was helping me build an empire. Every conversation that we had was about the streets, stacking our bread, who was a threat, and what plans we had to take over. It was what had made me loyal to her, even after she betrayed me and we weren't together anymore; I always looked out for her. The problem was, the more we were about our business, the less we took our time to truly enjoy each other. Our relationship was business all the time.

So when Amber came over to me, batting her eyes, flirting and playing around, I soaked it in. The time I spent talking to other women gave me a short reprieve from my dangerous lifestyle and allowed me the time to have fun. Amber was someone I'd seen a few times before and I knew I was playing with fire from the moment she sat down. She'd already made it obvious on a few occasions that I could have her pussy whenever I wanted it. She was serving it up for free. I didn't even know that once I'd taken it, I would have to pay with part of my life.

As I say in the car, I started the engine and then continued to sit, thinking to myself. So much had changed in the span of only a little less than a year.

A year ago, I didn't even know Sage. Tami was alive, I was probably fucking with some random broad, Kale was still my best friend, and Indie was answering my calls. Now, none of that was true. Tami was dead, Kale was in prison for killing her, I was engaged and about to be a father, and Indie was pretending like I never existed. I didn't know what happened after we spoke at the courthouse to make her want to avoid me, but I couldn't get in contact with her.

The night my case was thrown out, Sage had helped me

make a huge dinner and we waited for hours for Indie to show but she never did. I was confused. According to Sage, Indie had asked her to let me know that she would be at the house a few hours later and then never came. I sent her a few texts and called multiple times over the next few days until finally, one day, she returned my text with the exact same words she told me that I'd sent her.

Stop texting and calling me. I'm blocking your number.

After that, I tried once again and was hit with a text saying my number had been blocked. The message was clear: she wanted me out of her life. Maybe it was for the good. Indie and I had a connection and once I found out Sage was pregnant, she became a priority in my life. With the natural attraction that I had for Indie and the tension between her and Sage, there's no way that would have worked out peacefully. Not having Indie around was for the best.

I was about to pull away when I glanced down and saw Sage's letter peeking out of my pocket. With a sigh, I grabbed it and began to tear at the envelope to get it open. I wasn't at work yet, but I was on my way, like she asked. Plus, I had an hour and a half drive ahead of me. If she wanted me to read it during a time when I had nothing left to do but think, there was no better time than now.

Ink,

I love you more than life itself.

From the very first moment that I saw you, I knew you were destined to be mine. I tried to play it tough... I've never felt like that about someone before. But you saw right through the 'pretend me' from the beginning.

I guess that's why I love you so much. Or at least one of the reasons. I've been so tired of acting for so long. Pretending to be the perfect daughter, the perfect friend, and the perfect stepdaughter with the perfect life. To finally meet someone who could see the true side of me and still love me... that is priceless.

You once asked me if I thought I could be loyal and I told you that I could. Now that one of the hardest times in our lives is behind us, I hope you can see that I'll always be here for you. I'm thankful that you've decided to love me and I'm excited that I'll get to spend the rest of my life loving you.

Thank you for putting your faith in me. Thank you for creating a love that will not fail. Thank you for making me the mother of your child.

Love,

Sage

P.S. "Our love is right side up and as strong as a tree. Addicted to you, forever I'll be. I have you and you have me. Forever, until eternity. I'll always come back to you."

My blood froze in my veins, my heart beats slowed in pace, and I felt a thin layer of sweat begin to bead up at my hairline.

"Our love is right side up and as strong as a tree. Addicted to you, forever I'll be. I have you and you have me. Forever, until eternity. I'll always come back to you."

Those words were attached to a memory that I was able to remember for the first time.

With teeth gritted from an equal amount of anguish and confusion, I opened my car door. I swallowed hard, pushing the lump in my throat to my chest, then got out and began to walk towards the front door. The pressure made me feel like there was a weight on my head. Even sticking my key in the lock on the door and twisting it seemed like an impossible feat.

I pushed open the door, stepped over the threshold and closed it behind me, all the while staring at my daughter. She was jumping up and down on the couch, singing to the top of her lungs the theme song to some show with puppets and a Black DJ. It was a show that Tami had hated, but I'd always let her watch it anyway.

Careful to stay unseen, I slid past her and walked to the kitchen. When I arrived inside, Sage was still there. Her back was to me and she was humming some song that sounded slightly familiar as she washed dishes. I was standing not too far behind her, silent and watching intently. In my mind, I was wondering how much I really knew about the woman that I loved.

Still humming to herself, Sage turned off the running water and grabbed a towel to dry the dishes.

"Ink!" she exclaimed, jumping with surprise when she

turned around and saw me standing behind her. "Oh my god, baby. I didn't know you were still here."

Giggling to herself, she placed her hand on her belly and dropped her head as she took a moment to laugh. The soft ringlets on the crown of her head danced as she shook her head from side to side. Ever since I told her how much I loved her hair that way, she'd continued getting the hairstyle.

"You scared me to death." She laughed and ran her fingers through her hair. "Did you forget something?"

Ignoring her question, I began to step forward, closing the gap between us as much as I could until I was unable to walk any closer. The same perfume that had made my dick hard was now making me sick. There was a sour taste in the back of my throat, with what felt like a lump lodged right beneath it. I cleared my throat and fought through the wave of nausea that washed over me in order to speak.

"Tell me how you did it."

Sage's brows furrowed and her jaw slightly dropped in confusion.

"Huh? Tell you how I did what, Ink?"

I took a step closer, wanting to be sure that I was heard. She rested her hand on top of her belly and, for the first time since the moment she had told me that she was pregnant, I regretted that she was the woman who I'd chosen to nurture and grow my seed.

"Tell me how you did it," I repeated. "Tell how you killed Tami."

Chapter Thirty-Five

Sage

Before that moment, everything was perfect. Before that moment, I was the fiancée to a man whose child I was carrying. My bonus daughter was in the living room singing to the top of her lungs, and I was washing dishes from the breakfast I'd prepared on the first full day that we'd spend in our new home.

Later that day, I had a surprise planned for Tamiyah. She didn't know anything about it and neither did Ink.

After Kale was sentenced for Tami's murder, we were able to go on with our lives and things naturally fell into place. Tamiyah began to see me as her mother and our relationship grew quickly. It was almost like Tami had been gone years before Ink meeting me. In ways, I guess she had. It was no secret that she hated being a mother and rarely spent time with her child.

Even though that were true, I knew from personal experience that for a young girl, a mother is a person who could never be replaced, even if her presence was toxic in your life. I never considered my own mother as anything but a host but the fact that my father and stepmother pretended like she never existed, like she was some mystery woman, a ghost who had dropped me off and was done with me, had left a huge void.

For that reason, I wanted to make sure that Tamiyah was able to honor her mother and remember the good memories, however few there were. So, unknown to her and Ink, I had made sure to take down the memorial they'd made for Tami at the old house and I had brought it there. I was planning to take Tamiyah into the area behind the house that I used to play in as a child and place it there.

It was a forest of trees and I'd run away there to escape the hateful stares my stepmother shot my way when my daddy wasn't around. There was a small cave that I would hide in and make believe that I was speaking to my mother who, in my mind of make-believe, cared for and protected me. I planned to tell Tamiyah about the place and let her know that whenever she missed her mother, she could go there to speak to her. We would construct the memorial in a spot nearby and whisper a few words to update her on all the good things that had happened since she'd died.

I already had the spot picked out and I couldn't wait to take Tamiyah there. It was perfect. Especially since, unlike where they first had the memorial, that was actually where Tami's body was buried.

"Tell me how you did it. Tell me how you killed Tami."

It took a moment for me to register what Ink was saying because his tone, body language, and the angst I saw in his expression didn't seem to match his words. Though tense, his voice was even and calm. But his eyes were tapered at the ends, as if suppressing his rage.

"Ink, let's not talk about this now." I cut my eyes to the wall, reminding him that Tamiyah was only on the other side.

"Don't worry about my daughter," he said in a way that made me feel like I'd been cut. "You need to worry about what I asked. Now answer me."

He moved forward and grabbed my arms, squeezing them so hard that my skin began to burn. My bottom lip trembled as I looked up in his eyes, trying to read his thoughts.

"Speak!" He gritted through his teeth.

"I—I..." I licked my lips as tears pooled in my eyes. "I didn't do anything!"

"You're a fucking liar!" he hissed, and his fingers dug even further into my skin.

Tears stung my eyes and I bit down on my bottom lip as I tried to break away. He held on even firmer, and it took Tamiyah running into the kitchen before he reluctantly let me go.

"Mimi Sage, is everything okay?" she asked, looking from Ink to me.

Accusations of what she assumed he'd done to me were all in her eyes. I noticed it and so did Ink. I'd won over his daughter to the point that, if she thought he was causing me harm, she was ready to come to my defense.

"Yes, it is, baby," I told her, rubbing my arm while trying to blink back my tears. "Why don't you go outside and play for a little bit? I bought you something. Go check under the dining room table in that bag."

"Yay!" she screamed before doing as I'd asked.

The entire time she was gone, Ink's eyes stayed on mine,

shooting rays of hatred and anger into my face. I felt a sudden sharp stabbing feeling in my stomach and winced. With my hand on my belly, I was able to force a smile on my face just as Tamiyah came back into the room.

"You got me skates! Thank you!" She ran over to me and wrapped her arms around my waist. "I love you, Mimi Sage."

Wiping a tear from my cheek, I hugged her back like it would be my last time.

"I love you, too."

She left and Ink and I sat in silence until the moment that we heard the front door slam behind her. That time, I was the first to speak.

"Ink, listen to me, please. I'll tell you whatever you want me to say, but—"

He lifted a hand in the air to stop me.

"You made my daughter love you. You made her love you after you took her mother from her."

My heart felt like it was breaking into pieces. My entire life I'd always felt like I wasn't wanted by the ones I loved the most. My father, being that I was his only child and he was a man bound by his sense of responsibility, raised me because he had to. He gave me as much love as his guilt would allow him to, but it never was the way a father should love his child.

My stepmother was the closest thing I had to a real mother and I wanted her love so bad that it hurt. She never accepted me, and she made it clear that my presence caused her constant pain. Even when she spoke to me, she did it in ways that seemed more like she was speaking to herself, never actually addressing me like I was actually in the room. There was only one time I could remember her actually speaking directly to me like I was a person—a real person with real feelings and not a problem my father had created for her to tolerate.

"*Not everyone is meant to be a parent, Sage. Your mother definitely wasn't. You don't understand it now but some people are more valuable dead than alive. When you weigh all the destruction they cause to others and how much pain they bring to the lives of everyone around them, you see things differently.*"

With tears in my eyes, I sat silently with my head bowed as she continued. In the corner of the room were my suitcases filled with everything I would need for the camp that my father was sending me to. My stepmother was standing in front of the mirror ahead of me, putting makeup on her face so that she could be flawless for my trip to the airport.

"*A rotten person doesn't just destroy themselves; they bring everyone else down with them. Your mother tried to destroy a lot of lives: mine, your father's. Before she was killed, she tried to destroy yours.*"

My head snapped up and rage filled my eyes.

"*No, she didn't! She said she wanted to fight for me. She wanted to get me back.*"

My stepmother whirled around and frowned as she eyed me with her upper lip curled in disgust.

"*And what could she have given you for the exchange? You leave your life here and for what? To slum it in the projects with her? She had no money, no home to put you in. She just wanted to pull you into her misery so that she could use you to maintain leverage over a man. You were nothing but a guaranteed child support check as far as she was concerned. She was an evil woman and there is no cure for that. But now that she's dead, we can all move on and live our lives without the threat of her ruining our happiness."*

I hated hearing it at the time and it only made me hate my stepmother even more once she'd said it. It took over a decade for me to realize that what she'd said was true.

Tami was a poison. She was an evil woman who was destroying the lives of everyone around her. Ink was an amazing man who she refused to let go because he didn't want her. Like my mother, she was miserable and wanted him to join her in her misery. She had used Tamiyah like a pawn, never really seeing the value in the child who loved and needed her.

The night at the shop when I kept Tamiyah busy as Ink fought with her outside, was when I began to form the basis of my plan. When I looked in Tamiyah's eyes, I saw myself—what I could have become if my father had never taken me in. Her eyes were dark and sad, full of confusion over the rejection of her mother. She felt like something was wrong with her. Like something *had* to be because she was a child that not even a mother could love.

By the time I picked her up from Kale's house, I'd already determined that he would be the one to take the fall. In my mind, he was no better than Tami was. Instead of being a loyal friend to her, he was contributing to her sickness and dysfunction by supplying her drugs. Instead of being a loyal friend to Ink, he was betraying him by fucking his ex behind his back... and had been for a long time.

I knew the day that Tami showed up at Ink's house that I had to get things done and had to do it fast. There was one thing I knew about toxic people and I'd learned it firsthand—they had a hold on the ones who loved them. It was the way they were able to bring them down. Tami had a hold on Ink and, no matter what she did, he would always help her if she asked for it. And she would never stop asking.

That day, I could see it in his eyes when I looked at him. Tami said she wanted his help and even though he would reject her for the moment, it wouldn't last. She would be a constant source of turmoil in his life until the day she died.

Ink had already given me an idea about how to do it. He told me about the roofies and, when you had money, everything came easy. After Tamiyah was in bed, I slipped one in his drink and waited for him to finish half of the glass before I pretended that I was leaving for the night. The drug was so powerful that Ink could barely walk me to the door and nearly stumbled over his own feet when he tried to kiss me goodbye.

Not too long after, I knew that he would fall into a sleep so deep that not even the entire percussion section of a high school band could have awakened him. After driving a few circles around the neighborhood, I doubled back and crept in through the basement door, which I'd previously unlocked. I found Ink passed out in the living room, sleeping so soundly that I panicked and had to stare at his chest for a few seconds to make sure that he was still breathing.

Once I slipped his phone from his pocket, I held it in front of his face, and peeled back his eyelids to allow the facial recognition software to grab a positive scan.

I need to see you. I'm sorry about earlier. Tell me where you are so I can help you.

With that text sent to Tami, I didn't have to wait too long

before she responded back. She was desperate, so eager for the attention of a man that she wasn't good enough for. A man who pitied her but would never love her back.

Pretending to be Ink, I told Tami where to meet me and when. I'd already scoped out the motel and knew it was the perfect place to help someone get away with murder. Ink was right about one thing; no matter how much of a junkie she was, there was no way she would be caught dead in a place like that. Well... not if it had been up to her, anyway.

Junkies, pimps, prostitutes, and dope boys were their main clientele and, for that reason, they made it easy for them to feel at ease with breaking the law. The front desk clerk barely paid attention, didn't ask to see ID and the security cameras were connected to a cheap mainframe right behind the front desk. I made a mental note to bring a cup of coffee with me to destroy the system on the night I would put my plan into action.

Two hours before the time I told Tami to meet me at the hotel, I paid for a room in her name. When she arrived, I was already inside. The first time, I sunk the knife into her fast. I had been panicking and was losing my nerve but once she saw me, it was too late to change my mind. The knife made a sickening, squishy sound when I pulled it out and Tami and I both gasped at the same time when a rivulet of blood began spilling from her insides.

She raised her head to look up at me and there were tears running down her cheeks.

"How could you..." She made a panting sound as she struggled to pull air into her lungs. "Why would you do this to me?"

Her eyes bugged, stretched wide with grief as the realization hit her. There was no way she was making it out of there alive.

"I—I'm pregnant."

That definitely wasn't something that I had expected to hear.

"Is it Ink's?"

She shook her head. "No. I—I... I don't know whose it is."

I expelled a breath. Another child that she was going to bring into the world and, unlike Tamiyah, this one wouldn't have had a man like Ink to save it from its mother. How selfish could she be to become pregnant with another child when she didn't even love the one she already had?

After that, finishing the deed wasn't quite so hard. Grabbing her phone, I texted Kale until I was able to convince him to come by. It was risky, but even if he didn't show, I had a plan for that, too.

With that part done, I had to move quickly. Using the anger I'd kept buried inside for so long as fuel, I stabbed her over and over again until I was almost covered with her blood. Every day of my life I was plagued by the 'need to please' disease, making me feel as though I had to be perfect in every and any part of my life but, when it came to that, I acted out of pure emotion. I relinquished all control.

Once it was over, I felt victorious. Maybe that was how my stepmother had felt. All that was left for me to do was get away with it.

By the time that Kale made it to the motel, Tami was dead but knowing what I did about him and his connection to her and Ink, I counted on him leaving and staying silent about what he'd seen. I also counted on him suspecting Ink for her murder, driving a much-needed wedge between them. Turns out, I was right on both counts and, thanks to the video that I discreetly took of his departure from Tami's room, I had everything needed to cover my crime.

Once he was gone, I took my time rolling her body up in an old comforter, taping it up and after much struggle, I was able to get it in the trunk. Tami was petite and curvy but, in death, she was like carrying a bag of bricks. I drove to my house in the mountains, swapped cars, and then returned to Ink's home.

While I drove, I fingered Tami's diamond ring in my pocket. It was dumb to have it on me, but I'd been unable to stop myself from keeping it. Ink had given it to her when he loved Tami enough to make her his wife; I wanted the same *so* bad. It hurt me to my core when I had to give it to Dyano, but he'd told me that it was a necessary part of my plan.

I almost stopped him before he bumped into Kale at the courthouse and slipped it into his pocket. It wasn't until I saw the look on Ink's face when it fell out that I knew I'd made the right choice. Dyano was right, but I knew he would give me good advice. He was loyal to my father through friendship and his guilt for being involved in my mother's murder made him loyal to me.

Putting Tami's blood on Ink wasn't originally part of my plan. It was initially an accident.

When I pulled in his yard, I panicked after seeing him face down in the snow. I thought maybe I'd drugged him to the point that he was dead. I freaked out, forgetting that my clothes were still soiled and that I hadn't yet showered. When I helped him up, the blood smeared onto him.

"You came back..." he had said, giving me a drunken, lopsided grin as I struggled to pull him up from the snow. He was still fairly warm, letting me know that he hadn't been lying there too long.

"Of course, I did," I told him. "I'll always come back to you. It's like a poem I wrote for you one day. Do you want to hear it?"

Nodding, he grinned harder and rose to his feet, leaning against me as I helped him in through the basement door. While we staggered through the snow, coupling our strengths together to overshadow our weaknesses, I recited a poem that I'd written for him.

"Our love is right side up and as strong as a tree. Addicted to you, forever I'll be. I have you and you have me. Forever, until eternity. I'll always come back to you."

He was so heavy that it was all I could do to get him inside and, once he stumbled in and fell right into the chair at his desk, he passed out again. He was like dead weight and there was nothing I could do. I left him there.

I started to pull off his clothes but then something occurred to me. That was the perfect opportunity for me to prove my loyalty. If I held onto everything I had to set up Kale, Ink would be the #1 suspect. He would be in a position where the entire world, himself included, thought that he had committed the terrible crime. Everyone would believe that he was guilty.

Everyone except me. It was the ultimate show of loyalty.

"I would never do anything to hurt Tamiyah," I told him with tears running down my eyes. "We are a family. She's happier than she's ever been. Isn't this what you wanted for her? Tami was a junkie. She didn't even want to be her mother. But

I do. I want to give her everything that no one ever gave me."

Anxious to feel his touch, I reached out for Ink. He stepped back and shook his head.

"People change, Sage. No matter what, you don't have the right to take a life."

My mouth almost dropped open at the double standard. The position he was taking was in direct contrast of the things I knew about him.

"You've never told me all the details about your past life, but you said enough," I began, pointing my finger at him. "No one can make a name for themselves in the streets without, at one point in time, taking a life. Isn't that what you said? That's how you earned respect, right?"

I saw his pupils darken as he processed what I was saying.

"That's not the same thing."

"Yes, it is." I lifted my chin in defiance. "And if you can do that for something like respect, then what's wrong with doing it to protect your own child from being continuously hurt by a mother who will never properly love her?"

Conflict and confusion passed through his eyes. I watched him as he ran through his thoughts and then I saw his gaze dropped to my stomach, where I was carrying what would be his first son and only biological child. Now was the time to weigh his options. He was hurt, angry, betrayed, and a lot of other things, but I was hoping he would get over it and realize that everything I did had been done out of love.

"Did you kill her? Were you actually the one who took her life?"

Raising his head, he looked me in the eyes and, for the first time since the day I had met him, I was able to read him clearly. He wanted me to lie. He couldn't live with the truth. Truthfully, I couldn't either because it was clear that Ink would never be happy with me if I told him that I was the one who killed Tami. Maybe that was how my father felt when he lied to me.

"No," I said, letting the words out along with a heavy breath. "I didn't kill her, and I didn't have anything to do with whoever did. I just strongly feel like it was for the best."

A long silence settled between us as he scrutinized every part of me, reading me like a book as he searched for the truth. Then, finally, he ran a hand over his face, shook his head, and sighed.

"Okay." He sniffed and nudged the tip of his nose with his finger. "I have no reason to think you're not telling the truth. But I don't want to ever talk about this shit again. I can't do it any other way."

I blew out a breath of relief and felt fresh tears come to my eyes. Even while I was willing myself to stay calm and collected, some part of me thought that I had made a mistake and was going to lose out on yet another chance at true love.

Taking slow and careful steps towards him, my heart swelled with joy when he didn't move away. I wrapped my arms around him and hugged him tight, silently thanking God for small blessings when Ink returned my embrace.

"I love you so much." Sniffing, I wiped at the tears running down my face.

"I love you, too," he replied.

Still in his arms and with my head on his chest, I frowned.

I couldn't count how many times Ink had told me that he loved me, but I did know that every time he had said it, I'd felt the truth of it in my soul. That time I didn't.

"I'm going to work. And... I'm going to take Tamiyah with me."

"Huh?" I pulled away and searched his face. "Why? She can stay here; I have the whole day planned."

Ink shook his head and, though he hadn't shed a single tear, he looked a little red around his eyes.

"You've been working really hard and I want to give you a break. Take some time to yourself to relax, take a bubble bath or some shit. Anything."

I lifted one brow. "And will you be back?"

"Of course." He kissed me on my forehead and nodded.

Then he pursed his lips into some dull version of a smile and added, "I'll always come back to you."

"Okay." I ran my hand over my head and sucked in a breath before pushing it out in a whoosh of air. "Let me pack her a few things."

Bypassing him, I walked slowly to the stairs and headed up to Tamiyah's room, mentally making a list of everything she would need throughout the day. It wasn't until I was almost to the top that I looked down at Ink. He was sitting down in a chair with his head down and his face in his hands. It was a show of vulnerability and grief that he was allowing to come through because he didn't know that I was watching.

Will he ever forgive me?

Only time would tell. It would be difficult for the next few weeks, maybe even a month, but once the baby came, our love would be renewed. Our child would make everything right. And once that time came where we were finally one again, completely in sync and just as in love as we had been before that day, I would never do anything to jeopardize our love again.

I had to make sure he didn't find out about the other thing I did.

God, please. Please, don't let him find out about Indie.

Note from the Author

Thank you for reading!

I truly hope that you enjoyed this novel. When coming up with the storyline, my intention was to challenge myself with a multi-layered character, but to also write the novel in a way that was unpredictable and would inspire discussion. I hope that I've been able to achieve that!

As a romance author, I love happy endings (and I know readers of romance do as well), but the question is ... did this one really have a happy ending? Sage was able to get what she wanted (a family of her own), Tamiyah got what she needed (a loving mother who would do anything for her), and Ink wanted a loyal and devoted woman by his side... so does it matter how it was obtained?

Even in the most cherished love stories, there are not so good parts that are ignored in order to celebrate the incredible love that was birthed through the tragic times. Do you think that Ink can overcome what Sage has done, in her deadly pursuit of happiness, and move on?

Leave a review--I'm eager to know your thoughts!

Make sure to visit me on www.porschasterling.com and join my mailing list to keep up with everything that I have going on. No matter what, I always have another book in the works and you don't want to miss it! Text PORSCHA to 25827 for notifications on new releases.

Until we meet again, happy reading!

XOXO,

Porscha Sterling

Connect with U s

Visit us online at
KensingtonBooks.com
to read more from your favorite authors, see books
by series, view reading group guides, and more.

Join us on social media

for sneak peeks, chances to win books and prize packs,
and to share your thoughts with other readers.

facebook.com/kensingtonpublishing
twitter.com/kensingtonbooks

Tell us what you think!

To share your thoughts, submit a review,
or sign up for our eNewsletters, please visit:
KensingtonBooks.com/TellUs.